TAMARILLO TART

SOUTHERN LIGHTS 2

JAY HOGAN

SOUTHERN LIGHTS PUBLISHING

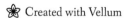 Created with Vellum

For my family who read everything I write and keep on saying they love it all, blushes included.

ACKNOWLEDGMENTS

As always, I thank my husband for his patience and for keeping the dog walked and out of my hair when I needed to work. And my daughter for all her support.

Getting a book finessed for release is a huge challenge that includes beta readers, editing, proofing, cover artists and my tireless PA. It is a team effort and includes all those author support networks and reader fans who rally around when you're ready to pull your hair out and throw away every first draft. Thanks to all of you.

CHAPTER ONE

"WHAT DO YOU MEAN YOU WON'T BE ABLE TO MAKE IT?" STEF jumped back to avoid a dark blue van with "Martin's Stables and Tours" plastered on its side as it pulled into One Mile car park, a cheery hand waving through the windscreen. *Goddammit.* It was the last thing he needed—a fucking Pollyanna.

"It appears he's here," Stef grumbled, watching the van do a slow circuit looking for a parking space. At nine a.m., the small car park was already bulging at the seams—something that came with being less than a ten-minute walk from downtown Queenstown and having one of the best free views of Lake Wakatipu and the surrounding mountains.

Today the glacial waters ran a vivid blue, not a ripple in sight under a cloudless autumn sky, and everyone had their cameras out. When Stef flew down to meet the man who'd snagged his best friend's heart, and taken Tanner fifteen hundred kilometres away to the bottom of the South Island, he'd expected much cooler temperatures. Instead, it was surprisingly hot for March—although minus the subtropical humidity of Auckland, which was a blessing.

"This whole thing was your boyfriend's idea, Tanner. I'm so

pissed at you right now. I only agreed on sufferance because... well, because I wanted Ethan not to think your best friend was a prissy dork. And I was trying to be good about it. I got us T-shirts and everything. You can't just abandon me. I don't do this outdoor shit, you know that."

He stubbed his shoe angrily into the gravel and did his best to ignore a cute Korean couple taking selfies in their matching honeymoon outfits barely a metre away. They were perched precariously on a big rock at the edge of the lake with the frigid waters behind them, and Stef was pretty sure he was gonna have to rescue their butts if they didn't watch what they were doing.

"I didn't exactly have a choice, did I? And what the hell... T-shirts, Stef? I think the less I know about those, the better." Tanner paused and took a breath.

Damn. Stef knew Tanner genuinely felt bad about pulling out. It was just... ugh, fuck it. It had been four months since Tanner had shifted south to follow his heart in the shape of one cute-as-hell Ethan Sharpe, and Stef had missed his best friend way more than he'd expected. And yeah, maybe he was just being a jealous prick over this new guy who was front and centre in Tanner's life—a guy Tanner was head over heels in love with. But Stef couldn't deny how much he'd been looking forward to getting a bit of one-on-one time with his best friend, just the two of them, and now...

"Look, I've already spoken to the tour guide. I can't help that Sophie's got gastritis and can't do the teleconference pitch to the Belgian team. I can't just blow them off. This is my *business*, Stef. We need that contract."

Stef knew that. Of course he did. He just... "But horses, Tanner? Horses! Dear God, the only thing that made that idea even bearable was the chance to see you as fucking awkward and uncomfortable for two days as me. What am I going to do on a fucking horse trek on my own?"

"You won't be on your own."

The tourist couple broke into a fit of giggles, and Stef glanced over to catch them leaning back and nuzzling while still trying to take a selfie. It had "tourist disaster" written all over it.

"Whoa, whoa," he called out.

"Stef?"

"Hang on," he told Tanner and walked over to the couple, gesturing to see if they wanted him to take the photo. They nodded enthusiastically, and he took the phone while they got themselves positioned. He snapped a set of photos, and they thanked him and moved on, still giggling. He watched them go and felt a slight tug at his heart. Okay, so he could admit to a little bit of envy. There, he'd said it.

"Sorry," Stef said into the phone. "Just averting an international incident. *Korean couple suffers death by selfie at New Zealand tourist hot spot.*"

"What the...? You know, forget it. I don't want to know. But getting back to me not being there, you know damn well I would've taken the quad bike option if I'd organised it. But Ethan raves about Cass, the guy who runs this tour. He leases one of Cass's horses every now and then to ride up Paradise Valley—says the views are breathtaking. He was trying to do something special for you since you're an *LOTR* nerd and all."

The van had finally finished its circuit of the car park and scored a potential win opposite Stef, where a red Mazda was pulling out. The driver whipped in to steal it before anyone could beat him to it. Switching the engine off, he turned and gave Stef yet another friendly wave.

Ugh. That much chirpiness wasn't natural, and Stef distrusted the guy on principle. He was still suffering whiplash from the fact that people in this small town actually said hello and smiled when they passed you on the street. It was enough to give a born-and-bred Auckland boy palpitations.

"Okay, okay, I'll do it." For Tanner and Ethan's sake, Stef would give this guy Cass the benefit of the doubt, but he wasn't promising anything beyond that. From ten metres away he couldn't see much more than sunglasses and a wide-brimmed cowboy hat. Stef didn't swim in the rugged-outdoorsy-type pool, so it didn't bode well. "Well, fuck me."

"Ugh. No, thanks."

Stef winced. "Yeah, well, ditto. But the guy in the van's dressed like a damn cowboy... in New Zealand, for fuck's sake. Are you sure he's not a complete tosser? And by the way, don't ever mention my name and the word 'nerd' in the same sentence again, you toad. I might be a fan of the books, but I am no fan of horses and you damn well know it. Colossal, unpredictable creatures with mouths full of nasty-arse teeth. The closest thing to a horse that interests me in *Lord of the Rings* is Aragorn's leather breeches and the removal of same. Why on earth did you agree to this nonsense?"

He missed most of Tanner's answer because right then the van driver's door opened and a pair of... *fuck me sideways*... cowboy boots appeared, followed by two long... *damn*... very long, lean, shapely legs, and a tight, well-rounded arse, all housed in soft faded denims, A snug black T-shirt over a fit torso just topped things off nicely, and...*holy moly*... Stef thought he'd be forgiven a swoon... if he did that sort of thing... which he didn't... ever.

The guy pulled off his hat and banged it on his thigh, sending a cloud of dust skyward as he ran his fingers through a mass of strawberry blond hair that hung in unruly waves past his ears. So, okay then, maybe Stef could be persuaded to revisit the whole cowboy vibe thingy with a more open mind.

Cass pushed his aviators onto his head and reached to get something from inside the van, and those damn denims stretched and the T-shirt rode up to expose a band of smooth, tanned skin... and Stef was sold. The tour was definitely starting to look up—although with Stef's luck, the guy was likely just the driver and the tour guide would turn out to be some sixty-year-old dude with a comb-over and bandy legs.

"Stef, dammit, are you even listening to me?"

"Of course I am," Stef lied, watching the driver re-emerge with a clipboard in his hand.

"He's right there, isn't he?" Tanner chuckled. "And you're drooling yourself into a frickin' puddle. Ethan told me he was hot."

"Mmm-hmm, maybe. Still not happy with you." But if this *was* in fact, the legendary Cass, then damn, he had to be six foot six at the minimum, and Stef was feeling distinctly happier. A bit of eye candy to even out the inevitable horror of the next two days was more than welcome.

Turn around, turn around, and... ah, there he is. Swimmer's shoulders, trim waist, all that wild hair falling around a sharpish jaw, and a slightly crooked nose that looked like it might have seen at least one fist up close and personal in its thirty-something years. So yeah, cowboys were apparently trending. Stef swallowed hard and tried not to look like a complete gaping dork while attempting to pick up the thread of Tanner's harping in his ear.

"And I agreed to this nonsense, as you call it, because Ethan went out of his way to get us on this damn tour, you ungrateful sod. He was so damn excited. If you think I was gonna stamp all over that, then you're batshit. I love the guy, *and* I live with him. So I don't care if you fall off the horse every ten minutes and you come back with its teeth imprinted on your back, you will not say anything bad about it to him, understand?"

Shit. I was possibly being an arsehole. "Of course I bloody won't. What do you take me for?"

Stef watched as Mr Hot and Handsome made his way to the back of the van, leaned casually against the rear door, and eyed him with one brow raised and a glance at his watch. Stef held up a finger, and the man locked on to the bright green nails and bit back a smile. *Huh.*

"I bet you rolled over like a lamb when he suggested it, though, didn't you? Probably sucked his dick as well." The comment was loud enough for half the car park to hear—including Cass, who simply snorted and checked his clipboard.

Tanner was unrepentant. "That and everything else I could get my hands on. Look, Stef, Ethan promised the horses are nice. They're not going to bite you. Cass will set you up on the beginner's one. It's only a few hours in the saddle the first day—"

"Oh. My. God. A few hours! I can already feel the chafing."

"—then an overnight at some historic shepherd's hut and back down the next day. And just think, you get to see the Lothlórien forest, the Ithilien Camp site, Isengard, the Misty Mountains, the filming location for the refugees of Rohan, and loads more. Come on, you must be gagging for that."

Stef's raked his eyes over the mouth-watering man standing opposite. He was certainly gagging for something. "Maybe. Not that I'll be able to enjoy any of it, because I'll have left half the skin of my arse on the fucking saddle."

The sexy cowboy shook his head in amusement.

"You sure this *Cass* can be trusted?" Stef eyeballed the man in question, well aware he could hear everything Stef said.

Cass smirked, and it looked good—too bloody good. "Standing right here," he pointed out.

"Was that him?" Tanner asked in disbelief. "Please tell me you're not having this conversation where he can hear you."

"Every damn word, and you still haven't answered me. I want him to know you'll sue his fine arse to hell and back if he tries to put me on anything that even remotely looks at me sideways."

That earned him a rumbling belly laugh from Cass, who then spun on his heel and waved Stef to the passenger seat. "Get in, Princess, or we'll be late. I won't let any harm come to you from the nasty-wasty horses. Nice to know you like my arse, by the way."

Cass made his way to the driver's door and got in, leaving Stef's jaw on the floor... again. *What the hell?*

Tanner choked back a laugh.

Stef narrowed his eyes and lowered his voice. "Is this dude gay? Did you guys fucking set me up? If you think for one minute—"

"We're not setting you up. And I have no idea if he's gay or not. What the hell does it matter, anyway? Hang on—"

Stef could hear Ethan chattering in the background before Tanner came back on.

"Ethan says he isn't gay. He was even married for a while, to a woman—"

Stef scowled. "*Pfft*. Like that means anything."

"Just go on the damn tour for heaven's sake, will you? Make my boyfriend happy. Make *me* happy. Have some fucking fun if it fucking kills you. Fill your fanboy bucket with all things *LOTR* and then come home. I promise you won't have to see another damn horse for the rest of your stay."

"Says the man who promised me he hadn't set me up and then volunteered me up on stage to that hypnotist two years ago, in full violation of our specified no-humiliation bro code. I still can't look at a doughnut without popping a boner. Completely ruined one of my all-time favourite foods."

Tanner chuckled. "It was your birthday. And you gotta admit, it was fucking hilarious."

"It was fucking mortifying."

The van backed out, putting the driver's window right alongside Stef. Cass rolled the window down. He was wearing his aviators and a shit-eating grin. He proffered his hand through the window. "I'm Cass, by the way. Get in."

"Stefan or Stef, take your pick." Stef's hand was briefly enveloped in the other man's warm, dry... huge clasp. He grinned. "Big hands, big..."

"Gloves," Cass answered and released Stef's hand.

The man had a sense of humour, at least.

"So"—Cass studied him with a gentler eye—"are you gonna trust me and get in, or am I gonna have to break it to Arwen that you stood her up?"

"Arwen?"

"Your horse."

"Are you kidding me?"

Cass arched a brow. "It's a theme, what can I say?"

Stef cranked his own brows lower into his this-guy's-clearly-a-fucking-weirdo territory. "You know I should pull out on the basis of that horrifying tourist-trap decision alone, and yet somehow I'm oddly charmed and terrified in equal measure."

He relayed the information down the phone. "I'm riding a horse called Arwen, Tanner. Did you fucking hear that? That must qualify as cruelty under the SPCA rules, right?"

Cass bit back a smile. "Is there a problem with the name?"

Stef locked on to those sea-green eyes and couldn't hold back a grin. God, the man was gorgeous. "Nope. But she'll be the first and only woman I'll ever ride." He cocked his head. "Just saying."

Tanner spluttered through the phone. "Stef! You did not just say that."

Cass barked out a laugh. "I'll be sure to warn her. Would you rather I gave you Gimli?"

It was Tanner's turn to laugh.

Fucker. "Ugh, all that hair." Stef shuddered.

"Thought as much." Cass ran his eye over Stef, who felt the sudden urge to straighten his jacket and tidy his hair. "By the look of you, I'd say you've spent one or a hundred hours in Auckland's day spas getting all shiny and shit, right?" He nodded to the passenger seat. "Now hang up and get in, Romeo. I have two more to pick up."

Stef opened his arms and looked down at his skinny black jeans, red Converse with rainbow laces, cropped black leather jacket, and Katy Perry T-shirt. "What's wrong with how I look?"

Cass eyed him up and down before locking gazes, and Stef could've sworn the air between them crackled. *Straight, huh?*

But Cass's gaze slid away. "You look... fine. I just hope you brought something else to ride in."

Stef waved his hand dismissively. "Hey. Don't let this hideously on-trend guyliner fool you. Beneath these designer clothes and mort-gage-worthy hair products lurks the soul of a true adventurer."

Cass rolled those delicious green-as-fucking-gables eyes.

"But if you're asking if I'm particular, then hell yeah, and I make no apologies for it."

"Didn't ask you to."

"But I'm no fanatic. I just think if everyone put in a bit more effort, the world would be a much more scenic place, right? Take you, for example." He gave Cass an approving once-over. "I never imagined I'd have a soft spot for cowboys. But you, good sir, have changed my mind with one tap of those sexy boots."

"Goddammit, Stef. Stop flirting." Tanner hissed through the phone. "You'll embarrass the poor guy."

Stef tilted his head and studied Cass for a second. "Oh, I think Cass can handle a bit of flirting, right, Cass?"

Cass said nothing.

"I'm gonna take that as a yes." Stef winked at the man. "And I do indeed have my rough clothes packed. I'm not ridiculous. Well, mostly not." Stef patted his blue backpack with its "Smile If You're Gay" logo.

Cass snorted. "Good to know. Now, get in."

"You heard the man. I'll call when I get back, *if* I get back." He raised a brow at Cass. "I assume there's no cell service where we're going?"

Cass shook his head.

"Figured. God, I must be out of my mind." He turned his attention back to Tanner, who sounded like he was about to lose his shit completely. "And I'll hold *your* boyfriend to blame if good old Cass here turns out to be a serial killer. Check his stuff for my TAG Heuer. No psychopath is gonna walk past that trophy opportunity, right?"

Cass threw open the passenger door for Stef. "I said, get in. And TAG Heuer can suck eggs. Give me a Hublot every time."

Stef's eyes widened. "Holy crap, Tanner, did you hear that? A Hublot? The guy's a philistine. I'm doomed."

"Yeah, yeah, we love you too. Now go and try and have a good time."

Stef pocketed his phone and got in the van. He belted up and then eyed Cass with a critical gaze. "A Hublot? Really?" He dug in his bag for his sunglasses. "Man, you're gonna regret owning up to that. I have two days to enlighten your arse."

Cass grinned and threw the van into gear. "Are we still talking about watches?"

Stef's gaze jerked sideways, but Cass had his glued to the road. *Hmm.* Stef wasn't going near that one with a barge pole. He thumped his hand twice on the dash and pointed forward. "Wagon ho, Cowboy. I thought you were in a hurry."

Cass rolled his eyes skyward and pulled out into the early morning traffic. "I'm gonna regret this, aren't I?"

Stef flashed him a wicked grin. "There's every possibility."

Cass's second clients were two late twenty-something brothers who were celebrating their construction partnership landing a lucrative apartment deal in town. They looked about as mismatched as a pair of brothers could be, not that it was any of Cass's business. But they were both skilled riders, which meant Cass would have plenty of time to coach their less-than-accomplished companion. The tour normally took six people, but Cass had kept it to four for this run—three now—for the very reason of Stef's beginner status. It would give Cass time with the newbie. He cast a sly eye at the handsome man and wondered if that had been such a good idea after all.

Ninety minutes after the pick-up he pulled into the kilometre-long driveway of Martin's Stables and made his way up through an honour guard of yellowing cedars to the 150-year-old homestead he shared with his father. The sprawling weatherboard house with its eighteen-bay stable block off to one side could have done with another lick of green paint on the windows and doors and a refresh to its red corrugated-iron roof, but they'd managed to get the cream walls finished over summer. The rest would have to wait for spring.

Extending and upgrading the stables had been more important, with two large movie shoots in the works for the upcoming winter.

Cass had already been approached to house some of the horses and assorted livestock for one of them, and the other was still under negotiation. Film industry contracts were lucrative when he could get them—the difference between just surviving the season and making enough to invest in upkeep and extension of the property, in a climate that could rip the hope from you in the space of few winter storms.

High-country sheep farming wasn't just tough, it was brutal. And although Cass's father didn't rely on that income any more, the farm having been reduced to hobby size—if several thousand acres could be thought of as hobby size—bad weather still led to an interrupted tourist season and impacted cash flow for both of them. Cass's accounting business was a godsend when that happened.

All in all he made a good living, if not a lavish one, and it meant his dad got to stay on the property his father had worked before him. Farming wasn't a lifestyle Cass wanted for himself—he was a horseman pure and simple, minus the sheep, thank you very much. But he liked that he could support his dad, and they rubbed along well enough. God knew what would happen down the road when his dad got too old or wanted to sell. Cass just hoped he'd have enough money tucked away by then to buy him out and keep the land to run his horses. He didn't want to even consider the alternative.

Most businesses and farms around Glenorchy were like theirs and benefitted from the film companies' hard-on for the beautiful valley in some way—from the local café to landowners, accommodation options, fuel services, everything. And film companies seemed to love the down-home nature of the community where people weren't fazed by the likes of a few Hollywood stars wandering their farms and streets. They had to wait in line for a coffee the same as the rest.

Cass pulled up in front of the old house and smiled as the chatter between his clients fell blissfully quiet in the face of what Cass thought was arguably one of the best views in the district. The silence in the van spun out, and he smiled. No one arrived at Martin's

Stables and *wasn't* impressed with the view—even Stef took a long few beats to simply stare and appreciate the outlook through his passenger window.

And Cass took advantage of those same few beats to appreciate *him. Damn.* Stef Hamilton was striking—sleek shoulder-length hair that shone as it if belonged in a damn shampoo ad; wide hazel eyes that glittered with a Pandora's box of mischief; a tight, fit body with just enough muscle to smooth out the angles; fine features; a sharp jawline; and a pair of drive-you-wild dimples put there as a direct temptation from the gods. All wrapped up in a packet of flay-you-alive sass and vinegar that was pretty much Cass's catnip, as it turned out—which was news to Cass. He'd always had a soft spot for similar types to himself: big, lean, earthy guys—sass not included. Go figure.

Mind you, Stef swung an attitude that punched well above his weight, so there was that. He was also a bit of an enigma—something Cass had cottoned on to almost immediately. Stef played the part of the unapologetic city boy with style and finesse and an acid tongue to boot.

But for some reason, Cass was convinced that's exactly what it was: an act, a role Stef stepped into and wore like a second skin. The way he moved with choreographed disdain written into every step as if daring others to respond. As if he'd been there for the half-time team huddle and taken the coach's words to heart: the best defence is a good offence. And if Cass was reading it right, he suspected few people who knew Stef would even guess at the lie. He was good, Cass gave him that. It was hard to see the joins. But if you looked close enough, they were there.

Cass had a knack with horses and could read one a mile away. And since the first moment he'd seen Stef standing in the car park, with attitude to burn and a judging eye for anyone who came within spitting distance, Cass's instincts had screamed that this particular horse had a whole lot of trust issues simmering just beneath all that prickle and sass. It set him to wondering about things he had no right to. Stef was in Cass's care for two days only. Cass needed to remember that.

The trouble was, Stef rattled something tantalisingly familiar in Cass's chest—something he hadn't shaken the dust off in quite a while, and he didn't know quite what to make of that. Hell, he'd all but told Stef he wasn't straight, and where the hell had that come from? His own father didn't yet know, but that was a whole other bag of snakes. Not an intentional secret as such, just grief he could do without. No one in his tiny, gossip-ridden corner of paradise had any idea. Glenorchy was just too damn small and its farming community too tight to have ever made that notion comfortable. Besides, he'd gone and married his teenage sweetheart, so it seemed like a lot of unnecessary bother after that.

Then he'd damn near gone and spat it out like it was as natural as could be, to a man he didn't know from a bar of soap. And Stef hadn't missed it, of that Cass was sure. At least he'd had the grace not to push, and Cass could leave it to rot as an unanswered question between them, where it belonged.

Only two days and Stef would be gone. Perfect. Until then, Cass just had to keep a lock on his fucking tongue, and dick, and every other damn shred of man-loving equipment he possessed. *Yeah, good luck with that, bozo.* It wasn't like he didn't scratch that itch if it needed it, because he did, a few times a year at least. But that was lust, or need, or just plain jizz-turning-to-fucking-concrete desperation.

This reckless, warm, want-to-get-to-know-you-and-not-just-fuck-you attraction shit? *Hell.* He hadn't been attracted to a guy, or girl, like that in a long, long time. Fucking years, if he was honest. Yet for some reason Stef pushed all those buttons—buttons Cass thought he'd excised from his soul for the sake of his sanity. And yet now? Jesus, he really shouldn't be allowed out. *Look at the guy. What part of learning those soul-destroying, painful lessons years ago did you not understand?*

"Come on." He waved the three men out of the van and over to where the edge of the lawn sloped away. "You can get good photos from here."

Nestled into the foothills of the Southern Alps, their farm sat high above the entrance to Paradise Valley, commanding a staggering view over the confluence of the Dart and Rees Rivers and the wide delta complex they formed before spilling into Lake Wakatipu. There was nothing flash about the homestead. It was clean and tidy and worked, for the most part, although it needed an injection of cash if it was going to last into the future: a new kitchen, bathroom, a few walls opened up to the views and the light. Cass could see it all in his head, just not in his bank account. Uncertainty about his dad and the future of the property meant overinvestment was a risk, so he stuck with the needs of the business.

Leaving his clients to their ogling and camera snapping, Cass glanced over to the old couch on the covered front porch, and his mouth tugged up in a smile. Man, he loved that porch. Most evenings found him there, sucking on a beer regardless of the weather, staring across the valley, not even knowing what he was looking at half the time. Just the sheer wonder of it, all of it. The river, the basin, the mountains, the sky, the... silence. Born and raised in the valley, he'd lived there thirty-six years—bar a brief university stint in Wellington. The land filled Cass in a way he'd never understood until he left it behind, and he wasn't moving again any time soon. Nope. He had no intention of making the same mistake twice. He just needed to remember that.

"Hey." Stef appeared alongside, and slid his phone back in his pocket. "I have to say I wasn't expecting this. Point to you, Mr Martin."

Cass laughed. "The big-city boy is impressed? I'll count that as a win."

"I never said I didn't love a great photo opportunity," Stef protested. "I just prefer not to view it from the top of a living, breathing, walking mountain of muscle... with teeth. Did I mention teeth?"

"Several times. You get bit as a kid?"

Stef's expression closed, and he turned back to the river. "Nope. I just find it... unnerving. I'm a city boy, born and bred."

"You do realise this is a *horse* trek, right?" Andrew griped from behind his brother's shoulder. "You *are* gonna be riding, in case you missed that part." He gave a disgusted shake of his head.

Tomas elbowed his older brother sharply. "Shut up."

Andrew returned a scowl with a nasty edge to it. He was a towering, beefy—though not unattractive—sandy-haired man who looked like he'd been born with a hammer in his hand and a stick up his butt. And there was a perpetually mean sharpness to his expression, as if the world owed him a living and was behind on the payments.

Unlike his friendly brother, Andrew had taken one look at Stef and his "Smile If You're Gay" bag and Cass swore he heard the clank of gears as that nasty upper lip notched up in a distinct sneer. Stef hadn't seen it, though he was unlikely to have missed the transparent way Andrew did everything in his power to avoid shaking Stef's hand, or touching him at all for that matter.

In the end, Cass had stepped in with a formal introduction and forced the issue. *Fuck him.* Put on the spot, Andrew had caved with the briefest handshake known to humanity and promptly turned his back.

Arsehole. Just what Cass needed. The overnight tour was rapidly headed down the barrel of being one of *those*: a guy he was attracted to and had to stay the hell away from and the risk of outing himself over the same, while simultaneously having a homophobic arsehole to account for. Awesome.

"The ad said the tour accepts all levels of ability." Tomas gave Stef a warm smile. "I'm sure you'll be fine. We'll all look after you."

Cass's eyebrows nudged together in a small frown at the *we* part of that sentence. From the minute they'd met, Tomas and Stef had engaged in endless meandering chatter about Auckland, music, clubs, and every other fucking thing in a way that had started to grate on Cass's nerves because... well, because it wasn't fucking Cass that Stef was talking to, was it? Ridiculous didn't even begin to cover it.

But Tomas was willowy and more handsome than his brother, two factors that hadn't escaped Cass's attention. Nor Stef's it seemed —judging from the appreciation Cass had witnessed when they'd been introduced. Dark hair fell over dancing blue eyes in glorious ringlets, which clearly drove Tomas to distraction as he was forever tugging on them, and his mouth seemed perpetually locked in a wide grin... unless he was looking at his brother. Then the grin shuttered, and he seemed to collapse in on himself, growing smaller in the space he occupied, though it didn't stop him backchatting the man.

That was families for you.

Stef shrugged off Andrew's dig with a grin that turned slightly wicked. "The *horse* part of the tour wasn't exactly my idea. Something with a little more piston power between my legs would have been more my style. But my best friend's *boyfriend*"—he paused for effect and held Andrew's eye—"organised the whole thing as a gift because yeah, I might be a bit of a Tolkien fan. But Tanner had to pull out at the last minute, so... here I am. And I have actually ridden before."

That was news to Cass.

Andrew snorted in disbelief, and Tomas arched a brow. "Really?"

Stef fished for his phone once again, and Cass could see he was biting back a smile.

"Well, kind of, almost." Stef held the phone up between them. "Do you mind?"

Cass shrugged, feeling his cheeks heat. "Um, yeah, go ahead."

Stef beamed, snapped the shot, and repocketed the phone before continuing his explanation. "I dated this show jumper a few years ago"—he winked to Cass before turning back to face the others—"and he um, led me around on his *mount*... once or twice. It was an... exhilarating experience." He turned a brilliant smile on Andrew, who instantly flamed, spluttered, and nearly swallowed his tongue.

Cass almost wet himself holding back a laugh.

Tomas didn't even try, much to his brother's chagrin.

"Shut it." Andrew shoved Tomas none too gently.

Tomas shoved him right back. "For fuck's sake, lighten up." He spread his hands dramatically. "Brothers, right?"

Cass shrugged. "Wouldn't know." His rear-view mirror had been full of the young man's hands constantly on the move as he chatted with Stef, who'd spent most of the drive half turned in his seat to face Tomas. And why the hell that bothered Cass so much was a question he was steering well clear of.

"You should offer him a refund," Andrew suggested snidely. "He's clearly pissing himself about the whole thing."

Fuck. Cass was running at a loss on this one to start with, but the man had a point. Stef *was* nervous, that much was clear. He gave a reluctant nod and locked eyes with Stef. "Ethan wouldn't want you to go just for his sake," he said. "I can get Dee to take you back into town."

Stef frowned and shot a nervous glance to the stables, where a half-dozen horses looked on with benign curiosity. One of those green fingernails found its way between his teeth, and he chewed absently on it while his gaze panned to take in the view once again, dragging slowly over Andrew Murchison in the process before completing the circle to land back on Cass.

His finger left his mouth, and Cass saw the second his shoulders steeled in defiance.

"Hell no." He flashed those fucking dimples Andrew's way. "I wouldn't miss this for the world. It's got fun written all over it."

Cass seriously doubted Stef felt that at all, but props to him for carrying it off not too badly.

"And I'm looking forward to you boys giving me tips on how to improve my, um... riding skills, so don't hold back." He raised an insolent eyebrow at Andrew, who glared sullenly in return.

Cheeky bastard. By the look on Andrew's face, the gauntlet had been laid down. At this rate Cass would be mainlining caffeine by the time they returned, trying to keep both men in their corners.

Done with Andrew, Stef turned that discerning gaze to Cass. "Those two stops you made on the way here—the view out to Isengard from Glenorchy, and the site of Faramir's battle with the oliphants at Ten Mile Delta—"

"Twelve Mile Delta."

"*Twelve* Mile Delta," Stef corrected himself. "They were magic. If those and this view are anything to go by, I definitely want to see the rest. Besides, I wouldn't give Tanner... or others"—he paused pointedly—"the satisfaction. He'd give me hell for the next ten years, and don't tell him, but I'm trying to make a good impression on the new man in his life. It's kind of a big thing, and he deserves to be happy. So, as long as you don't mind sticking close to my unseasoned arse, yeah, let's do this."

Did I mind? Like hell. And okay, trying to impress the friend's boyfriend was hella cute. So the guy was nice as well as hot. Just fucking dandy.

CHAPTER TWO

WHILE THE SMALL GROUP FINISHED THEIR ELEVEN A.M. ploughman's lunch courtesy of Dee—Cass's local supplier—and then organised their overnight gear into saddlebags, and Stef got changed —who knew how long that was gonna take—Cass tended to the horses. He had them tied in an organised line so he could systematically work his way through the prep and didn't forget anything. Although experienced riders got to look after their own mounts during the tour, Cass liked to get them ready at the start just to be sure all the equipment was on board, safe, and strapped well. The horses knew the drill, resting in the shade with their heads down, feet stamping and tails flicking at the clouds of irritating flies that always hung around stables.

Gimli carried most of the gear, and if the brothers turned out to be as skilled as they claimed, Cass would allocate the job of leading the pack horse to them, initially at least. That way he could focus on Stef... as if he needed a reason. *Ugh.*

Cass was halfway through the saddling when the screen door slammed open and Dee emerged with an armful of containers. She crossed the browned-off back lawn to the back door of the canopy on her electric blue Ford Ranger, kicking up dust with every step. Cass had never seen it this dry in the valley. The bright side? The olive trees he'd planted the previous year were doing well, and he hadn't seen a mosquito or sandfly in weeks. Still, he'd packed a fuck-ton of repellent just in case.

"They're nearly done in there." She jerked her head back towards the house. "I'm gonna head on up to the river crossing and get those stores for your dinner and breakfast over on the flying fox," she said, loading the containers into the truck. "And you must need some hay up at the hut soon. Your dad and I can get that done when he's back, if it suits, before the rains hit and the quads can't get up the river track—we'll get it supplied to last the winter. Tomorrow's late lunch provisions are in your fridge. Texas chilli and noodles. They should love it."

"You're a star," Cass replied, hauling the girth tight on Arwen. The mare grunted and stamped her hoof in disapproval. "Suck it in, sweetheart." He patted her belly. She snorted loudly, and he got the buckle hauled up another two notches. "Good girl." He stroked the sleek warm run of her neck, then hung over the fence to watch Dee put the last of her gear in the truck.

"And Dad will enjoy the run up to the hut. He hasn't been for a while. Can you stock the canned goods while you're at it?" He glanced at the sky. "I hope this damn heat eases. The horses did it hard last time. The river's edge stop just doesn't have enough cover. I'll use the forest one instead and get them under some shade. If the boys want to cool off, they can hike the five minutes it takes to get to the swimming hole."

Which was something Cass *wouldn't* be doing if there was any chance in hell that Stef was gonna be waltzing around in swimming trunks. They'd all been told to pack them, and Cass hardly needed to see the man half-naked on top of everything else. He pushed off the fence and ducked under Arwen to finish tightening Gandalf's girth.

"I'll add canned goods to the list." Dee closed the Ranger's canopy and walked around to lean on the driver's door. "And walking to the river will only make the swim better, if the water's even deep enough."

"Yeah, it's as low as I've seen it in a long time," Cass called over Gandalf's withers. "We need some damn rain."

Dee studied the light puffs of clouds on the western ranges and frowned. "That's global warming for you. Never known it not to rain at least once a week around here in March. But apart from that electrical storm a couple of weeks back, we've had nothing. Still, they're forecasting some for tomorrow evening, so don't dilly-dally on the way home, sweetness. The ground's so damn hard any decent rain is gonna run right off it. Use the satphone if it looks dodgy on your way down."

"I will." He rubbed Gandalf's ears, and the horse batted him with his nose. "Usual drill if we get caught out. We'll use the supply track on the other side of the river and meet you at the road bridge. But if it's fine and we get time, I want to take them to that lookout on Cranberry Bluff. There's still some manuka flowering there with this long summer. Looks beautiful. And no-one with bee-sting allergies this time."

Dee laughed and brushed away a fly from in front of her face. "Yep, that was a doozy. At least he had his EpiPen with him. Not that he told anyone about the allergy beforehand." She wiped a smudge off her driver's door with a bit of spit and her finger. "By the way, Carol called last night to say your dad's sweating his socks off over at McKenzie's muster. Same time last year they got snowed on in the high grazing runs the first night—half froze to death. This year it's a damn sauna."

Cass laughed. His father hated the heat—bred for the mountains and snow with crampons for toes, he'd always told Cass growing up. "They doing okay?"

"Of course they are. You know that lot."

Cass had ridden in enough of the McKenzie annual musters to have more than a good idea of what that entailed. "Nothing but a bunch of old men and trouble."

She laughed and swung herself into the cab, switched on the engine, and popped the window down so she could lean through it. "That they are. Nine landowners and ten days, with nothing but a gang of dogs and a lot of bullshit to throw around as they bring down a mob of 30,000 merinos for the winter? Hell yeah, they're trouble. Still I'll be glad to see him home safe. Your dad's getting a bit old for all that. His hip will give him trouble for weeks."

"Don't let him hear you say that."

Dee's gaze narrowed. "Don't you say nothing."

"I promise. One day down, nine to go. He'll be home soon enough." Cass moved back to the first horse in line and began adjusting all the stirrup leathers to the approximate length for each rider. "You need to get a ring on that finger, Dee. You're way too soft on him. Then you can tie him to your damn bed and know exactly where he is."

He glanced over in time to see her smile fall and could've kicked himself. *Shit.*

"Yeah, well, you know how that goes."

He nodded. "I should've kept my mouth shut." Dee and his dad had been an item for over five years, but his old man was just dragging the chain. If he wasn't careful, he was going to lose her. She'd lost her first husband in a boating accident fifteen years before, owned the local café and supplied all their tour provisions, with a side order of keeping his dad's bed warm several times a week. They were great together, and Cass loved her to bits, but for some reason Sean Martin had it in his head that Dee didn't see him in a long-term marriage kind of way.

Anyone with half a brain could see that was a mile from the truth, but Sean was stubborn as a mule and twice as thick when it came to women, Cass's mother included. In fourteen years of marriage, Sean hadn't even taken her on holiday, and Liz was a townie through and through, unused to the rural life. When Cass was twelve, Liz had finally given up waiting for the romancing to begin and left for someone who was more interested in providing it.

Having said that, she'd stayed in his life, still lived only a couple of hours away, and was all up in Cass's business more than he liked, so he had little to complain about. But when he was twelve, well, that was another story. Back then he couldn't get past the why of it all... or the bone-crushing hurt when she said she was leaving. Not that he'd wanted to leave the farm, but fuck, she hadn't even asked.

"Forget about it." She cleared her throat and glanced back at the house. "But while we're on the subject of relationships, it must be time for you to pay a visit to your mates up north again—have some fun, be a bit rowdy, get laid maybe."

Cass nearly choked on his tongue. "Now I know you didn't just tell me to get laid, Mrs Wright."

Dee snorted. "I damn well did. You've been far too cranky for your own good, lately."

Cass shoved some horse treats in his saddle bag and buckled the strap. "I do just fine."

"Yeah, right. You spend too much time on your own, Cass. You've been back a long time now, and the only friend I've known you to knock around with is Graham from Hopkin's station. And he's about as much of a hermit as you. There's still some of your old school mates kicking around Queenstown, you know. You could get in touch."

Cass said nothing. Those were mates whose friendship Cass had no interest in rekindling. He wasn't that guy anymore. Not to mention all those *mates* had known Tricia as well, and Cass wasn't keen on any of his business getting back to his ex-wife. Graham was an Aussie import, a bit of a loner and a horseman just like Cass. They understood each other, and that was good enough for Cass. So what if they only saw each other every couple of months. Cass did a ton of socialising with all the clients that passed through his doors. It was more of a problem getting enough peace and quiet.

Dee grinned. "Okey dokey, this is me taking the not so subtle hint to drop the subject. So, on another note, I see you've got a virgin on this tour."

Cass fumbled the stirrup leather, and Arwen turned her curious horsey eye on him as if to ask what the hell he was doing.

Dee flashed him an amused look. "Stef. He's never ridden before, right? Whatever did you think I was referring to, Cassidy Martin?"

Cass scowled, damn sure he was flushing beetroot, and wondered not for the first time just how much Dee knew or had guessed about him. She was a shrewd, worldly woman who'd seen a lot of life pass through her café, not to mention a gossip network that rivalled the Kardashians'.

"He'll do fine. I have a feeling about him." He managed to get Arwen's stirrup leather sorted to his satisfaction and swept his hand over the mare's sleek chestnut flank. She turned her head and nickered. He grabbed a stiff bristled brush and ran it through her mane till it fell like satin on her neck.

"And what exactly *is* this feeling you have about me, country boy?"

Fuck. Cass's gaze jerked to the back porch, where Stef was leaning against the veranda upright wearing a cheeky smile. He'd changed, and Cass couldn't keep from returning the smile as he took in the fresh outfit.

With his hair tied back off his face in a long glossy tail, decent short-heeled boots for riding, and a pair of faded, loose denims hanging from those tempting, lean hips, Stef almost looked like he belonged in the country. Almost. Until you registered the green fingernails and the fitted, colourful T-shirt with "Brokeback Since Way Back" in large lettering across the chest.

Holy Mother of God. Cass snorted and shook his head.

Stef spotted Dee and sent her a wave. "I hate to burst your bubble, sugar, but the last time the word virgin was legitimately applied to me, I had acne on my chin and had just received a *D* on my English assignment on great English poets. Apparently, Rodney P didn't count."

Cass chuckled and moved along to his tall grey mount, Gandalf, who nuzzled against his side with undisguised affection. "Wow, shocker."

Stef glared in mock affront. "Hey, you're talking about the godfather of British hip-hop. The man knows how to throw down a rhyme, so show some respect."

Dee threw the truck in gear. "On that note, I'm off. Have fun." The Ranger looped past the stables and headed down the drive, followed by a cloud of dust.

Stef wandered to where Cass was finishing tightening the straps on Gandalf's bridle. He stopped well short of the fence and watched him work.

"You finished lunch quick," Cass commented.

Stef shrugged, slipped his hands in his pockets, and rocked on his feet, looking like some twelve-year-old caught out in a lie. "Don't tell Dee, but to be honest I only picked at some cheese. Ethan cooked pancakes for breakfast, and I wouldn't want to lose my girlish figure." Stef patted his very flat stomach.

Cass's mouth ran dry.

"The other two look like they've settled in for the long haul. I doubt there'll be a potato chip or crust left by the time they're done scoffing. You breed them big down here. Although I'd need a more detailed examination to verify the accuracy of that assumption, of course."

Cass rolled his eyes at the less-than-subtle innuendo. "You let me know how you get on with that, won't you?"

"Mmm. You still haven't answered my question, by the way... this *feeling* you supposedly have about me." Stef batted his lashes and smiled charmingly.

He looked ridiculous, and Cass had to laugh. "Jesus Christ, I hope that works better for you in Auckland's bars than it does down here, Romeo."

Stef narrowed his gaze. "I've had no complaints."

Oh, Cass just bet he didn't. If there was one thing Stefan Hamilton wasn't lacking, it was sex appeal. The guy could melt your briefs straight off your hips at twenty feet without even breaking a sweat, and Cass doubted a night spent with him would be easily forgotten.

"Be that as it may," he said with a grin. "I only meant that I think you'll do better riding than you expect to. I have a sense about these things." He stood back and ran his eye over Stef, delighted to see the other man look slightly uncomfortable for a change. "You look... balanced when you move, like your feet know where they're going before your head even thinks about it, and believe me, that's not as common as you'd think."

Stef's smile went flat, and there it was, another tantalising glimpse of the man behind the veneer.

"Yeah, well, gotta love an optimist," he said. "A smart man wouldn't take that bet. But, um, thanks anyway. I'm not your outdoorsy type, in case you hadn't guessed. And if my feet really knew what was best for them, they'd have hightailed me outta here when you made the offer, in case you missed the part where my agreeing to keep going was mostly a big fuck you to Mr Arsehole in there." He jerked his thumb in the direction of the house. "So I apologise in advance for all the extra effort I'm gonna cause you. I hate to say it, but the dickhead was probably right." He shrugged apologetically.

Cass's brows notched together. "I bet you're a good dancer, right?"

Stef nodded warily. "I've been told, I guess."

Oh, Lordy. And there was a whole other rabbit warren of imagery to fall into: grinding, holding, moving up against each other. *Goddammit.* Cass pursed his lips. "Exactly. So, as I said, I think you'll be surprised."

Stef blinked slowly, then looked away. "Well, I guess we'll find out, won't we? So, this all belong to your family?" His gaze swept the yard and the towering ranges behind the farmhouse.

Never let it be said Cass couldn't take a hint. He did his own sweep of the scenery. "Used to, pretty much. Or at least, sixty thousand acres of it did, on my dad's side. Mum didn't push for her share when they split, which was good of her. She had her own business. Dad sold thirty thousand back to the government about ten years ago to add to their conservation plot. High-country sheep farming is a tough life, and since I was never interested in the farming side as such, Dad needed to make it manageable for himself, especially as I wasn't living here for a few years."

Cass grabbed a brush and gave the gelding's mane some much needed attention. It wasn't one of Gandalf's favourite things in the world, and he stomped his feet to show his displeasure.

Cass talked as he brushed. "The conservation lark was a good option, but he also sold another twenty thousand to a neighbour who'd been asking him for years. That left him with ten thousand to play with, on which he runs a small, high-quality merino flock aimed at the top fleece dollar. But it's only really pocket money. The bulk of our income is from the tourist trade and the film contracts, which we split. I lease out our grazing and stables if they're needed by the film companies and do some on-site animal management as well. With the tours, I do the actual tour guide thing, though Dad can if he's needed, but he mostly sees to keeping the hut stocked and the equipment clean. I help him with the farm if he needs it, bring stock down from the high country and stuff like that."

"So, you're still a farmer, then—a cowboy, even?"

Cass grinned and lifted Gandalf's shaggy front hooves one at a time to pick the insides clean. "Not sure my dad would agree with you. I'm actually a chartered accountant."

Stef sucked in a breath. "You're kidding me. Now that, I would never have guessed. You kind of look the full cowboy package." His gaze slid over Cass like warm butter.

"Is that a nice way of saying I'm a bit too country for a university degree?" Cass eyed him steadily. "You need more than a few brains to farm this land, you know. I'm running three businesses. It helps."

Stef's mouth fell open. "Whoa. No. Shit. Sorry. I didn't mean that at all. It's just that you seem to... *fit* here, I guess. Like it's... I don't know, a part of you. I can't imagine you in a big city at university."

Out of the mouths of babes. Cass stretched his back and sighed. "You're right. I do fit here, although some days I feel like a total fraud. But university wasn't so bad. I had a good time."

Stef gave a wry smile. "I'm pretty sure everyone feels like a fraud at some point, no matter what they do."

"I guess that's true." Cass moved down the line of horses, negotiating around Eowyn's generous butt and trailing his hand over Gimli's warm flank. The pack horse was well strapped and ready to load. Cass didn't normally take an extra horse, but he had some replacement equipment for the hut. It meant no one would have to carry their own gear this trip, which was an added bonus. He kicked the dirt from his boots and leaned on the fence.

Stef joined Cass on the other side of the fence and sent him a shining look. "Well, you don't look like any accountant I've seen."

Cass shrugged. "Maybe not, but the number crunching keeps my accounts afloat and me independent. I love the farm, but farming's not my life, not in the way it's my dad's. All *I* really need is a house and some stables."

He caught sight of Stef's T-shirt once again and cracked up laughing. "And what the hell are you wearing, by the way?"

Stef brushed imaginary dust off the front of the T-shirt and managed to look suitably offended. "I bought a few for the trip as a kind of joke. They were supposed to embarrass the hell out of Tanner, and quite possibly you. Now? Well, if they earn me a smile like the one you just gave, it'll still be money well spent." He waggled his eyebrows.

"Has Andrew seen it yet?"

Stef snorted. "What do you think?"

Cass didn't even need to think about it. "I think you took the first opportunity you could to shove it in his face."

Stef laughed. "And you'd be right. It was fucking glorious. He took one look and damn near choked on one of Dee's epic pickled cucumbers. I told him he needed to be careful and maybe practice a bit before he attempted an uncut one—"

Cass snorted.

"I, um... offered to give him a lesson."

Oh God. Cass would've paid good money to see that.

"Do you get many like him?" Stef asked, a slight frown dipping between his eyes.

"No, thank God. If he's a bother, just let me know."

Stef shrugged. "I can handle him."

Cass caught Stef's eyes and grinned. "Now that's a bet I'd definitely take." He dropped his gaze as Gimli shoved his nose through the railings to reach for Stef's pockets.

"Whoa." Stef jumped back. "Is he trying to bite me?"

"No. I suspect he's after a treat. What've you got in there?"

Stef scowled at the horse. "See what you've done?" He delved into his pocket and pulled out a roll of peppermints. "Guilty as charged."

Cass huffed. "No wonder. Horses love peppermints."

"Really?" Stef studied Gimli with interest. "Huh. Seems kind of a low bar to set on the treat ladder. Should I, um, offer her... or him... one?"

Gimli nodded his head shamelessly, and Stef laughed. "Him, and maybe later. He's only allowed a couple of sugar treats a day, and it's not good to reward pushy behaviour."

Stef's green eyes danced. "Oh, I don't know. I've found pushy behaviour to be extremely rewarding at times." He let his gaze linger on Cass for a few seconds before his cell buzzed with a call. He turned away to take it, but not before flashing those dimples at Cass one more time.

And God help him, but Cass felt the tug down to the stitching in his jeans. He sucked in a deep breath and mentally slapped himself.

"Hey, you."

Stef's voice held an affection and warmth of familiarity Cass hadn't heard from him. The boyfriend, maybe? *Ugh.* Pathetic, much?

He busied himself and tried not to make it too obvious, but it wasn't his fault Stef hadn't moved out of hearing range. Maybe Stef *wanted* Cass to hear. Dear God, could he be any more narcissistic?

"Yeah, I'm here now. Did Tanner call you?" There was a pause as Stef listened to the answer. "Mmm, I wish you were here too. It would be a lot more fun with two of us..." He turned and sent Cass an apologetic smile. "But I'll take lots of photos, okay? And we can talk about it when I get home."

Cass frowned. It was an odd way to talk to a boyfriend, if that's who it was. His chest lightened at the thought and he chided himself. He shouldn't feel relieved. A boyfriend in play would at least cut off the oxygen to this ridiculous little crush he was feeling.

"I'll make sure to tell him." Stef's gaze held steady on Cass, who'd given up pretending he couldn't hear and was just waiting by the fence. "No, he said he's gonna look after me." Another pause. "Yes, I trust him." He rolled his eyes at Cass.

"Really? You don't need to—. Argh, whatever, I'll put you on." He held his phone out to Cass. "He wants to talk to you."

Huh? Cass's eyes popped. "Me?"

Stef sighed dramatically. "Just do it. I'll never hear the end otherwise. You've no idea how persistent he can be."

"Who?" Cass opened his hands, at a complete loss.

"My big brother, Benny."

His big... what the hell? Cass stared at Stef. "Your brother?" he mouthed silently.

Stef shrugged and waggled the phone. "Just take it."

Ugh. Cass took the phone and held it to his ear like it might bite. "Hello?"

"*Hi. Are you Cassidy? Tanner said your name was Cassidy.*"

Cass took a minute to process the slightly odd comment, aware of Stef watching him closely. The voice on the other end certainly sounded old enough to be Stef's brother, but there was a... young quality about it. "Yes," he answered. "But most people call me Cass."

"*Well, I like Cassidy. Cass sounds like a girl's name.*"

Cass bit back a smile.

"You're not a girl, are you?"

"No, I'm not a girl." He glanced over at Stef and winked. Stef's shoulders relaxed, and Cass couldn't help but feel he'd passed some kind of test.

"That's good, because Stef doesn't like girls. Not like that, I mean."

Cass snorted. "So you're saying Stef likes *boys,* then?" He eyed Stef pointedly, and the man's eyeballs nearly popped out of his head.

"Give that here." Stef reached for the phone, but Cass ducked out of reach.

"Yes, he does, but Mum says he makes horrible choices. Dad says his boyfriend radar sucks big hairy balls—"

"Big hairy balls, huh? That's too bad," Cass repeated in complete seriousness, his eyes dancing Stef's way. God, he was gonna give the man hell for the next two days.

Stef lunged and got his hand on the phone, but Cass white-knuckled it and held on, tipping it slightly so they could both hear. Stef leaned in, putting their ears dangerously close together, and Cass caught a whiff of coconut body wash that somehow bypassed his brain and short-circuited all the way to his dick.

"Benny, shut up. What the hell are you telling him?" Stef flushed a shade of crimson rarely seen in the valley.

"I'm making sure he'll look after you. He needs to know stuff."

"Not *that* stuff."

"Why not? You're not in the wardrobe—"

"Closet, dude, I'm not in the *closet.*" Stef turned a pained look Cass's way and mouthed the word "Sorry."

Cass merely grinned. The whole thing was so fucking sweet, he could feel the cavities popping in his teeth.

"That's what I said. Anyway, Cassidy might be able to find you someone down there. Mum says there aren't a lot left in Auckland you haven't—"

"Stop," Stef interrupted, much to Cass's disappointment. "Don't say it. I know what Mum says, okay?"

Cass was nearly pissing himself trying not to laugh, and Stef fired him a glare with enough venom to strip the skin clean off his back. Cass smiled back sweetly, which didn't win him any favours. He could live with it.

"*Are you angry with me?*" Benny's voice wobbled.

And Stef nearly crumpled against Cass. "No, tiger. Never. How could I be angry with you? You're the best big brother ever."

"*Really?*"

"Really."

"*Okay, then. Is Cassidy there?*"

Cass turned his head. "Yes, Benny, I'm here."

"*Tanner said I could trust you.*"

"I, um, hope so. Yes, you can."

"*Did you know there was a man called Butch Cassidy? He was a cowboy too. But that was a long time ago. He's dead. Dad says we don't have cowboys in New Zealand, but he must be wrong, because you're a cowboy, right?*"

Cass's heart squeezed.

Stef caught his eye and nodded.

Cass got the message. "Yes, I guess I am, kind of?"

A bubble of excitement sparked through the line. "*See, I knew it. I can't wait to tell him. But you'll take care of Stef for me, won't you, Cassidy? He's scared of horses, silly billy. But he's brave, and he'll do everything you say.*"

Cass fired an amused glance at Stef, who mouthed, "Don't even," before Cass could run with it.

"I promise I'll take care of him, Benny. And it's good to know he'll do what I say— Ow!" He rubbed the spot where Stef had just knuckled him.

"*Okay. Thank you, Cassidy. Bye.*"

And, oh God, Cass wasn't at all sure he wasn't going to tear up. "Bye, Benny." He handed the phone back to Stef, who wandered well out of eavesdropping range this time. Whatever they talked about, Stef returned to the corral a few minutes later misty-eyed.

"Thanks for that," he said quietly, leaning on the railing.

"You kind of dropped me in it." Cass walked over from where he'd been filling the troughs.

"Yeah, I know, but I thought you'd do okay winging it," Stef shot back, unrepentant. "Benny doesn't need an *introduction*. He's a person and my brother."

Shit. Totally deserved. "I'm sorry. That was pretty ignorant of me, right?"

Stef returned a faint smile. "A little, but you're forgiven. Benny's the best. He's a year older than me, and yes, he has Down's syndrome. My mum was a huge Abba fan. My younger sister's called Frida."

"Shouldn't that have made you Bjorn?"

Stef's mouth quirked up. "Yeah, well, I lucked out there. Dad put his foot down. I mean, think about it. Gay, fem, and named Bjorn? Holy fuck, that would've turned a difficult adolescence into a veritable shitshow. I have much to be thankful for."

Though on opposite sides of the fence, they'd somehow managed to creep towards each other till their hands were almost touching, and Cass slid his into his pockets and took a step back.

Stef gave a wry smile and once again disarmed all Cass's defences without even trying.

"Well, Benny clearly thinks the world of you," Cass murmured. "You two seem to have something special."

Stef's face lit up. "He does, and we do. But he's also way too protective of me, which isn't always so easy to live with. Case in point. But he has a bullshit radar like you wouldn't believe. What Benny said about my boyfriends? He was right. He and Dad hated them all, and I should've listened. Could've saved myself a lot of heartache. Not to mention Benny has a fuck-ton more common sense than I do, as you heard."

"He lives at home?"

Stef shook his head. "Nah. He lives in a group home and has a job at a café not far from there. He's kind of great, and he, um, seems to like you."

As opposed to how Benny felt about Stef's boyfriends. The implication hung between them, but Cass wasn't about to touch it with a ten-foot pole, and thankfully Stef let it go as well.

Cass cleared his throat and began gathering the covers and grooming equipment to return to the barn. "So, um, I think we're ready. How about you get the others?"

"Oh, right." Stef shot a glance to the house, then back to the horses, looking less than enamoured with the idea.

Cass reached out a hand without thinking and gave Stef's forearm a squeeze. "Hey, you'll be fine. I'll be right alongside."

They locked gazes for a few seconds, then Stef nodded and sighed. "Okay."

He headed back to the house, and Cass could finally breathe again. It wasn't getting any easier to ignore the strong attraction he felt toward the feisty man, and the thundering drums of trouble were fast approaching. Four hours old and his ridiculous crush was already sliding sideways into affection. What the fuck was wrong with him?

Hell, he'd taken a year to fall for his damn ex-wife. So what if this guy was already under Cass's skin? There was nowhere for any relationship between them to go, and Cass wouldn't risk that, not again. He needed to keep his infatuation to a few what-ifs and wishful thinking, period.

Yeah, good luck with that.

CHAPTER THREE

IT DIDN'T TAKE LONG TO GET THE BROTHERS MOUNTED ON THEIR horses and ready to go, with Cass doing his best to ignore the sour look of disapproval on Andrew's face whenever Stef came into his line of vision or shared something funny with Tomas. Because, of course, Tomas and Stef were chatting up a storm just as they had in the van, and even Cass was getting a little riled, though for entirely different reasons. He appreciated that Tomas was likely just trying to keep Stef distracted—the mounting panic on Stef's face was kind of hard to miss—but yeah, Cass was a bit... well, jealous. *Fuck...* Yeah, he was jealous. There, he'd said it.

Between Andrew's redneck attitude and his own adolescent dramatics, God help them all over the next two days. Happy trails.

On the bright side, the brothers seemed more than competent in the saddle. Cass had watched as they put their horses through their paces in the training arena for a few circuits so he could be sure, but they were fine. Their matching bays, Bilbo and Eowyn—the whole *LOTR* name thing had been Cass's father's idea, one Cass had thought was ridiculous but the tourists ate up like fucking elven bread—were settled on the bit, ears twitching, calmly following their riders' instructions. All of which were a good sign the men were sending the right messages about who was in charge.

Cass had a couple of back-up horses if he'd needed to swap them out, but the boys looked good. The same couldn't be said for Stef, who'd yet to even venture through the gate into the corral. He was still busy eyeing Arwen from the other side of the fence like she was last week's meat patty sitting in the fridge and turning green around the edges.

"She hates me." Stef leaned over the fence and tilted his head slightly. "Is that normal?" He pointed to the foam gathered around Arwen's mouth.

The mare's soft eyes widened a little at his looming approach, but other than a glance Cass's direction as if to ask, "Who's the clown this time," she stayed perfectly still. In the six years Cass had owned her, Arwen had never been a less than gracious hostess to any of the greenhorns she'd had to endure on her back.

The same couldn't be said for Cass. There'd been more than a few riders who'd been lucky to make it back to the farm in one piece, and not from anything the horse had done to them. He rolled his eyes and undid the latch on the gate. "She doesn't hate you. And she's just been chewing at her bit, is all—it's only saliva."

Stef fired him a dubious look. "That's what they said about Cujo."

Andrew grunted in derision and said something under his breath that Cass was glad he missed, or he might have been forced to confront the man. He was pretty sure a showdown was on the cards at some point over the next two days. Andrew wouldn't be able to keep his mouth shut.

"Get in here." Cass waved Stef inside the corral and shoved a helmet into his hands. "Put it on, and stand on the far side of Arwen."

Stef held the helmet at arm's length as if it were riddled with disease and arched an are-you-fucking-kidding-me eyebrow at Cass.

He ignored it and said, "Not negotiable. Everyone wears one, even me. We clean them regularly, and your hair will survive." He

knocked on his own wide-brimmed leather hat to show its solid inte-
rior. "What would Benny say?"

Stef narrowed his gaze. "You play dirty."

Cass had a hundred and one responses on the tip of his tongue
and none of them appropriate. "Whatever works. Now, come on, let's
get you mounted so we can get going." It was out before he realised,
and sure enough...

Stef flashed him a flirty smile, then leaned in to whisper as he
sauntered past, "I bet you say that to all the boys."

Cass felt his cheeks flame but said nothing. No one picked him as
anything other than straight 90% of the time. And the other 10% was
because he was aiming to send those exact signals. He wanted to
believe that Stef simply flirted with anyone, any time he thought he
could get away with it. But Cass suspected it was actually because
Cass was failing dismally to keep his own attraction under wraps,
waving it like a goddamn rainbow flag above his head. All he needed
was for Andrew to twig and the whole excursion could end up in a
downhill slide into shit town.

Stef made a wide arc around Arwen's haunches, the stiff set of his
shoulders undermining his attempt to appear even remotely relaxed.
He was far, far more nervous than he was letting on—scared, even,
and it brought Cass back to earth with a guilty thud.

Stef was his fucking client, not some potential hookup, and he
deserved the best Cass could offer, not this cheap adolescent
behaviour currently on display.

Arwen turned her head and nodded enthusiastically at Stef's
approach, her bit and bridle jangling in her mouth.

Stef froze at the sound. "Wh-what does that mean?"

"Oh, for fuck's sake. This is too fucking painful." Andrew reined
his horse back over to the training ring and began a wide, lazy circle.

Good riddance.

"Ignore him." Tomas shot a glare at his departing brother's back.
"Arsehole is his middle name, but he's not usually as bad as this."

Cass and Stef exchanged a pointed look. *Yeah, right.*

"Um, you sure about that?" Stef eyed Tomas dubiously. "I know he's your brother, but he clearly has a problem with me. And if he keeps this up, I won't be concerning myself with protecting his—or anyone else's—feelings, understand? I have an untapped reservoir of arseholery in my own tank, and right now his name is written all over it."

Tomas lifted a shoulder in defeat. "Hey, you'll get no argument from me. I'm sure he'll deserve it, because... you're right, he's an arsehole most of the time." He flashed them a quick smile. "But he's a good builder, so there's that. And in case you're wondering, we don't share the same views on... well, you know."

Stef's expression softened. "That's pretty obvious, and... thanks."

Something passed between the two that Cass didn't quite understand, and the next thing he knew, he'd crossed the distance between them and taken Stef's hand in his.

Stef froze at the touch.

"Here." Cass flipped Stef's hand, placing a small carrot in his palm. "Hold your hand out, keep your fingers straight, and she'll lift it right off. No biting. Promise." He dropped his hand and stepped back.

Stef nervously licked his lips, and Cass tracked the movement.

"She won't bite," he repeated. "Consider it a getting-to-know-you gift. Make friends with her."

What felt like a week later, Stef finally nodded. "Okay." The nervous flicker in his eyes remained, but he took a step towards Arwen, hand outstretched, and offered her the carrot. She extended her neck until her soft lips quivered on his palm and gently took the treat, crunching it enthusiastically.

"And the crowd went wild!" Cass broke into applause, and Tomas joined in.

Stef's face split into a broad smile. "Hey, how about that. She didn't bite."

"Jesus, you guys, can we get going already?" Andrew hauled back up alongside the corral.

Cass ignored him and clapped Stef on the back. "Of course she didn't bloody bite. How the hell would I keep my business if my horses mauled every tourist who fed them a carrot?"

Stef didn't move a muscle, staring at the mare with childlike wonder, and Cass barely suppressed the urge to throw an arm around him.

"Her nose. Damn, it's like... velvet." Stef reached tentatively for another brief touch then whipped his hand back. "And those whiskers. They tickle. I hadn't expected that. She was so gentle taking it. I barely felt her." He took a couple more steps till he was almost at Arwen's shoulder, then spun to face Cass. "Can I pat her?"

"Of course." He stepped up beside Stef. "Start with her neck and shoulder, like this." He ran a hand down Arwen's neck. "Nice firm strokes, so she doesn't have to wonder what you're doing."

Stef didn't pick up on the opening Cass had given him. Instead he stretched his arm and ran the flat of his hand smoothly down Arwen's neck exactly as instructed, completely focused.

Arwen cast an approving glance back, and Cass swore she almost purred. The mare was an attention whore of the highest order—a trait she likely had in common with her new rider. They might prove an even better match than he'd hoped.

"You're such a good girl," Stef murmured, taking a step closer to Arwen's head. "We're friends, right? You gonna let me ride you?" Arwen turned her head and offered Stef her long nose for a scratch. He obliged immediately. "Oh, you like that, huh? Can't say as I see the attraction, but hey, each to their own. No kink shaming here."

He leaned in and took a sniff. "Hey, she doesn't smell as bad as I thought she would."

"I'm sure she's relieved," Cass teased and shared a knowing smile with Tomas. But when he looked back, Arwen had lifted her twitching nose almost to Stef's shoulder. Cass shot to attention. "Uh. Stef, you might want to—"

Too late.

The mare sneezed, and several long, shiny strings of equine snot landed on Stef's chin and neck. He froze mid-scratch, eyes scrunched and lips pursed, as the Murchison brothers doubled over in hilarity.

Cass's own laugh threatened to choke him, but he stomped it down and slipped to Stef's side. "She, um, has a sensitive nose. Scratching tends to make her sneeze."

Stef slowly opened his eyes and stared at Cass, making no attempt to hide his suspicion. "No kidding. A fact you could have mentioned earlier, I'm thinking."

He lifted the hem of his T-shirt and wiped his chin and neck while Cass tried desperately not to gawk at the miles of creamy skin the act exposed. Not to mention the smattering of dark hair that ran from a lean, fit chest with one exposed, eminently lickable, dark-brown nipple down a flat belly and into those loose fucking jeans that hung about his hips just begging for attention. Nothing but full-blooded sexy man, all. The. Way. Down. *Holy shamoly.*

"Aw, man, that was epic." Tomas wiped at his eyes.

Even Andrew took a moment to calm down. "If nothing else, I have to admit he has entertainment value."

Ignoring Andrew, Stef sent Tomas a baleful look. "That was a set-up. I'm not sure how he did it, but I *will* find out."

Somehow Cass found the strength to drag his gaze from those damn jeans and raise his hands. "Not at all. I'd take it as Arwen's official blessing—"

Stef's eyes popped comically. "Have you lost your damn mind? Your horse snotted me, Cassidy. In what universe is that a blessing?"

"Hey, you survived, didn't you? And you came away from a close encounter with a set of horse teeth, none the worse for wear."

Stef's eyes went wide, and all colour fled his face. "Holy shit, I did, didn't I? Her mouth... it was right in front of my face. She could've... if she'd wanted to..." He deflated against Arwen's shoulder without realising what he was doing, and when she twitched, he jumped back and eyed her warily—but not with the same fear Cass had seen five minutes earlier. "Okay, so maybe she doesn't hate me."

"There you go." Cass threw the reins over Arwen's head and

unclipped her lead. "Now you two have made friends, we can get going. The hut where we're staying has a great outlook and gets rave reviews from our clients, but it's across the river, and we need to get there before the light fades. We'll stop for afternoon tea on the way, and since it's hot, we're gonna head for one of our most-talked-about film locations and get some shade for the horses—the elven forest." He waggled his eyebrows, and Stef's eyes flashed with excitement.

"Lothlórien?" He beamed at Cass.

Holy shit, it was like having a damn kid along for the ride, and Cass couldn't stop the smile that split his face in return. "Is that good enough to get you up on this horse?"

"Hell yeah." Stef reached for the saddle, and Arwen chose that moment to give a botfly an annoyed flick with her tail, catching Stef's back in the process. He shot sideways like a rocket—straight into Cass, who froze on the spot, Stef's groin hard up against his thigh. A few inches to the left and things could've been interesting.

"Oops, um, sorry." Stef pushed away, looking anything but.

Cass closed his eyes, took a deep breath, and willed his body to behave. Thank Christ the brothers were behind him. It was going to be a long, long trip.

"So, um, where do you want me?" Stef deadpanned, and Cass gave him a much-deserved eye-roll.

Had he mentioned *loooong*?

"Well?" Stef studied him innocently, looking like butter wouldn't melt in his mouth.

He counted to three and shortened Arwen's lead rope to steady her. "Turn around and grab a big handful of her mane with your left hand—"

Stef looked aghast. "But that's... won't it hurt her?"

Holy Christmas crackers. "Not if you don't pull it out."

"Oh, right." He shot Cass a concerned look. "Is that, um... a possibility?"

"No. I'm kidding. You can't... *ugh*, just do it."

"Come on. Get on with it," Andrew grumbled.

"Just give him a minute." Tomas pushed his horse forward. "You'll do great," he told Stef.

"Fine." Stef scowled at Cass. "But no more kidding." He grabbed the mane as instructed.

"Now put your left foot in here—" Cass held the stirrup for Stef, who slid his foot inside. Arwen took a small step sideways, and Stef hopped to keep close.

"Hey, what's she doing?" He turned a panicked eye over his shoulder.

"It's fine. She's just getting her balance. Now, with your right hand, grab on to that horn on top of the saddle."

Stef arched a brow. "The horn, huh? This hard, round handful, right?"

Cass snorted. "That's the one."

"Aw, you put a sheepskin on the saddle for me."

"I did. You can thank me later."

Tomas chuckled.

"These are Western saddles," Cass explained. "They'll hold you better and are more comfortable over long distance, though you'll still feel it tonight. You just need to lift your leg a little higher to get over the back of it, the cantle. Now, I'm gonna be close in behind you so you can't fall back, and on the count of three you're gonna pull yourself up and swing your leg over. I'll guide you if you need it, okay?"

Stef turned his head sideways a fraction. "I'm always down for a bit of... guidance," he said so only Cass could hear. "Just saying."

Cass almost spluttered. "Good to know." *God help me.* "Now, here we go. One, two, three—"

Stef hauled himself up and over while Cass directed his butt into the saddle with a guiding hand on the small of his back... okay, so maybe a little lower, sue him. Then he stood back and eyed the slightly unnerved look on Stef's face. "There, you did it. You okay?"

Stef sucked in a deep breath, took a look down and around him, and seemed to calm himself. "I think so."

Just then Arwen swivelled her butt, took a single step back, and

Stef white-knuckled the horn like the apocalypse was upon them all. "What the hell? You've got her, right? Don't let go!"

"I do, and I won't. She'll stay on the lead." Cass smiled indulgently. "But you can take up the reins, like this." He worked them into Stef's unclenching fingers. "Relax."

"Easy for you to say."

Arwen turned her head, and if that wasn't a giant eye-roll, Cass would eat his hat.

He patted Stef's hand. "Keep them loose, just a gentle connection with her mouth. She's more English than Western trained, and if you gather them up too tight, she'll either think you're getting ready to stop or that you're about to ask her to speed up—"

Stef turned a horrified look Cass's way. "Speed up? No, no, no. I definitely don't want her to fucking speed up. I told you I'd be crap at this."

"And I said you'll be fine. I'll be leading you from my horse until you get comfortable—"

Stef's eyes blew wide. "*Pfft.* You keep taking those drugs, sunshine, 'cause that is never. Gonna. Happen."

Cass chuckled. "You'd be surprised. I'll talk you through the steering bit as we go. I bet it won't be long till you're fine to go mostly on your own on a long lead, with me alongside."

Stef eyeballed him in disbelief. "On my own? You are joking, right? You don't... I can't... just no. Tanner barely lets me drive his car on my own, and you want me to drive, *ride*, a horse? What if I screw up? What if she—" He straightened in the saddle and gave Cass a sanctimonious smile. "What would Benny say?"

Cass let out a little laugh. "Really? You're going with that?"

Stef tilted his head. "Damn right."

"Who's Benny?" Tomas asked.

"His brother," Cass answered without taking his eyes from Stef. "And I think *Benny* has more faith in you than you think. Shall we call him?"

Stef swallowed hard and his gaze slid away. "No. He thinks I'm a fucking superhero. No need to disavow him of that erroneous impression if we don't have to."

Cass smirked. "Superhero, huh? Is that *except* for the part about your crappy boyfriend radar, where he thinks you suck—"

"—big, hairy balls," they finished together.

Tomas roared with laughter.

Stef's grimace had a distinctly sour edge to it. "Yes I'm well aware what Benny thinks. Now, can we move on from that, please?"

Riling Stef had a lot going for it, but Cass decided to give him a break. "We can." He took Gimli's lead along with Arwen's, vaulted on to Gandalf, and slowly headed them all out of the corral, with Stef rigid as a steel bar in the saddle.

Tomas sidled Eowyn alongside Arwen. "Relax," he told Stef. "Take a big breath and sink into the saddle. Drop your shoulders... and... there. That looks much better."

"I take it the princess is finally ready?" Andrew griped, drawing Bilbo alongside. "We shouldn't have to wait like this. We paid good money."

Cass turned to face him and kept his voice low. "Everyone paid good money. And I told you when you called that I had a beginner booked on these dates, and what that would mean. I gave you the option to choose a different time."

Andrew gave a disdainful snort. "These are the only free days we had available."

Cass held his temper. "Then don't complain. But since you know the area, if I decide you can ride as well as you claim, you'll be able to keep your own pace within reason once we get off the road, as long as you stick to the track and keep circling back to touch base. I'll let you know when I've watched you for a bit."

Andrew glared sullenly. "We'll be fine."

"I'll decide that. But to start with, I'm gonna let you two take Gimli on the long lead. He's used to carrying gear, so you'll have no problems, and it'll give me a bit more freedom with Stef while gets comfortable. But keep some distance from Arwen, will you, till Stef gets the hang of things? Her and Bilbo don't always agree on things, but as long as he doesn't crowd her, she's fine. At the end of the driveway we'll turn right. Keep to the verge all the way up the road to the track at the far end, and stay within fifty metres so I can see you."

"Fine." Andrew took the other lead and pulled to the front. "Tomas, come up here."

Tomas answered his brother's summons, with an apologetic smile at Cass as he trotted past.

Cass shook his head. Andrew Murchison was a flat-out pain in the rear end, and keeping him busy with Gimli would at least keep him out of Cass's hair for a while.

He threw a smile Stef's way, pleased to see him looking a least a little more relaxed. "Ready, John Wayne?"

Stef narrowed his gaze. "Way too soon. And no. But don't let that stop you. Go on. Let me know when we get to the wow-this-is-fun part. I'd hate to miss it. And remind me to tell Tanner he owes me his arse in a sling."

Cass spluttered. "Wow. An image I could've done without."

Stef pursed his lips thoughtfully. "Mmm. And not one likely to happen, because... well, boyfriend." He shrugged. "And also, ew... though I could be convinced to watch if Ethan—"

"Nope. Nuh-uh. Not listening." Cass tugged on Arwen's lead, and they moved off down the driveway with Stef rocking gingerly in the saddle and looking about as comfortable as a man heading to his execution.

By halfway down the driveway he'd at least unglued his eyes from the death grip he held on the reins and the saddle horn, and looked up. "Hey," he said. "Maybe this isn't so bad, after all."

Cass grinned to himself and began to relax.

At the two-thirds mark of the driveway there was a little rise to negotiate with a lot of weathered potholes. The horses knew it well and daintily sidestepped their way through the warren of ruts. Or at least they all did except Arwen, who, for the first time in Cass's memory, tripped on the edge of one and took a slight stumble. Of course she fucking did.

Stef pitched forward on to her neck and then tipped alarmingly sideways, flinging the reins and making a grab for Arwen's mane—a successful one, thank God. He scrambled upright and threw Cass a reproachful glare. "See? I can't do this. I need to go back—"

"Are you still in the saddle?"

Stef scowled. "Just."

"Then sit up and relax. You're making her tense. In an hour you'll be an old hand at this and be glad you didn't give up." Arwen was much closer to bored than tense, but Stef didn't need to know that, and Cass had a plan.

"What do you mean, tense?" Stef eyed the mare nervously. "Did I hurt her? I told you she hates me."

"Nothing like that, and would you stop saying she hates you. But the more relaxed you are, the more relaxed she'll be. You get uptight, she gets uptight."

"Think of it like sex." Tomas had come back to see what the problem was. "Horses feel your energy and then respond accordingly. You want her to enjoy herself and give you a good ride, not get all tight and anxious, you have to trust her. You relax, she relaxes."

Stef side-eyed the younger man with horror. "I don't know who the hell you've been sleeping with, sunshine, but I'll tell you one thing for free. If you think this is anything like sex, I really feel for you. You need to raise the bar, sweetheart."

Cass choked out a laugh and nudged Gandalf on. "Come on, let's pop your cherry, city boy."

Stef threw him a filthy look and was still muttering to himself as they headed out between the honour guard of poplars. "Think of it like sex? What the hell is wrong with you people?"

CHAPTER FOUR

OKAY, SO THE HORSE THING WAS TURNING OUT BETTER THAN expected—not that Stef would be saying those words out loud any time soon, at least not if Cass was within hearing distance. He was looking far too pleased with himself as it was. With Arwen's lead in hand, he'd ridden alongside Stef until they'd arrived at the afternoon tea spot, whistling snippets from some maddening tune straight out of Nashville, as if he could see into Stef's brain and read how much he fucking hated country music. Give him techno or hip-hop any time. And when Stef had finally caved and asked what the hell the song was, Cass had slid him a sexy victor's smirk, informed him it was "Good Ride Cowboy" by Garth Brooks, and continued on with the torture. *Cheeky fucker.*

But yeah, as it turned out, Stef was actually enjoying himself. Go figure. The scenery was all towering mountains, braided rivers, and quiet country roads just like the movies—one of the highlights being the slice of trail past Diamond Lake, which was drop-dead gorgeous. It led to one of the original homesteads in the area, the surrounds of which played host to the location shoots for *The Desolation of Smaug* and Beorn's house from *The Hobbit*. Stef could almost imagine the four of them carrying the ring towards the Misty Mountains. Which raised the intriguing question, to whom would he allocate which roles?

Stef himself was Frodo, of course, but with a fuck-ton more style and sass. If anyone ever needed a queen on his side, it was that poor hobbit. Which meant Cass should theoretically have been Sam, but just no. There were all sorts of reasons *that* didn't work in Stef's head, not the least of them being that if there was a single character in the movie who didn't do it for him, it was Sam Gamgee. No disrespect to Sean Astin, but Stef had always thought Sam was a whining pain in the neck.

Now Aragorn, oh yeah, he could work with that. He cast a side-ways glance at Cass and... *fuck*... yeah, that did nicely. Tomas was of course Pippin, the ever-cheerful mischief-maker, and as for Andrew? Hey, who was Stef to argue with typecasting? Gollum or Worm-tongue, no question about it.

Stef's arse was holding up surprisingly well with the extra padding of the sheepskin Cass had provided, and if the special treatment had earned him a laugh or two from the builder brothers, well, fuck 'em. Stef figured his fine rear end had done a damn sight more miles than theirs over the years, and in ways he bet they wouldn't want to think too closely about. He wasn't going to turn down the opportunity to keep it in pristine condition.

But the biggest surprise of all? He'd managed to master the whole horse-steering shit pretty damn quickly. Cass was a patient teacher, and once Stef had settled enough to not have the whites of his eyes showing, Cass had started class. It turned out to be not nearly as terrifying as Stef had thought.

Bar a couple of rookie mistakes—who would've guessed that leaning forward meant "go faster" in horse lingo and leaning back and sitting heavy, meant slow down—he was doing quite well. Sitting up straight not only solved both those problems, but also avoided Stef being thrown forward with his balls banging on the damn saddle horn—a win all round. He was going to have bruises where he didn't need them, that was for sure.

Cass still kept hold of the long lead, of course, but two hours in and Stef had found himself pretty much riding—read slow walking— on his own. Cass had reached over for a high five, told Stef how well he was doing, and apparently meant it. The unexpected praise did floppy butterfly things to Stef's stomach that he didn't want to look at too closely, although even now he still suspected Arwen was only biding her time. Given the whole sneezing thing, he figured she was just letting him get comfortable until she could catch him off guard again. But he had her number, and they'd be having a talk.

Before they stopped, Cass suggested he try going solo after the tea break, untethered from Cass's hand but with the rope still slung over Arwen's neck just in case. If Stef didn't feel exactly thrilled about the idea, he was at least game enough to give it a go—a decision that earned him a bright smile from the sexy cowboy, and an answering twitch south of his belt.

He knew better than to get all wistful about straight or even curious boys and their wicked eyes, but for some reason this partic- ular one had got under his skin. Not least of all because Cass just didn't smell straight irrespective of what Ethan thought, which was why Stef kept pushing the man's buttons. He wasn't averse to a little fun in the mountains if Cass was on board with the idea, but he didn't want to read things wrong either.

Regardless, whatever that cowboy was wearing needed to be bagged and tagged, because holy shit, that smell was addictive. He'd found himself, more than once, angling Arwen closer to Gandalf just to catch a whiff. Any subtlety of movement implied was laughable consid- ering how little control Stef actually had over the horse—crashed their legs together on occasion was closer to the truth. Either way, he got his reward: leather, citrus, grass, and something earthy that just reeked of country boys throwing hay bales around in a shed with no shirts on and a lot of muscle happening, and wow, that went nuclear fast.

But watching Cass ride had been... sexy, and enthralling, and had he mentioned sexy? It was like watching a dance—Gandalf responding to signals from Cass that Stef was totally oblivious to. And when he asked Cass about it, Cass had talked about guiding his horse with his seat—his arse—shifting weight, small nudges of his thighs and calves, a toe, a heel, a little bit of pressure on the neck from a rein. But it was all a secret code to Stef, whose own effort with the reins more closely resembled one of those YouTube videos of white-gloved traffic conductors in rush hour.

"You ready for coffee?" Cass slipped alongside Stef on the fallen trunk, startling him from his musings. After two hours of riding, Cass had led them into the welcome shade of the beech forest, then sent them off to stretch their legs while he set things up for the afternoon tea Dee had prepared.

"Son of a bitch." Stef slammed shut the notebook he'd been sketching in while his heart took a few beats to calm down. "Warn a guy next time, will you? Are the others back?"

The brothers had taken a walk to the river to cool their feet and possibly even take a dip. Stef had thought for a second about how close those mountains were, calculated the likely water temperature, and declined with a horrified, "I have no words for how ridiculous that suggestion is."

"I told them forty minutes, so they have a bit of time." Cass stretched those long legs of his out, well past the ends of Stef's toes.

"Jesus, those things need their own damn post code," Stef muttered.

Cass chuckled and ran his hands the length of his thighs. "Yeah, they do have a tendency to get in the way sometimes."

Stef eyeballed him. "I just bet they do."

The corners of Cass's eyes crinkled in amusement. "So, how are *your* legs holding up, amongst other parts of your anatomy?"

Stef ran his hands down his thighs. "Better than I expected, to be honest, but I'm guessing by the way everyone keeps checking that I'm in for a rude awakening later? As for the other parts—we'll have to wait and see, but I'm thinking the same applies."

"Maybe." Cass picked at a few impossibly green fern fronds growing out of the rotting trunk. The air in the forested glade had a sweet damp smell at odds with the blistering temperature beyond its borders. He offered Stef a fern and the tiny act stirred something unexpected inside Stef. *Huh.*

He accepted with a nod and twirled it between his fingers, avoiding Cass's gaze.

"Some handle it better than others," Cass explained. "But yes, I'd expect you to feel *something* tomorrow. It's like leg day on steroids. You'll feel it in your butt, thighs, and hips. Unless you ride, it's not a position they're used to on a daily basis."

Stef looked over and cocked a brow suggestively.

Cass shook his head. "Nope, don't even go there. But you seem to be enjoying it, or at least I hope you are?"

Stef's gaze drifted to the magical dell. Broad, sturdy tree trunks climbed skyward to split the emerald canopy, while the sun painted the ground and greenery at their feet in wide golden shafts, and the distant rumble of the river as it tumbled and spilled over rocks provided the perfect sound track.

He sighed. "Yeah, I'm having a good time—a really good time, actually. But don't go telling our revered tour guide, or it'll go to his head and we'll never hear the end of it."

Cass snorted and elbowed him gently. "Mum's the word. And a *good* time, huh?"

"*Really* good," Stef corrected.

"Still, I'll have to see if I can improve on that. We at Martin's Stables aim for amazing, at the very minimum."

"Oh, amazing?" Stef smiled. "Them's big words, Mister. I seem to recall my last boyfriend promising something very similar, which only goes to show just how disappointing life can be."

"Ouch." Cass laid a hand on his chest. "Should I take that as a personal challenge?"

Stef shifted slowly to face him. "Now, that depends on if we're still talking about the tour here, 'cause I have to say, Cassidy Martin, you're sending off all kinds of contradictory messages." He let that sink in for a minute.

Eventually Cass's gaze slid away. "The tour, of course."

"Hmm. Of course." Stef thought about challenging him but didn't. What did it matter? Cass didn't owe him any explanation. He blew out a long sigh and stared up at the canopy instead. "It sure is beautiful here. I can't believe I'm sitting in the middle of the Lothlórien Forest and it looks, well... exactly as I imagined, actually. And somehow that only makes it more amazing—"

"Hah! There you go—amazing. I knew you'd say it." Cass licked a finger and gave himself a point.

Stef narrowed his gaze. "Don't get cocky. This forest is none of your doing. But yeah, when you see the movies, you tell yourself that it's all remastering and special effects and shit. And then to come here and find out it's actually just as beautiful in the flesh, that kind of blows your mind. I can imagine Galadriel coming out of those trees barefoot, silver dress billowing—"

Cass shot a silencing finger up in the air. "Listen—you hear that?"

Stef snapped his mouth shut, and bright, musical birdsong filled the space. "What is it?" he whispered.

Cass leaned over, and Stef breathed him in.

"A bellbird. They're common around here, but the forest acts like a kind of amplifying chamber. The birds always sound like they're just on your shoulder—children's voices, tiny wood fairies singing in your ear."

Oh. Stef turned and laughed softly, his lips inches away from Cass's cheek. "I think you've been smoking too much of that Hobbit pipe-weed. But it's a nice thought."

Cass let out a slow breath. "You can find magic in lots of places, don't you think? These forests are old. Who knows what they've seen. Maori used to come through here in search of pounamu—greenstone—there were lots of camps. You can feel it in the air, a sense of the sacred. It's just... different in here."

Stef stared at him for a long minute, caught somewhere between amusement and admiration. Did anyone really talk like that? Well, Cass apparently did. And that just made the man infinitely more interesting. Alarm bells went off in his head, but he let them go.

He turned back to the glade and let the bellbird song slide around him like a child's promise. He drank a lungful of cool, damp air, and something deep in his chest unfurled and stretched a pair of fledgling wings. It felt... big. New. Peaceful. Strong. Yeah, sacred was a good word for it, even if it sat a little awkwardly in Stef's head.

The perpetual tension he seemed to carry in his body suddenly leached away, and he leaned back on his hands and stretched his legs, bringing his shoulder and thigh in contact with Cass's. The man flinched a little but didn't move, the heat of his body searing through Stef's clothing like a brand imprinting itself on his flesh. Stef should have moved away, but he didn't. Story of his fucking life.

Cass nudged his shoulder. "If it was truly Lothlórien, then it would be a magical realm, right? So, what would you wish for?"

Stef snorted. "Aren't you supposed to wish for endless wishes?"

Cass turned and tut-tutted. "Elven rule number one—no wishing for endless wishes. But today's your lucky day; you get another chance."

Stef turned and inclined his head to acknowledge the honour. "Well, in that case, I'd wish for..." He paused to think, and a predictable image of Paul popped into his head accompanied by the usual what-ifs. But then, not so predictably, it disappeared and another answer came unbidden. "This," he said, surprising himself.

Cass's brows bumped together. "The forest?"

"Yes. No. I mean this *feeling*, what this place *brings*—or maybe it's what all places like this bring. If I could carry that feeling around with me, I think I'd make better choices in the future. I want less... regret in my life."

He felt Cass's eyes drilling into him, but the burning in his own stopped him from turning to check, and he looked away.

"I would never have picked you for a romantic," Cass said softly in his ear. "I'm not sure if that's my lack of vision or your determination to appear like you don't give a fuck—sorry, that wasn't very professional."

"Fuck professional." Stef laughed. "And yeah, I guess I'd own that. I am, or at least I *was*, a romantic. Too much of one, if I'm honest. Not great for protecting your heart, as it turns out. And by the way, there must be some serious witchy-woo-woo shit in this place, because I don't talk like this, ever. And it's going to stop right now—after *you* answer the same question, of course. So come on. Your wish? Cough it up."

Cass's head tipped back to let him gaze at the canopy above as he took a minute to reply. "I'm not sure what it means that I don't have an answer for you right on the tip of my tongue. I should, right? It would seem natural that everyone would have something they'd wish for, if they only had the chance. Maybe I'm just not a romantic like you."

"Yeah, nah. Don't believe that for a minute." Stef pushed off his hands and threw Cass's fern leaf back at him. "How can you live with all this on your doorstep"—his arm swept over the glade—"and not believe in romance, or at least the possibility of it, even if it's only with your horses or your sheep." He raised his hands. "Hey, I'm not here to shame."

A smile dangled on the corner of Cass's mouth. "Yeah, gotta love a stereotype. Well, I would've said I was a romantic once, but not anymore."

Really? Stef didn't believe that for a minute. No one spoke like Cass had without having romance in his very bones, and that didn't just disappear. Stef had learned that the hard way. "I sense a story there."

Cass eyeballed him, guarded. "Do you, now?"

Stef let it go. "But you still haven't answered the question. What would you wish for?"

Cass leaned forward to study the damp ground between his feet and forked his fingers through his hair. "I think I'd wish for this place to stay like it is, untouched and... magical, so that people like you"—he turned and locked eyes with Stef—"could come here and find a way to make better choices and have less regrets. Then maybe they could teach me how to do the same."

Well, shit. Neither of them looked away, and when the silence became too much, Stef broke it with a horrified chuckle. "What the hell? Look at us. We should make wristbands. WWGD."

"WWGD?"

"What would Galadriel do?"

Cass threw his head back and laughed. Then he nodded at the notebook still clutched in Stef's hand. "You keep a journal?"

Stef fingered the notebook, his cheeks warming. "Nah. It's my, um, ideas book, I guess you'd call it. I'm a jeweller by trade, and patterns or ideas can sometimes just pop into my head. A new line or... something. I had a few when we were riding, and then, um, this place..." He waved his hand around. Could he look any more of a fool?

Cass reached over and turned Stef's chin to face him. "Why, you're blushing, Stefan Hamilton."

He jerked out of Cass's hold. "*Pfft.* I am not. Don't be ridiculous. The light in here's fucking with your eyes."

"Riiiight, of course it is. Can I take a look? Or is it top secret?" Cass nodded at the notebook.

Stef closed his eyes for a minute to stomp on his immediate urge to say, Yes, look to your heart's content and flay my insides open while you're at it. *No one* got to see Stef's notebook, not even Tanner. Half the stuff in it never saw the light of day, and the other half often bore little resemblance to what might come from it: lines, vague colour palettes, and disconnected phrases that meant nothing to anyone but him.

He frowned. "I don't, um... at least I never..."

Cass's expression immediately became apologetic. "Shit, I'm sorry, it's fine. I didn't mean to pry—"

"No, it's okay. It's just kind of weird for me. It's nothing but a lot of lines and silly shit."

"I doubt anything in there is silly, but I understand. Come on, let's go get that coffee. The boys should be back."

"We are. Thought you'd abandoned us." Tomas appeared through the trees with damp hair and a bright, smiling face. Andrew followed behind, and though not as openly cheerful as his brother, he looked refreshed and the most relaxed Stef had seen him.

They came to an abrupt halt and stared around at the small dell. "Wow, this place is amazing."

Cass sent Stef a pointed look. "See, amazing. What did I tell you?" He headed off back to where the horses were tied, and Stef rolled his eyes.

"Oh, for fuck's sake," he called to Cass's back. "They're clearly not thinking straight. That water had to have been all of minus five degrees. Their balls are probably still up around their tonsils holding out for rescue." He turned to the brothers but focused on Tomas. "And seriously? We need to have a chat about keeping our tour guide's ego in check. I'll expect you to follow my lead."

Cass called over his shoulder, "I heard that."

Cass really needed to get his head out of his arse before things got out of control. He was clearly doing a shit job of flashing his straight card, because Stef didn't look like he was buying a single bit of it. *And why was that?* He hardly needed to wonder. He needed to stop reacting to the sexy man as anything but a paying client. Yeah, good luck with that, because no matter what he did, he couldn't seem to take his eyes off Stef. That previously sleek dark hair was now adorably tousled and slightly matted from the riding helmet, and a smudge of black guyliner had found its way over the curve of his right cheek. He looked like he'd just rolled out of bed, and it had been all Cass could do not to reach over and lick the smudge clean before getting to work on licking everything else as well. Instead he'd just pointed it out and watched a slightly flustered Stef deal with it himself.

And what was with the whole damn group therapy moment they'd shared in the forest? He should've just called the guy over for coffee and left him. But did he do that? No. He sat beside Stef, *close* beside him, and talked, and not just about the bloody weather.

So, now he was interested in way more than just fucking the guy. Cass wanted to know what was in that bloody notebook, wanted to ask Stef about his jewellery line and how he'd even got into that, because that was no regular career. He wanted to know about the quiet romantic who sounded like he'd had his heart trampled on and the types of decisions he didn't want to regret any more. And nothing, *nothing* about any of that fit with Cass's immediate life plans—or the long-term ones, for that matter.

Stef was a big-city guy—in his own words, born and bred. How many times did Cass need to have his heart pummelled before he got the message? Did he want to fuck Stef? Hell yes. That wasn't the problem. He'd fucked enough guys since his divorce without it being a problem, though none from his tours, obviously. *Obviously*, he reminded himself, because... well, unprofessional, dipshit.

But Stef was different. Cass damn well knew that fucking Stef wouldn't end with that. He'd want more. *That* was the problem. Stef was the first man or woman who'd had him interested since... well, since fucking forever, and that was after only half a damn day. Could he be more of a fool?

They finished their afternoon tea and managed to demolish almost every one of Dee's famous cherry doughnuts. Cass made sure to repeat the flavour several times as he handed them out and was rewarded by a subtle blaze of pink on Stef's cheeks at the saddle-virgin innuendo. But Stef got his own back by claiming the last doughnut as his rite of passage, wrapping it and tucking it in his jacket pocket for later. When they filed out of the magical forest with full bellies, cooler bodies, and rested horses and headed north-east towards the Dart River crossing, even Andrew appeared in a good mood. Things were looking up.

A welcome cool breeze funnelled through the valley as they followed the river trail up to the crossing. Cass drew everyone's attention to Mount Earnslaw and its ranges to their right, Tolkien's Misty Mountains. They couldn't have asked for a more perfect day. He did this trip twice a week and never tired of it regardless of the weather, but on a flawless day like this there was nowhere in the world he'd rather be. And this trip it wasn't just about the scenery—well, at least not *that* scenery.

"So the Dart and Rees Rivers drain into Lake Wakatipu, right?" Stef ambled alongside Cass while the brothers brought up the rear with Gimli in tow. For all intents and purposes Arwen seemed contented with her hugely inexperienced rider, apart from the odd glance Cass's way as if to say, Are we there yet?

Stef, on the other hand, had taken a bit to lose the startled possum-in-the-headlights expression when he realised Cass had been serious about him going solo. But it faded as Arwen stepped into her role beautifully and Stef finally began to relax. He actually had a good seat on him and balanced well in the saddle, which realisation took Cass's thoughts spiralling to other ways of being seated, but there you go. No one said he was an angel. He thought Stef would probably make a good rider if he kept at it.

He leaned across and patted Arwen's neck. "Yes. Five rivers feed into the lake, and only one drains out. That's why we get flood issues in Queenstown after heavy rain. It's a glacial lake, about eighty kilometres long, and because of its odd S shape it even has a kind of tide or standing wave, where the level rises and falls ten centimetres every twenty-five minutes or so."

Stef's eyes widened slightly. "No shit. Huh. That's pretty weird, I'll give you that. I bet there's a Maori legend about it, right?"

"Either of you two locals know it?" Cass called back to the brothers. "Don't let me down here."

Andrew snorted something no doubt derisive, and it was Tomas who answered. "There was a woman kidnapped by a giant taniwha. Her lover saved her, but he was worried the taniwha would come back, so he set fire to it while it was asleep on its side. It burnt right into the ground and melted the surrounding snow, which then filled the crater, making Lake Wakitipu. The taniwha's heartbeat is what causes the rise and fall of the lake."

Cass stuck up his thumb. "Go to the top of the class."

Andrew trotted up on the other side of Stef, and Arwen flattened her ears.

"Just keep him back a bit," Cass warned Andrew, though he was pretty damn sure the man hadn't forgotten. The guy was shit-stirring. "Don't upset her."

Stef jerked his head sideways. "What do you mean, upset her? Is she—"

Stef never got the chance to finish his sentence, because Andrew suddenly swung his horse, causing Bilbo's hip to connect with Arwen's flank. She in turn stretched her neck towards him and delivered a swift nip to his shoulder. Bilbo kicked out with one back leg, and Arwen shot sideways into Gandalf, pushing Cass right off the trail.

If Stef hadn't grabbed for the horn of his saddle, Cass would likely have needed to pick him up off the dirt. As it was, Stef kept his seat, but Arwen opted to put some distance between her and Bilbo and popped into a dead-slow trot, sending Stef bumping around in his saddle and hanging on for dear life.

Fuck.

"No-o-o-o-o-o. Cass! What do I do?" Stef shouted back in horror. "Holy shit... H-help! C-Cass, get your arse up h-h-here and d-d-do something... Easy, girl... Oh m-m-my God.... How d-do you ride this ridiculous sh-shit... Cass!"

"Stef, hang on!" Tomas immediately kicked Eowyn into a trot but Cass waved him off.

"No. Stay back," he warned. "That goes for your brother as well."

"But he's gonna fall—"

"I'll handle it." Cass left Tomas fretting and trotted up alongside Stef. He slowed to keep pace but left Arwen's reins where they were. It was actually pretty damn funny, and it was all Cass could do not to laugh. Arwen was in no danger of bolting—she was too much of a lady. What she wanted was distance from the other horse. In truth, she was barely bumping along and Cass really wanted Stef to learn how to settle her back down. It would give him confidence and a sense of accomplishment.

"Okay, calm down. I'm not gonna let anything happen to you." He flashed Stef a reassuring smile, which didn't go down well.

Stef turned an incredulous look on him. "Then f-fucking s-stop her!" he stuttered through the bouncing.

"You can do it yourself—"

"N-no, I f-fucking c-can't. Cass!"

Cass grabbed the long lead from around Arwen's neck but left it loose. "There, I've got you if I need to. Now, drop your weight into your butt so you sit heavier in the saddle, and you won't get bumped around so much—but don't squeeze with your legs, 'cause that'll only make her go faster."

Stef threw a dagger glare at Cass that left little to the imagination, but he did as he was told and slumped into his seat. The bumping settled, and he immediately looked less likely to teeter sideways.

"Okay... drop my weight—got it. No squeezing—got it. Now what?" Stef still looked a bit spooked, but he was listening.

"Relax your lower body a bit more till you roll with the trot rather than bump. Imagine trying to push your arse right through the saddle to the ground. Then you can let go of the horn and slowly, gently pull her up with the reins, keeping your legs off her flanks."

Stef turned a horrified look Cass's way. "Pick up the reins?

You've got to be kidding me. If I let go this saddle, I'm a goner. I'll look like a fucking waffle on the ground, with hoof prints all over me."

Cass snorted. "You can try using just one hand, but it'll be tricky to shorten the reins if you need to. Just give it a go. I won't let anything happen."

Stef stared at Cass as if homicide was becoming a very real option. "Alright, but don't say I didn't warn you." He blew out a breath, dropped his weight, let go the horn, flailed his hands in panic for a moment till he got his balance, then calmed himself and gently pulled on the reins. Arwen's ears twitched, and her gait slowed to a comfortable walk.

"Yes!" Stef patted the mare's neck and then fist-pumped the air. "Holy shit." He spun in his seat to face the brothers, who were still keeping a respectful distance. "Did you see that, motherfuckers? I did that." He eyeballed Andrew. "And don't think I don't know you did that deliberately, arsehole."

Andrew sent him a sour look. "Don't be ridiculous."

Stef flipped him off. "Well, it didn't work, did it? Because this boy can riiiide." He jiggled his arse and immediately had to grab the horn to stop himself tipping over.

Cass broke into laughter and nestled Gandalf closely alongside Arwen to trap Stef's leg so he couldn't fall. "Take it easy there, Cowboy." He reached across and clapped Stef on the shoulder. "You did well."

Stef threw him a shit-eating grin. "I did, didn't I? Hell yeah, I'm a cowboy. Yippee-fucking-ki-yay."

"Yeah, well, just keep hold of those reins, and let's get to the hut in one piece."

"Yes, sir." Arwen reached for a mouthful of grass in passing, and Stef promptly nosedived on to her neck.

Cass grabbed the back of his T-shirt just in time and hauled him back into the saddle with a grin. "Yippee-ki-yay, city boy."

Stef's cheeks pinked, and he leaned forward over Arwen's neck.

"You and I need to have another chat," he whispered. The mare's ears flicked back and forth, and Cass could've sworn he saw her smirk.

───────

This section of the river was perfect for their crossing: still at its summer low, barely up to the horses' knees, and about twenty metres bank to bank. They let the horses quench their thirst. Cass stayed close to Stef so he didn't tip head over arse when Arwen spread her front legs and dropped her head to drink. But he needn't have worried—the rookie took it in his stride, looking a little nervous but following instructions and leaning back in the saddle till she'd had her fill.

"Right, it's gonna go like this." Cass gathered everyone's attention. "Tomas and Andrew will go across first, and I'll follow, bringing Gimli. Once you lot are safe on the other side, I'll come back for Stef. Got it?"

Everyone nodded.

"Dee has ferried our supplies across on the flying fox up there." He pointed to the heavy-wire-and-pulley system that spanned the river about thirty metres away. "All we have to do is collect them and then head up the track for about forty-five minutes to our rustic overnight accommodation. There's a grill for some steaks and even a light beer or two once we're there. The hut sits just above the treeline. You can see all the way across to Mount Earnslaw and halfway down the valley to the delta, so get ready for another spectacular view."

"We're okay to cross this on our own if you want," Tomas offered. "And we can manage Gimli as well."

Cass shook his head. "Thanks, but you guys are my responsibility. It's not a commentary on your skills, just the way it has to go." They offered no further argument and set about handing Gimli's lead over before waiting for the all-clear to cross.

Cass pointed Stef a little further up the bank, away from the river's edge. "I'll get you to wait up there till I get back. Hop off and let her graze a bit on the end of her lead."

"Um, just *how* rustic are we talking," Stef asked, eyebrows drawn. "I mean, are we talking 'futon not inner sprung' kind of rustic? Or 'lucky if you get a mattress at all' kind of rustic?"

Cass bit back a smile.

Tomas clapped Stef on the shoulder as he walked his horse down to the river's edge. "I suspect, oh precious one, that the correct answer falls somewhere between the 'you might be better off standing in a corner for the night' kind of rustic and 'there's a prize for who has the most bruises in the morning' kind of rustic. Right, Cass?"

Cass sent Stef an apologetic smile. "Pretty much, sorry to say. Consider it another cherry popped. Now let's get going." He waved the brothers ahead into the river, leaving Stef calling to their backs.

"Bruises? It can't be that hard to get a few mattresses up there. Are you batshit? I don't need any other cherries popped, thank you very much. And people pay for this? Goddammit, Tanner, you and your boyfriend are gonna owe me big time."

As tempting as it was to look back and catch Stef in his full, adorable fury, Cass kept his eyes on his other guests until they were safely across. The current was gentle and the horses sure-footed in the stony riverbed. They'd done this crossing hundreds of times. When everyone was safe under the shade of a large red beech tree on the other side, he headed back to collect Stef, who was shoving something back in his pocket and looking anxious. "You sure there's not another way to do this?"

"You'll be fine." Cass helped him back up into the saddle. "I'm gonna lead you across. All you have to do is hold on." He remounted Gandalf and nudged him down to the river's edge. Arwen shadowed him happily.

"If anything happens, I just want you to know that you have a fine arse to follow," Stef commented drily. "And I'll have gone to my grave a happy man."

"No one's gonna die, but, uh... thanks. I think." Cass chuckled. "Now just hold on to the horn and let me do all the work."

Stef flashed him a coy smile. "Not the first time I've heard that."

Cass rolled his eyes skyward and shook his head. "Do you ever stop?"

Stef's smile turned wicked. "Now where would the fun be in that?"

Cass sighed. "Okay smart arse, watch closely. If Gandalf steps into a hole, or stumbles, you'll need to brace in case Arwen does the same."

Stef gave a sombre nod. "You have my undivided attention. As I said, that's one epic arse."

Okay, maybe not so sombre. Cass stepped Gandalf out into the river, his hooves making a hollow clatter on the stones. He swore he heard the staccato opening lines of "Bubble Butt" being sung softly behind him, but when he swung around to where Stef was following on Arwen, the man was all innocence and batting lashes.

Cass flipped him off with a smile and gave a tug on Arwen's lead. Stef tensed with the mare's first few steps into the water, his knuckles whitening around the saddle horn when Arwen's hoof slid off a mossy rock, but other than that he said nothing. By the time they'd picked their way across the river and up on to the far bank, he was calm and relaxed, and Cass felt a moment of... pride. *Ugh.*

Tomas applauded loudly, and Andrew shook his head in disgust.

Stef beamed at the younger brother and took a dramatic bow. "And that, gentlemen, is how it's done."

CHAPTER FIVE

THE HEAT OF CASS'S EYES ON HIM, SCORCHED STEF'S BACK AS
he rubbed Arwen down and settled her for the night. And if he put a
little extra swish in his butt as he worked, that was only because it
helped him do a better job, right? When Cass said they all had to
tend their own horses, he'd nearly thrown up on the spot. Getting
comfortable riding at a walk was one thing; getting all up close and
personal with the creature's legs and feet and that bloody piece of
torture equipment called a tail that stung like fuck when it caught
you across the face was an entirely different matter. But Cass had
explained exactly what he needed to do, and Stef didn't want to give
Andrew the pleasure of another I-told-you-so moment.

And Arwen was a sweetie. Despite his best intentions not to, Stef
had grown to appreciate the ridiculous animal. She was a lot like him,
he decided: stubborn and cheeky as all hell. He'd even been feeding
her secret titbits of cherry doughnut over the afternoon. But the
sneaky animal hadn't taken long to figure the trick out and had
rumbled his pocket more than once in the last few minutes, trying to
help herself. Case in point, as yet again he nudged her velvet nose
aside from his jacket.

"You'll lose that girlish figure of yours," he scolded. "The rest is for tomorrow, *if* you're good to me. No more of that bone-rattling trotting shit."

She nickered and lifted her chin to rest on his shoulder, charming him in a flat second. "Goddammit, if you snot me again, horse, there'll be nothing but a cold shoulder in that pocket tomorrow, just saying."

Her lips quivered in his hair, and he shivered at the sensation. "Get off me. Any more of that and you'll get more than you bargained for. Don't tell anyone, but that's a sensitive spot. You know how it goes."

She nickered again and dropped her nose. "Okay, okay." He scanned the area, dipped his hand in his pocket, and retrieved another doughnut morsel. "But there's no more till tomorrow, so you better make it last."

He picked up the brush to attend to Arwen's mane and sneaked another glance at Cass while he was at it. Cass was bent over the stone firepit, that prime arse pointed right in Stef's direction, looking too fucking sexy for his own good. God help him, the man was delicious, and Stef could swear there was an "Eat Me" sign stuck to the back pocket of those snug-as-fuck jeans. Or maybe not, but a boy could dream, right?

For all of the spectacular scenery he'd delighted in that day, Stef's gaze had been continually drawn to the tall drink of water with emerald eyes and unruly strawberry blond hair, sitting astride an equally tall, grey shadow of a horse—looking far too fine to be anything but trouble to Stef's heart.

Even if Cass wasn't straight, he likely wasn't out, or at least he wasn't advertising it in Stef's direction. Which, okay, dented Stef's ego just a smidgen. *Goddammit.* Why now, and why *this* man? If there was a more unsuitable guy for Stef to get a crush on, he couldn't think of one. They had zero in common and fifteen hundred kilometres or so between them. *Fuck.*

"Get out of there." He pushed Arwen's inquisitive nose from his pocket for the millionth time so he could finish brushing her mane.

She pulled back a little but left her head slightly turned so she could study him with a soft brown gaze. It occurred to him that horses really did have beautiful eyes.

He rubbed her forehead affectionately. "You need a treatment on this," he deadpanned, fingering her forelock. "It's as dry as a drag queen's humour. You have to take better care of yourself. Tony would crack a fit if he saw this. That's my hairdresser, by the way. Camp as a row of tents, but don't tell him I said that. Nice guy—I said quit that." Arwen had the bottom of his pocket in her mouth yet again, attempting to chew through to the treat she was sure lay inside.

He dropped the comb and worked his pocket free from her teeth. *Teeth.* He gulped and took a step back, then reconsidered. She'd had all day if she wanted to bite him. He stepped back in, picked up the brush, and finished the last section of mane. "There. You're beautiful again. More than can be said about me. Don't tell your boss, but it's gonna take me a week at the spa to recover. I doubt he'd understand. Goodnight, sweetheart." He cast another sneaky look around, then dropped a kiss on the mare's neck.

"I saw that," an amused voice called from the fire pit.

"Goddammit." Stef spun to find Cass standing with a beer in one hand and a platter of raw steak in the other, wearing a wicked grin plucked straight out of Stef's filthy mind. "Yeah, well, don't go getting all jealous. Much though it pains me to admit, it was the best kiss I've had in months." He rubbed Arwen's nose one last time and ducked under the corral fence.

While Cass finished preparing to cook, Stef ventured inside the hut to clean the worst of the day off his skin. He smelled like a farm-yard—more precisely, like the manure *in* a farmyard, and that was putting a bright face on things. Funnily enough, he didn't mind the scent of Arwen; it had an earthy, sweetish edge that reminded him of... Cass, actually. No surprise there, since the guy was around the animals all day, but Stef hadn't expected to find the stench of unwashed quadrupeds sexy. Another of life's eternal mysteries sent to vex him.

The hut amounted to little more than the name had promised: corrugated iron and stone walls with a large covered wooden deck out front and, horror of horrors, a long drop toilet out back. Stef had never seen one, let alone used one of the monstrosities. Cass had provided detail—too much detail. Stef figured if God wanted humanity to use long drops, she wouldn't have invented heated toilet seats with built-in privacy music—and he was desperately trying to figure how he could manage to continue that state of affairs without doing his colon irreparable damage. It would be a close call.

The deck had a selection of seating arrangements, from tree trunk benches straight out of a film set to a couple of collapsible deck chairs that would've been at home in any cheap camping supply store. But the setting was nothing short of spectacular.

They'd ambled up the track from the river for around forty minutes before exiting just under the treeline, where a collection of stunted beech trees and other determined bushes still managed to survive. A small space had been cleared around the hut to house a run for the horses and a smaller corral, but it was the view from the deck out front which stole the air from Stef's lungs. It faced south-east back towards the lake, with a broad view over Paradise Valley and across to Mount Aurum.

Inside, the hut smelled of leather, sweet hay, dust, horses, and the unmistakeable musk of men, which was the only upside as far as Stef could tell. About eight by eight metres, it had a large latched window, a few stacked cots in the corner—those bruises were looking more likely by the minute—a wall of storage cupboards, hooks and saddle racks for all the gear, boxes of bottled water, a wood burner ready to go with an ample supply of stacked wood both inside and out, and a few bales of hay set out as seating around a table.

No shower, of course, that would be too much to ask, but Stef had anticipated that particular snafu and had stashed a packet of lemon-infused wet wipes in his saddlebag. Tomas snorted when he saw them, but then hung back and mucked around with his belongings a little too long to be entirely innocent, and Stef realised he'd have to watch himself. The questions around that boy's sexuality were growing by the minute, and the increasingly irritated glances Andrew was throwing his younger brother hadn't gone unnoticed either. If Tomas wasn't out, it didn't take a rocket scientist to figure out why. Jesus George. Trust Stef to end up on a trek with two closeted gays.

Following a pointed look, Tomas eventually ran out of reasons to hang around, and Stef was able to set about raising the grooming tone of the camp by about 500%. Then, feeling semi-human once again, he grabbed a paper bag from his pack and emerged from the hut to a choked laugh from Cass that he suspected was due to his clean T-shirt, which read, "Cowboy Butts Drive Me Nuts." That would teach the man for flashing his arse Stef's way.

He batted his eyelashes at Cass as he walked by and kept his voice low. "Just saying." Then he grabbed a beer from the cool bag and gingerly eased his backside on to one of the sawn rounds of tree trunk by the fire. His inner thighs and pelvic bones were starting to ache like a motherfucker, and it didn't bode well for the morning.

The care he put into getting himself down to a sit, however, hadn't gone unnoticed, and Cass bit back a smile while Andrew looked like it was the best damn thing he'd seen all day.

"You'll wanna take some ibuprofen for that before you go to sleep," Cass said. "And I hope that's not alcohol." He nodded to the bag in Stef's hand. "There's a lot of riding left tomorrow."

Stef studied the bag with a degree of disappointment. "I wish I'd thought of that option, but no." He opened the bag and handed it around. "First of the season. My brother packed them for me, seeing as how it's too damn cold down here to grow the things. That fact alone should automatically disqualify anyone from living here."

Tomas peered inside the bag. "Tamarillos? You're kidding me. You brought *tamarillos* on a horse trek? Not to mention... ew. Nasty-arse fruits."

Stef snatched the bag from him. "Heathen. That ignorance only goes to prove how backward you lot are down here. This little miracle of nature is packed with antioxidants and vitamins, not to mention if you moosh them up and smear them on your face it works like a facelift. You'll save a fortune in Botox later."

Which earned him a round of choking laughter from all but Andrew, who simply glared.

"Holy shit, where did you say you picked him up from?" Tomas snorted.

Cass wiped his eyes. "He's friends with a mate. What can you do?" He smiled Stef's way. "Go on, toss us one. I'm quite partial to the messy buggers."

Stef nodded in approval and pitched a Tamarillo which Cass caught with one hand. Then Stef eyed the surly man sitting across the fire from him. "Last chance, Andy."

"It's Andrew, meathead."

Stef's gaze never wavered. "I know it is."

They locked gazes for another few seconds before Andrew grunted and turned away. "Keep it."

Stef smiled. It was a victory of sorts. "Your loss." He turned to Cass, making sure he had the man's eye before he bit down into his own plump tamarillo, sending red juice dripping down his chin. He then pulled the fruit apart and sucked the flesh off the skin, maintaining eye contact all the while.

Cass swallowed like he had a Mack truck stuck in his throat and turned away to take a bite of his own.

Stef smiled to himself, threw the red skins on the fire, and wiped his hands down his jeans. "My mother makes this amazing tamarillo-and-brown-sugar-custard tart."

The corner of Cass's mouth twitched. "Tart, huh?"

Stef narrowed his gaze. "Yeah, well, not gonna deny it. But that little taste explosion is fucking sex on a fork." He waggled his eyebrows at Cass. "I'll make sure to send you some."

Cass swallowed hard and Stef grinned to himself. *Gotcha.*

He and Tomas chatted for a while as Cass cooked and Andrew pouted. What the hell Tomas was doing in partnership with his surly arsehole of a brother, Stef couldn't fathom. He couldn't imagine running a business and having to deal with that level of redneck shit on a daily basis. He had to assume Andrew wasn't the face of the company.

And while Stef felt as out of place around the cowboy campfire as a drag queen on a rugby field, he didn't hate it as much as he'd thought he would. Aside from the smell of unwashed bodies, they were all easy on the eye, so that was a bonus, and it was freeing to not feel like he needed to be on point all the time. Andrew would rather he curled up and died, which invited zero fucks to give on Stef's part, and Tomas and Cass seemed to have no expectations of him at all. It was a refreshing change from his usual social gatherings, where people seemed to rely on him to turn up in something provocative and then provide the witty banter and snarkful repartee that kept the evening entertaining. Not saying he didn't enjoy it, but it was... exhausting.

Tomas eventually gave up on trying to engage his brother in conversation and moved to take the seat alongside Stef, after pulling it closer... a lot closer. It appeared he wasn't the only one with a crush. Cass glanced their way, a deep crease between his brows, and Stef bit back a grin. *Aw, fuck it.*

He leaned closer to Tomas and asked him to pass the bowl of mixed nuts. Tomas did, holding it while Stef pretended to sort through and pick out his favourites, an act that brought their heads close together. Stef stole a glance through his lashes and saw Cass watching them from the grill, that frown of his dredging a little deeper. Hmm.

Then he heard Tomas breathe him in and immediately sat back. *Oops.* Stef didn't want to encourage him. Nothing against Tomas, he just didn't hold a candle to the man who currently held Stef's attention like a magnet.

Conversation over dinner flowed easily, with a fair bit of crude hilarity that even Andrew seemed to appreciate, and the food was pretty damn good. Thick steaks, potatoes in the jackets with sour cream, and the requisite baked beans—poshed up with some chilli and herbs.

Stef learned that Andrew and Tomas were thirty and twenty-eight respectively, had grown up on a farm—hence the riding skills—had lived in Southland all their lives, and had been in business together for four years. The tourist boom in Queenstown had meant lots of building work for them, although things had slowed the last year—hence the celebration for winning the lucrative apartment contract.

Cass talked a little about the history of the Glenorchy area and how originally all the land east of the Dart River, over two hundred thousand acres, had been leased by just one man, William Rees—hence the Rees River. Stef found the whole story fascinating, not to mention the man telling it. Rees and another pioneer had apparently flipped a coin to see who got which side of the lake, and that was that. *Holy fuck.* No wonder the local Maori tribes didn't stand a chance.

The region went through phases of farming, mining, and even a gold rush, but as early as 1860 it was already playing host to tourists brought by settlers writing home to Europe and raving about the scenery. Stef could hear the pride in Cass's voice when he explained that the Routeburn walking track, starting in his very own Paradise Valley, was one of the ten classic hikes of the world, and the drive from Queenstown to Glenorchy, which they'd done that morning, was one of the top eight scenic drives in the world.

When it was his turn, Stef kept it safe, talking mostly about his jewellery business—his apprenticeship in an old Auckland firm where the grandfather was still handworking his own pieces and had ridden Stef hard to develop his skills, and a bit about his more recent expansion with his own commercial brand, *Stefan.* Cass had asked a million questions, which was flattering. Girls were always fascinated with jewellery, but it wasn't often men showed more than a passing interest—or they wrote it off as a predictably gay endeavour. Whatever.

Stef had been hooked from the minute his teenage self had laid eyes on his grandmother's 1920s gold-filigree-and-pearl flapper head-piece, and he hadn't looked back. These days his interests ran more to male jewellery and to all kinds of piercing items, but he was slowly making a name for himself, and an Australian company had recently bought the rights to a line of his cuffs and chains.

"Is that yours?" Cass pointed to the freeform silver plug Stef wore in one ear.

Stef fingered the earring and shook his head. "This was a friend's. These are mine, though." He pulled back the neck of his T-shirt to reveal his clavicle piercing, with its rose gold bar and titanium end balls. A two-centimetre-long delicate blossom fell from the lower ball, representing a week of painstaking work.

The brothers leaned in for a closer look, but Cass was on his feet in a second and all up in Stef's business in two.

"That's pretty cool." Tomas was so close Stef could've licked his ear.

"Can I take a look?" Cass eyeballed Tomas, who shifted away. Then he leaned closer and ran a finger down the etched leaf. "Is that a... wisteria flower?"

"Yeah." Stef shivered under the touch. "Benny loves them. They're his favourite." Cass's cheek floated just inches away, and that citrus earthy smell Stef thought he'd forever associate with the man drifted between them like one of those wishes they'd talked about in the forest. He closed his eyes and drank it in until a puff of air landed on his lips. When he opened his eyes he found Cass staring at him.

"So this is how you carry him with you?"

Stef nodded weakly and licked his lips. God, Cass's mouth was right there. All it would take is a slight lift, and...

"It's beautiful."

He was. And Stef was finding it all kinds of impossible to focus on anything else with the man centimetres away and the sheer level of heat simmering in those dazzling green eyes. His heart picked up and his cheeks ran hot and... *oh no. No, no, no.* He did not blush. Not for any fucking guy. A little pink, sure, maybe on occasion, but not a full-on blush. He narrowed his gaze and cleared his throat.

Cass blinked slowly, straightened, and returned to his side of the fire, and Stef was acutely aware of Tomas's and Andrew's eyes on the both of them. He wasn't sure how much they'd picked up on, but if their darted glances were anything to go by, they knew something was afoot. Tomas looked like someone had kicked his puppy, while Andrew looked just plain pissed—though whether it was at him or Tomas, Stef couldn't tell.

Stef caught Cass's eye, but Cass quickly looked away which allowed Stef to study his discomfort at a distance. He and Cass were going to have a come-to-Jesus moment pretty damn soon. Stef didn't like being toyed with, and he wanted answers. It might be the worst decision in the world, but a quick tumble in the hay at Cass's farm at the end of all this was sounding better by the minute. It wasn't like he'd be seeing Cass again afterward, so he had nothing to lose, right? But this is-he-isn't-he shit was driving Stef mad.

But it could wait a bit longer. He stretched his legs in front of the fire, ankles crossed, and raked his gaze over the tall cowboy. "Would there happen to be any dessert in that magical food box of yours?" he enquired with a waggle of his eyebrows.

Cass smiled and sprang into action, seemingly relieved to have something to do. Stef wasn't complaining—watching all that tight muscle shift and flex was rapidly becoming his favourite pastime. He drew up a list in his head of all the things he could ask Cass to help with over the next day so Stef could ogle at his leisure. It was a long, long list.

Dee's chocolate lava cake was possibly the best Stef had ever tasted, although that could be partly attributed to eating it under a calm, starlit sky, with Mount Earnslaw silhouetted in the distance and the river valley painted in moonlit stripes. Maybe there was something to this camping lark after all.

"Hey." Cass nudged Stef's foot with his boot. "You were a million miles away."

Stef looked sideways and couldn't help smiling. "Sorry. I was thinking."

A warm thigh pressed against Stef's other side, and he realised Tomas had sidled even closer while Stef had spaced out. *Goddammit.* That would teach him to try and be clever. He shifted away a fraction and hoped that conveyed his meaning without being a dick about it. Tomas frowned and leaned forward to poke at the fire.

Cass watched the manoeuvring with undisguised amusement. "Penny for them," he asked Stef.

Not on your nelly. Stef had been watching Cass collect and stack the dishes with rapt attention to every stretch of denim and flex of muscle on display. There wasn't enough time in the world for all the geography his hands and lips wanted to explore and chart on that mouth-watering terrain. Just thinking about it had his dick straining at the zip of his jeans, and there was no way he was sharing any of that, no matter how pretty the company.

"Nothing, really. Did I miss something?"

"I just said I'll leave you guys to wash up while I check and feed the horses for the night, if that's okay with you?"

"Oh, right, sure. Consider it done." But after a couple of failed attempts to get to his feet, Stef finally had to accept Cass's offer of help, his heart tripping as the other man's huge hand swallowed up his own. Vertical at last, he brushed himself off and slid Cass a wry smile. "I fucking ace this camping shit, right?"

Cass snorted as he left, calling over his shoulder, "Don't forget to take some ibuprofen, princess."

CHAPTER SIX

CASS SHOULD'VE BEEN IN BED HOURS BEFORE, BUT HE SIMPLY couldn't relax. He'd crawled into the sleeping bag on his cot only to find himself sandwiched between Stef and Tomas, something he suspected was Stef's doing to keep Tomas at a bit of a distance. The younger brother hadn't struck Cass as anything but straight at first, but there was no denying he seemed to have developed a certain starry-eyed attraction to Stef, one that had Cass squirming with a response far too close to possessive to be comfortable.

And he wasn't the only one to pick up on the little crush. Andrew had watched his brother on and off all through the evening, darting glances between him and Stef as if just waiting for a reason to say something spiteful. Luckily Stef didn't give him one, but Andrew clearly wasn't happy, and Cass couldn't help but wonder if this was the first time Andrew had asked himself that particular question about his brother. He couldn't imagine Tomas being out and Andrew being happy to live and let live, so it made more sense that he hadn't had a clue about Tomas... until now.

But if Tomas thought he'd been subtle, Cass suspected he'd been rapidly disabused of that notion once the dishes were done. While

Cass was finishing with the horses, he'd witnessed a heated conversation between the two brothers. Nothing Cass could hear clearly, but given the furious, disgusted expression on Andrew's face as he left for the hut, and Tomas's shocked and dismayed one as he stood by the fire and stared after his brother, Cass hadn't needed an interpreter.

Cass approached the younger man to offer an ear, but Tomas saw him coming and fled inside. Cass would try again in the morning, and if Andrew put a foot wrong between now and when they got back to the farm, Cass was gonna rip the bigoted arsehole a new one. Roll on tomorrow. Happy fucking days.

At least Stef didn't appear to return Tomas's interest, so there was that. It seemed pretty clear his interest lay in Cass's direction which was... flattering, and set off a ridiculous fluttering in his stomach. Hence the reason he was back outside under his oilskin coat with a blanket wrapped overtop, prodding the dying fire into life at one a.m. while freezing his damn balls off. If he had to spend another minute around the sweet notes from the bubble gum chapstick Stef seemed to apply in every spare minute, Cass was gonna blow a gasket from the frustration alone.

Not to mention Stef had fallen asleep facing Cass's cot. Of course Cass could've turned away and faced Tomas instead, but yeah, like that was ever gonna fucking happen. There was just enough moonlight for Cass to see the rise and fall of Stef's chest and to trace those fine features, relaxed in a way Cass had never seen when the man was awake. Stef always seemed to be on his guard, ready with a quick reply and keen to get everyone else on the back foot so he could keep the upper hand.

It had a charm of its own, but *this* version of Stef—this was all sorts of fucking trouble for Cass, who just wanted to haul the guy over on to his cot, wrap him in his arms, and keep the world at bay. Dammit if there wasn't something fragile about him in a fierce, paper tiger kind of way. And then there were those damn piercings. Cass couldn't get them out of his head... or help wondering if there were any more of them.

Knowing what to do about his inconvenient crush was the $64,000 question. Cass was pretty sure if he so much as squeaked that particular door open, they'd be having a bit of naked fun at the end of the tour. Hell, Cass could even ask Stef to stay the night, since his father was gone mustering for another week. He'd have all the time in the world to get acquainted with Stef's body art. Then Stef would go and Cass would be... what?

And that right there was the problem.

Cass knew already he wasn't going to be satisfied with a one-and-done with Stef, or likely even a short fling. But he also couldn't think of anyone less suitable for him to be interested in—city boy, horse shy, out-and-proud gay as a fucking Easter parade, and based at the other end of the country. A sure-fire way to find himself up to his armpits in emotional alligators. Been there, done that, got the T-shirt—not to mention the divorce. Best thing all around was to just enjoy the view and let it head on back to where it belonged, unmo-lested. *Yeah, right.* Which of course explained why he was sitting outside in the middle of the night, freezing his dick off and talking to himself.

"You looking to be alone, or did the fart haze finally get to you?" A hand landed on Cass's shoulder as Stef ever so slowly lowered himself on to the tree trunk alongside. "Man, I don't know what you put in those beans, but holy shit, those boys are rotten in there. Or maybe it's just you southerners? Should've packed my air freshener."

Cass snorted. "You bought damn near everything else. I mean, tamarillos? Who the hell packs tamarillos on an overnight horse trek?"

Stef managed to look affronted and amused at the same time. "I told you, they were my brother's idea. And no one back at lover's lane central liked them too much."

"You not a fan of your friend's new... arrangement, then?"

Stef raised a brow. "All the coupley shit, you mean? Nah, it's not that. I'm thrilled for Tanner. Ethan is really nice—"

Cass nodded. "He is."

"It's just a bit... intense, I guess." Stef poked at the fire. "Fuck, it's cold out here."

Cass took the blanket from his shoulders and draped it around the other man.

Stef tilted his head. He studied Cass from the corner of his eye and went to shrug the covering off, but Cass stopped him with a hand to his shoulder. "Take it."

Stef flashed him a grateful smile, edged closer, and pulled the blanket around both of them. "I vote we share."

Fuck. That was all Cass needed.

"Don't growl."

"I wasn't."

"You were. I won't bite."

"Says you."

Stef faced him with overly wide eyes. "Why, Mr Martin. If I didn't know better, I'd think you were nervous about being so close to me. Not sure whether it's because you don't trust me or you don't trust yourself."

Cass narrowed his gaze. "Why, Mr Hamilton. Be assured you have nothing to worry about. I'm a professional, and some of us don't find the need to hit on everything that walks on two legs." *Fuck.* He hadn't meant to sound such a judgemental dick.

"Ouch." Stef watched him closely. "There's a difference between light-hearted flirting and hitting on someone. I figured you'd know what that was. Maybe I was wrong. But just so we're clear, I don't cross that line unless I mean it. And let me assure you, *Mr* Martin, there is a very long list of criteria to be met before that happens. I think maybe I'll leave you to enjoy your fire."

He went to stand, but Cass grabbed his wrist. "Please, stay. I'm sorry. Clearly I turn into an arsehole after midnight."

Stef stared at him for a moment, the orange flames dancing in those hazel eyes in a way that made him seem almost wolf-like: a little predatory, a little *I wanna rub my smell all over you right fucking now.* Cass would've taken either and considered himself damn lucky.

Stef smiled coyly. "Okay, we'll go with that, for now. But there's a whole unfinished conversation that needs to be had between you and I about this issue, understand? Having said that, you're lucky, because I'm too sore and too damn tired to start it. But it's not over."

Cass chuckled and reluctantly let go of his arm. "I imagine not. By the way, did you take something for the pain?"

Stef winced and squirmed on his arse. "Yeah, fat lot of good they did me. I'm not sure I'll ever get feeling back in my tailbone, and my balls have packed their bags and headed for more welcoming accommodation. I don't know how you do it day in and day out."

Cass shrugged and threw another lump of wood on the now-blazing fire. "Let's just say my balls have had a long time to get used to it." Between the blanket and his oilskin coat, the heat was building to uncomfortable, but Cass wasn't racing to get free any time soon. Stef's warm body was all kinds of tempting as he leaned into Cass and sucked the heat from him as if they hadn't just met sixteen hours before.

"*Pfft*. I bet they just shrivel from the wear and tear till they're like hard little walnuts." Stef sounded genuinely concerned. "I bet they're tucked up inside your belly somewhere, immune to everything this country might throw at them—horses, snow, rocks, freezing rivers, everything. And I think you need to prove to me I'm wrong, just so I can sleep reassured on your behalf."

Cass tilted his head back and laughed. "Oh, you do, do you?"

"Absolutely." Stef nudged him with his shoulder. "Solely for the purposes of science and scholarship, of course."

Cass reached over to draw the blanket around Stef's shoulders a little tighter. "I think you'll have to take my word for it. My balls are soft, suitably sized, and geographically appropriate."

Stef pushed out his lower lip. "If you insist. Spoilsport."

"I do." He brushed a lock of hair from Stef's eyes before he could catch himself. *Jesus Christ.* He needed to stop touching the man. He dropped his hand, but not before he caught the twitch of Stef's lips. "I take it yours aren't all of the above, after today?"

Stef wriggled once again. "Are you kidding? They're all lawyered up and filing suit for wilful neglect and abuse. Let's just say they're, um, used to a certain level of consideration."

God, this man. Cass was struggling to not lose his shit completely. "Well, I apologise to your balls on behalf of the entire horse population of Southland."

Stef gave a curt nod. "Apology accepted." He dug at the burning logs with a long stick, wiggling his legs around till his merino-sock-covered feet were sat right in front of the heat.

Cass always provided the thick socks for his customers as part of the deal. They were no good for wearing in boots, but man, nothing beat them for keeping out the cold. And at these alpine reaches, even midsummer nights were on the chilly side.

"You did good today," he said, keeping his eyes on the fire and his thoughts on that slim molten rectangle where their bodies were aligned and touching.

Stef snorted. "You don't need to humour me. I know I sucked. Hell, I consider a three-star hotel roughing it. And I know the impression I give; poor little soft city boy with his eyeliner and nail polish, I'm hardly a poster child for Lumberjacks R Us." He stabbed at the fire, his lips set in a tight line.

"Hey, did I say that?" Cass leaned forward so their shoulders were touching. "So I grew up on a farm. I know animals and roughing it. But you should see me in the city—pathetic and floundering doesn't even begin to cover it. I wouldn't know my latte from my ristretto—"

Stef's lips twitched.

"You'd mow me down in Britomart Station while I was trying to work out which train to catch, then have to come back the next day to scrape my country arse off the pavement. I can't wait to get out of the place. But if I went up there with you, you'd look after me. Down here, I do the same for you."

"It's not the same thing. This"—Stef waved his arm to the hut and the horses—"this shit is fucking testosterone crap, right? And I know it doesn't mean anything, not really, but it still carries all those over-tones, and it's just another sucky way I don't tick the box. Even gays drool over that whole masc thing. Jesus, I'm what they mean when they say 'no fems' on Grindr, for fuck's sake."

Cass closed his hand over Stef's. "Stop and look at me."

Stef let the stick fall but let Cass keep hold of his hand. Then he begrudgingly turned sideways, eyes wary, and Cass felt the urge, yet again, to wrap his body around Stef and keep him safe.

Instead he said, "Look, I don't know who you've been listening to or where you got all this shit you just spouted, but I'm going to say it again, and this time you're going to hear it: You. Did. Great. Today."

Stef's brows knitted in a frown, and his eyes searched Cass's face for any sign he was being made fun of. Or at least that's what Cass guessed he was doing. Well, he wouldn't find it, because Cass meant every word.

He continued, "I've taken tours with first-timers who never got off the lead rope in two days. You were on your own in an hour. You didn't fall, you didn't spook your horse. You looked after her, including those bits of doughnuts and whatever else you've been feeding her from that damn pocket."

Stef regarded Cass with a decidedly unapologetic expression. "She was patient with me. She looked after me. She deserved it."

Cass grinned and squeezed his hand. "You looked after each other. You handled that river crossing like a pro—relaxed and trusted me to get you over. You helped with the food and the fire and brushed your horse down. She's comfortable with you, and that's no mean thing. Horses are sensitive; they don't give respect easy. They're big animals, and if they think they can get away with shit, they'll try it on. So I don't want to hear you say you suck at all this. Are we good on that?"

Stef stared at him for a long time, and Cass was worried he'd gone too far. Then Stef nodded, and he let go the breath he'd been holding.

"I, um, don't know what to say. But if you truly believe that, then yes, we're good. It's just, well, no one ever says stuff like that to me."

Cass shrugged and looked away. "Well, they should. You're tougher than you look, Stef, and tougher than you think you are. Hell, you've got your own business up and running. You just need to trust yourself more."

A heavy silence fell between them, and Cass guessed he'd finally gone and said too much, as usual. He had no right. He didn't know Stef well enough to make any of those broad statements. And, Jesus, who was he to talk? His whole life had been a chain of disastrous decisions all based around not trusting himself or that it was okay to want less than everyone else—or at least something different from them. He'd learned the hard way not to try to turn himself upside down just to make someone else happy.

Hazel eyes rested on Cass with something more than gratitude. "Ever since I was a kid, I was *that* gay kid." Stef's voice threaded softly between them. "Most schools had one, right? A bit fabulous, a bit precious, didn't like to get dirty, hair always styled just so, sarcastic and smarta walking fucking stereotype. You know the one."

Cass had to nod. He did. "Mark Wheeler. Nice guy, but yeah, what you said. He's now a costume designer with Weta Workshop, almost famous." He quirked up a smile.

Stef snorted. "See, I told you. Walking fucking stereotype."

"But that doesn't mean—"

"I know. I know. And to be honest, embracing it got me through those teenage years pretty damn well. When you already don't fit in, it pays not to give them further ammunition, so I avoided any activity that even remotely smelled of testosterone. I had a posse of bestie girl friends who were fierce and popular, so none of the real bastards messed with me for fear of pissing them off—but I didn't have a lot of guy friends, not till I left school. Which, honestly, probably didn't help with the whole Boy Scout–fail issue. It got me through, but it maybe stopped me from trying as well, if that makes sense?"

It did, and Cass's heart squeezed for the teenage Stef. Cass had had it easy in that regard. He'd passed as straight without a second look most of the time. "You have those friends now, though, right?" For some reason Cass really needed that to be the case.

Stef smiled. "Yeah, I do. But I still suck at the outdoors thing."

Cass opened his mouth to protest again, but Stef held up his hand.

"My last boyfriend was the outdoorsy type. Though to be fair, he was also a bit of a douchebag, even if it took me till the end to see it. At the beginning, and right up until the day he dumped my colour-me-surprised arse, I thought he was pretty cool." Stef's gaze slid back to the fire. "I thought I was in love with him, to be honest. We'd been living together three years." A flash of pain clouded Stef's expression, and he paused, watching the fire spark at his feet. "I was so naive."

Damn. Cass wanted the name of the man who'd put that defeated look in Stef's eyes.

"I had this whole future planned out in my head. I thought he was *the one.*" He snorted in self-disgust. "Talk about being played for a mug."

Cass watched him carefully. "Did he cheat on you?"

Stef looked up and shook his head. "Nah, nothing like that. Might have been easier if he had, though. No, he, um, was a nurse. Worked in a private hospital. Then one day he comes back to our flat and announces he's signed a two-year contract with Doctors Without Borders and he's off to Syria."

Cass gaped. "What the hell?"

"Right? I didn't even know he'd applied. He went through all the interviews and everything without saying a damn word. Said he just had to do it. That he loved me, but if he didn't take the opportunity he'd regret it for the rest of his life." Stef leaned back on his hands and stared at the night sky. "Clearly *leaving me* wasn't going to give him the same problems."

"Jesus, Stef. He sounds like a total arsehole."

Stef lifted a shoulder. "That's the problem. He wasn't, not really. He was a nice guy... well, kind of. I'd simply read him completely wrong. And see, here's the rub. I asked why he didn't tell me he wanted to apply—that maybe I could've gone with him, volunteered or something, I don't know. They'd probably have laughed me out of the interview, but I could've tried, right? I mean, fuck, I thought we were heading for the forever, white-picket-fence thing. But when I asked the question, he cracked up and said that I'd never have coped with any of it. That he'd spend all his time worrying about me—and he didn't want me trying to talk him out of it, so he decided it was easier not to say anything."

Not willing to risk betraying how furious he was, Cass kept his glare to the fire, but he couldn't keep the angry growl from his voice. "Easier for him, the fucker."

Stef looked up in surprise.

But, goddammit, Cass wanted a few minutes alone with Stef's ex. You don't want to be with someone? You want something different, you have a dream you need to live, you don't feel the same way? Then have the conversation, for fuck's sake. His ex-wife sprang to mind, but Cass shoved that nauseating thought back where it belonged, with all the other buried crap he had no time for.

Stef studied him with a curious look. "Yeah, maybe. But he was right. I do suck at all this outdoor stuff. When I read what Doctors Without Borders do and where they go, it was probably better that he didn't tell me."

Cass turned and eyeballed him. "I thought we'd been through this and established you don't, in fact, suck at it. You've just never tried it, right?"

Stef sighed and looked away. "So *you* say. And okay, if I can ride a horse, then maybe I have a tad more potential than I thought. But that doesn't mean I'm a good candidate for an NGO assignment in a war zone."

Cass nudged his shoulder, and Stef leaned into the touch enough for Cass to feel the warmth of his body. "No, it doesn't," he said. "But neither am I. Outdoor skills aside, I'm pretty sure I don't have what it takes to deal with all that. I'd come back a raging mess of anxiety and PTSD. I wouldn't cope."

Stef's brows crunched together as if that was a totally astonishing concept. "Really?"

"Really."

Stef gave a faint smile. "Huh. Not sure I believe you, but thanks."

"Believe me, I'm not brave in that way at all. So, is that what put the dent in the romantic?" Cass asked, and a crease formed between Stef's brows. He explained, "What you said in the forest, yesterday."

"Oh, right." Stef wrinkled his nose. "Yeah, pretty much."

Cass grunted and crossed his legs up under him to get them away from the heat. "Well, for what it's worth, I think you'd have made a good volunteer, once you got used to things. Better than me."

Stef cast an expression of total disbelief his way. "Nice of you to say, but it's a long way from barely learning to keep my gay arse on a horse to volunteering in a refugee camp. Unless they needed a nail salon, right? Or maybe I could use my jewellery skills. All those starving families lining up for ear gauges and piercings just to take their minds off th—"

"Stop it," Cass snapped.

And surprisingly, Stef did, shutting his mouth with a nervous glance Cass's way. "What?"

"You damn well know what. Stop dismissing yourself. I didn't say you'd find it easy, I said you'd be a good volunteer."

Stef opened his mouth again, but this time Cass laid a finger on his lips and... *shit*... they were as warm and soft as they looked. They also immediately froze with his touch, and for a second he couldn't tear his gaze from where they connected. Then he felt the heat of Stef's eyes and whipped his hand back. "Sorry." He cleared his throat at the roughness in his voice.

"Don't be." Stef let out a slow breath, his gaze locked on Cass. "I'm not."

Cass blinked and looked away, the fire, the touch of their bodies, the pleasing scent of the other man all crowding his senses and messing with his common sense. "Yeah, well, it shouldn't have happened," he muttered. "So like I said, I'm sorry. But I do want to answer your question about why Doctors Without Borders would be lucky to have you."

Cass faced Stef again. "You seem to like people, sass not withstanding—and I imagine that's actually not a bad thing to have in that kind of work. From what I can see, you read people a little like I read horses—using intuition mixed with a good dose of street smarts—but you're no pushover—in fact, you're a bit of a firebrand. Now, I don't know you that well, but I feel safe in thinking you also have a good heart. And all of that, is why I believe you'd do well."

Stef's mouth opened, then closed again. He shook his head and turned away. "I think your beer must have been spiked."

Cass's chest tightened. "Are you saying you'd take him back?"

Stef groaned. "God, no. And Tanner said much the same thing about me coping better than Paul thought I would. With the addition of cutting Paul's balls off and pickling his dick in sulphuric acid."

Cass snorted. "I like this Tanner."

"You would. Which is an excellent reason never to introduce you. I could see the two of you getting on too damn well, and I don't need another smart-arse in my life."

"How about another friend?"

Stef's head whipped around, and he stared at Cass for a moment before his expression softened. "Yeah, why not? Not that I'm down this way too often, but yeah, every gay man needs a cowboy in their life, right?" He fired Cass a wicked grin.

Cass snorted. "You get that I'm not really a cowboy?"

Stef gave Cass a shining look. "A boy can dream. Plus, you come pretty damn close."

Cass groaned. "You're gonna tell that to Ethan, and I'm never gonna live this down."

Stef waggled his brows.

"Ugh, I knew it. But seriously, you should learn to ride properly. There must be stables up your way—all those rich Remuera kids. And you seem to enjoy it."

Stef glanced behind them at the horses, and the corners of his eyes crinkled. "You know, I do enjoy it. Surprised the hell out of me." He turned and met Cass's eyes with a thoughtful gaze. "Do you really think I could? Not all horses are like Arwen, I'm guessing."

"No, they're not." Cass took Stef's hand without thinking and squeezed. "But no respectable instructor is going to put you on a difficult horse to start. And yes, I really think you can do it."

Stef dropped his eyes to where his hand sat enveloped in Cass's much larger one and smiled brightly. "So... maybe not so straight, then, Mr Martin?"

He looked back up, and for a few seconds Cass had no words, lost in the rich colours of forest and fire reflected in those eyes. Finally he chuckled. "Bent as fuck, Mr Hamilton."

Stef's lips twitched, and he reached up and pressed a chaste kiss to the corner of Cass's mouth, sending a herd of butterflies tumbling through Cass's chest and searing the taste of bubble gum chapstick into Cass's brain forever. Then, to Cass's surprise, instead of pressing for more, Stef pulled his hand free and got gingerly to his feet.

"I like you, Cassidy Martin. But if I stay here any longer, that friend basket you so nicely put me in isn't going to have a chance in hell of holding me. And I don't want you to do something you'll regret. Thanks for the pep talk. I appreciate it. See you in the morning."

CHAPTER SEVEN

STEF GOT THREE STEPS BEFORE A HAND LANDED ON HIS shoulder and spun him into Cass's arms. *Thank fuck for that!* He wasn't sure he'd have made it much farther before caving and running back like a fool, begging for Cass to please, please just kiss him, or let Stef blow him, or throw Stef down over the log and fuck him till the sun came up—preferably all three, and not necessarily in that order.

To hell with being friends. What on earth was Cass thinking? Stef could be friends with Cass about as easily as he could stop his dick from lighting up every time the other man walked within sniffing distance. So, yeah, there was that. This was way, way less humiliating.

"Why, Mr Martin, whatever are you doing?" He regarded Cass coyly through fringed lashes. The hard-to-get play might have worked better if Cass's gaze didn't have enough heat in it to support a solar system or two, turning Stef's mouth to sawdust and sending his cock to rigid attention.

"This." Cass lifted him off his feet, swivelled, and planted him on one of the sawn-off rounds, bringing the two of them almost eye to eye. And if anyone said Stef squealed, they were damn liars. Cass closed the distance between them until he was so far up in Stef's business he may as well have bought the lease and put his name on the sign out front, and Stef was so, so down with every aspect of that idea it was almost embarrassing. Then Cass simply stopped, his gaze locked on Stef, and waited.

Stef leaned forward and brushed Cass's ear with his lips. "You, um... need directions, there? 'Cause I'm an excellent navigator."

Cass leaned his cheek and nuzzled into Stef's hair, and... *holy shit*, Stef didn't think something so damn cute could be so fucking sexy. He pulled back and cocked his head. "If you're waiting for permission, Cowboy, you have it. So, how about you give me a taste of all those thoughts running around in that head of yours, and we'll take it from there."

Cass grunted, his pupils blew wide, and Stef sucked in a breath. *Finally.*

Cass slid one hand to cradle the back of Stef's neck while the other held him gently by the throat, and *holy fuck*, the subtle dominance cranked Stef's shit so hard so he could barely breathe.

Keeping up the soft pressure, Cass turned Stef's head from side to side, running his mouth and nose over every inch of Stef's throat: nibbling his ear, breathing through his hair, rubbing his cheek along Stef's temple, all the while murmuring how sexy Stef was, how beautiful, how hot, and all the delicious filthy and wonderful things Cass wanted to do to him, until the words had reduced Stef to a puddle of want, and need, and right the hell now.

It was like nothing Stef had experienced before, so fucking new he didn't know what to think—if he could've held a thought in his head. Which he couldn't, too lost in where Cass's lips would touch next, where his nose would brush, his cheek, that fucking sexy hum that rumbled in his throat.

He was being inhaled, tasted, savoured. It wasn't ravenous or devouring, it was... fascinating and adoring. As if Cass was captivated with the smell of Stef, the taste of him, the feel of his hair and skin.

And it was so fucking intoxicating to be thought of and explored like he was a delicious puzzle to solve, a cherished opportunity too good to miss—a fine wine, every aspect being fully appreciated before the first taste.

Most of Stef's lovers were turned on by the idea of subduing the sass in him, relishing the battle Stef offered just by being himself. But *this*? Stef didn't know what to do with *this*. Because in that moment Cass owned every bit of him, every square centimetre, every groan and flare of pleasure, and that was... well it wasn't how things went in Stef's world.

He didn't do that. Guys didn't get to overwhelm him, not even Paul. No one was worth that level of vulnerability. The slice of defensiveness in him as wide as a fucking ocean always kept him in the game, on top of the action. He topped from the bottom like a fucking champ—that was his signature. But this— *Put me under a microscope and map my DNA, bordering on worship? Holy hell.* This was a fucking drug with Stef's name on it, and he wanted nothing more than to lay himself out on a table and tell the man to have at him, he'd collect the pieces later—to give Cass whatever he wanted, whatever he needed as long as he kept doing *this*.

While Stef was battling the urge to pull away versus the one to rip the very clothes off his body and paint "Yours" all over it, Cass raised his head and drew their faces close enough to brush their noses two or three times. All done to that endless stream of soft murmurs and sweet nonsense that did Stef's head in. It was unexpected, and romantic, and sweet, and shocking, and hot as fucking Hades. He lapped up every second of it, while at the same time his head screamed "Danger" in tall, flashing, neon orange capital letters.

Then Cass closed the distance between them, covered Stef's mouth, and it was all over. His lips moved, warm and soft, and with a happy sigh, Stef melted like butter. When he licked along the seam of Stef's lips, Stef opened immediately, their tongues plunging alongside each other, desperate to finally, finally taste and explore.

Cass groaned and pulled Stef hard against him. There was no

mistaking he was as into this as Stef, his swollen cock pushing into Stef's stomach in a delicious tease that had Stef two seconds away from falling to his knees and taking the man down his throat without further ado.

That was if he could free himself from Cass's iron grip any time soon. One hand was still lightly wrapped around Stef's throat, while the other was on the move, down under the waistband of Stef's—thank Christ—loose jeans and barely there briefs, to cup his arse and haul him even closer. A finger slid into his crease, pressed on his hole, and... *dear God...* Stef barely recognised the needy moan he breathed into Cass's mouth.

Cass smiled against his lips. "You like that, huh?"

How he managed to say anything with his tongue far enough down Stef's throat to strike oil, Stef had no fucking idea. But the answering squeak he summoned in reply must've been enough to reassure Cass that Stef did indeed *like that*, and yes please, and a lot more, and right the hell now—because Cass promptly pushed Stef's jeans down a little further, pulled back and licked his fingers slow and filthy, and then inserted the tip of that middle sucker up where the sun don't shine. And this time Stef's whimper came in full Dolby surround sound and earned him an approving chuckle and a nip to his lower lip.

But holy smokes. Between Cass fucking Stef's mouth with his tongue, and Stef riding Cass's finger in his arse, it was nearly all over, Rover, without Stef even getting a single touch, let alone a lick, spit, and polish to his aching dick. *Nuh-uh. No way in hell.*

Stef tried to wriggle free but Cass had the grip of a sumo octopus, and a large part of Stef was more than happy to stay in his arms. What they had going on was all kinds of hot, needy, and intense, but it was also achingly insufficient to slake Stef's true desire. And in case Cass came to his senses and this was the only time Stef ever got him even halfway to indecent, he sure as shit wasn't gonna go out on a bit of schoolboy-level hot-and-heavy. He wanted at the very minimum a look, feel, and taste of the other man. Stef had many, many more boxes that needed ticking.

He finally wrenched his jaw free and shoved Cass back, which was easier said than done, given their vast difference in height and weight, and Stef's arse felt suddenly cold and empty. Cass smiled wickedly and took a step back toward him, but Stef used a hand on his chest to keep him at arm's length. They stood there, breathing heavily and regarding each other like a favourite ice cream just out of reach. Stef took a second to remember why he wasn't already tripping the light fantastic, getting messy in his jeans, and yelling the man's name, but then... *oh yeah, right...*

Cass pushed against Stef's hand.

Stef pushed back.

"Nuh-uh. Hold it right there, Mister. I'll admit you've got a good game going there... okay, a great game"—Stef cleared his throat and narrowed his gaze, trying to look a lot more convincing than he felt, because the truth was, he was two Cass sniffs away from a full roll-over-and-belly-up submission—"but if you think I'm gonna come in my briefs for you without even getting a gander at what's in those jeans of yours, or at least a finger or two on my dick, you need to think again."

Cass bit back a smile and pushed harder against Stef's hand. "Is that right? You think I've got game?"

Stef shored up his elbow and scrambled together a glare, which only earned him a flirty smirk in return. Admittedly he might have sold it better without the epic boner currently tenting his trousers, but yeah... good luck with that.

"You have excellent game," he confessed, and Cass beamed, eyes flashing like bright green jewels in the glow of the fire. *Goddammit.* "Stop that." Stef waggled his finger at the other man. "No more of this witchy-woo shit. I have standards. I have needs. I have a decent eight... well, okay, seven-inch warhead lodged in my pants that needs immediate attention, and I won't be distracted by any of your—"

"Seven inches, huh?" Cass's grin turned all shades of wicked, and he licked his lips slowly.

Stef's mouth ran dry. "Uh, yes. Absolutely. That's what I said, right? Yes, indeedy. You know, maybe even seven and a half with a good tailwind, and—wh-what are you doing?"

Cass wrapped a hand around Stef's wrist and leaned in till they were almost nose to nose. His tongue darted out and flicked over Stef's lips, and... *goddammit*, there went another whimper.

"You sure about not getting distracted?" He kissed the end of Stef's nose while moving Stef's hand from between them altogether. Of its own accord, the traitor circled Cass's waist till it found a generous handful of arse to maul, which earned Stef another one of those throaty growls.

"You like that, huh?" Stef threw Cass's words back at him, and that knee-dropping smile got another workout.

"I do." Cass pressed a kiss to Stef's lips. "A lot."

Stef rolled his hips forward till the solid length of Cass's erection pressed up against his own, and... *Oh. My. God*, it was in complete proportion with the man's towering height. His mouth watered at the same time as his arse tightened in a teensy shiver of nerves. He slid a hand between them to cup Cass through his jeans and squeezed firmly.

"My, my, Mister Martin, they sure grow them big down here."

A crease formed between Cass's brows, accompanied by a flash of concern. "Too much? You know you don't have—"

Shit. Not what Stef meant.

He stopped whatever was about to come out of Cass's mouth next with a kiss. "Hell no. I'm up for the challenge. We'll just, um, take it slow, yeah?"

Cass cast a nervous glance over Stef's shoulder to the hut. "Maybe it's not a good idea. I'm not so sure we should—"

Stef covered Cass's mouth with his own before he could get cold feet and say something ridiculous like they should stop. Which they should, of course... but hell no, and fuck that, and not on your fucking nelly, Mister.

"I want you," Stef whispered between kisses. "I don't care how we do it, as long as there's naked skin involved, a lot of friction, a digit or two would be fucking awesome if you could find it in you to deliver, and a mouth... holy shit, I have to stop talking or I'm gonna jizz where I stand."

Cass snorted, but Stef kept on kissing till he was sure he had Cass's attention back where he wanted it.

"So yeah, something like that... pretty please?" He stepped back and batted his lashes invitingly. "And sometime soon would be just grand. Do you need me to beg? Because I'd be totally down with that."

Cass sent another wary glance to the hut, then back to Stef, and the grin that split his face was breathtaking.

Stef did a mental fist pump. *Hell yeah.* This was gonna happen. He would've almost taken the bet that Cass was gonna bug out, but no, it appeared Stef was gonna get his hands on the sexy man after all.

Cass pinned him with a predatory look. "You're trouble, Stefan Hamilton—"

"Oh, absolutely." Stef slid up Cass's chest like a sleek cat till those long arms encircled him. "I'm so much trouble, like you wouldn't believe. Such a bad, bad boy." He angled his head and peeked up at Cass through half-closed lashes to give him a lazy smile. "But I'm worth it... if you can keep me in line." *Holy shit, what am I doing?*

Cass eyes widened, then he gave a slow, sexy grin. "Is that right? I'm not sure that's entirely possible, based on current data, but I'm up for the challenge."

Stef bit his lip and watched Cass's gaze track to it. *Oh yeah.* The man was fully on board. "Well, you can try."

Cass fired one last glance at the hut, then grabbed Stef's hand. "I'll do more than try. Come with me." He grabbed the blanket from the ground and hauled Stef around the back of the hut. There was enough watery moonlight to guide their feet all the way over to the lean-to tacked on to the horses' shelter that housed the feed bales and was well out of sight of curious eyes.

Hell yeah. Stef was so damn excited he nearly tripped over a coil of baling twine lying on the ground. Cass caught him just in time and swung him against the nearest hay bale, caging him in with hands on either side of his head.

Stef gave Cass a slow once-over, then took a look at the nest of bales that surrounded them. "Love what you've done with the place."

Cass snorted and hauled off his coat, throwing it to the ground with a decided thunk.

Stef raised a brow.

"Satphone," Cass explained.

Stef arched his hips forward to try and gain some friction. He connected with Cass's thigh, which in turn placed the man's thick cock hard up against Stef's stomach. *Damn he was big.*

Cass hissed and sucked in a breath.

Stef rubbed his nose up Cass's throat and nibbled his ear.

"Fucking oath, Cassidy. If this cowboy-in-the-barn shit wasn't one of my fantasies before, it sure as hell is now. So, now you've got me here, what are you going to do with me? And I sure hope the answer includes words like 'hay bale' and 'over' and 'fuck me,' or it's gonna be hella disappointing."

Cass kissed each of Stef's eyelids and then slowly worked his way down to his mouth. "Is that what you want?" He eyed Stef like he wanted to eat him alive. Well, Stef was down with that.

"Right now I'll take anything I can get. You've got me so worked up I've got steam coming out my arse, and—mmm—"

Cass's lips took over, and Stef immersed himself in a kiss that was as demanding and voracious as the others had been tender. Long limbs wrapped around him, and Cass's hard body trapped him against the hay, giving Stef enough purchase to swing his legs up to lock around Cass's waist.

"Jesus, you're so fucking tall," he mumbled, wriggling just enough to be sure Cass's hard dick was aligned nicely behind his balls, then sliding up and down all that tight denim. In the meantime they rediscovered each other's tonsils, and Stef found himself lost once again in everything Cass, including his smell—that blend of the earth and hay and the sweet edge of dessert. Delicious didn't even begin to describe it.

Cass dropped Stef to his feet and took a step back, pupils blown in the moonlight. "Okay, so I might need those damn clothes off before I rip them from your beautiful body." He cupped himself and squeezed.

Well, damn. Stef eyed him sideways, drew his wallet from his pocket and dropped a condom and packet of lube on the ground. Then he set about unbuttoning his jeans in no particular haste. Done with that, he turned ever so slowly until he had his back to Cass, at which point he bent over and slid his jeans down his legs to the floor before stepping out of them, giving Cass a front-row seat to his arse, which he then shimmied... just a little.

The strangled grunt his performance earned shot Stef's arousal from hot to incendiary, but he wasn't done yet. Keeping his back to Cass, he then hooked his thumbs into his briefs and slid them off as well, and just as slowly, standing to pull his T-shirt over his head to finish with a flourish. Then he turned, naked, and stood there with one hand on his hip while a crooked finger on the other beckoned to a salivating Cass whose gaze had locked on to Stef's cock in wide-eyed disbelief.

Stef allowed himself a satisfied smirk. "Cat got your tongue, Cowboy? You wanna pick that jaw of yours off the floor before you drown in your own drool... just saying."

Cass swallowed hard, blinked slowly, and cleared his throat. "You're, um... I mean, you have a... fucking hell, Stef..."

Stef cocked his head and raised an eyebrow. "You mean these old things?" He swept a hand over his junk, which sported a series of hafada piercings on the anterior of his scrotum just under his penis, so when it was erect the three intricate yellow, white, and rose gold rings were clearly visible. There was another bar in Stef's hip, and one in his pubes just at the base of his penis, though his penis itself was clear—he'd never felt the need to quite go there, but in the future, who knew?

He was used to getting a reaction—some guys thought it hot, some weren't so sure, most just thought he was fucking weird. But Stef loved them, and if Cass's lustful expression was anything to go by, it seemed the cowboy did as well. He could only pray he'd get the opportunity to show Cass just how the rings tickled all those sensitive nerves on the outside of his hole when Stef was balls deep inside him. Happy thoughts.

"Do they... hurt?" Cass looked at him anxiously.

Stef winked. "Only if you want them to. Now, are you just gonna stand there all night, or you gonna fuck my fine arse like I asked you to?"

Cass closed the distance between them in an instant, pushing Stef up against the upright stack of oversized rectangular hay bales so he could plunder his mouth and run his greedy hands all over Stef's skin. They found his arse, and fingers dipped into the crease to brush over his hole.

"Yesss." That Stef was naked and wrapped in Cass's fully clothed body was hot as all hell, and offered more than enough compensations for the scratchy rub of the hay on his skin. He slid a hand between them to close over Cass's straining dick, still trapped in his jeans, and gave it a firm squeeze.

"You're overdressed, Mister Martin," Stef said breathily. "Can I help you with that?"

"Soon." Cass stepped back and stared at Stef with a look that could've singed his eyebrows clean off. Then he reached down, grabbed the rug he'd discarded, and threw it over a single bale on the ground. "Sit," he growled.

Holy shit. Stef sat.

Cass walked up and put his groin at eye level with Stef, and Stef's mouth filled with saliva. Fuck, he couldn't wait. He wasn't usually into play like this, but son of a bitch, bossy Cass was a fucking wet dream.

"Undo me."

Stef did, then dropped his hands and waited, laser focused on the glistening wet patch at the front of Cass's tight black briefs. It was all he could do not to take that sucker down the back of his throat there and then. He loved giving head and was good at it, gag reflex be damned—something he was keen to show the man standing in front of him.

"Take me out."

Stef released Cass's impressive erection, slid those briefs down to his hips, and held Cass's pulsing cock by its base. He barely got his fingers around the monster, but he was past worrying about something as trivial as whether the fucking thing was ever going to fit in his aching hole. He'd make damn sure it did, even if he didn't walk straight for a month.

"Excellent." Gentle fingers threaded through his hair, and Stef turned his head to nuzzle Cass's palm. Cass stroked his cheek with his thumb. "Such a sweet man."

And damn if Stef's dick didn't jump to attention. He glanced up and caught Cass's smirk. *Fuck.* He hadn't missed that.

"Now, how about you open up and let me into that sassy mouth so I can fill it for you."

Stef pulled his lower lip between his teeth and winked. "Like I haven't heard that before."

Cass chuckled. "I bet you have. But did they have the goods to follow through?"

And if Stef whimpered, who could blame him? Cass was sinfully hot, he had a filthy mouth, and even though Stef was thirty-seven, Cass possessed one of the biggest dicks Stef had ever had the pleasure of entertaining, and, well, did he really need to add anything more? So he did exactly as instructed and swallowed Cass down the back of his throat and went to town.

Hands cupped his jaw, and fingers trailed over his face as Stef sucked and swirled his tongue around Cass's dick like it was his favourite ice cream. Cass groaned, reached to where his cock disappeared into Stef's mouth and slipped in a finger alongside. He left it there a few seconds, pulled it out, licked it, and just... *damn.*

Stef stopped sucking, dropped his hands, Cass's cock still filling his mouth, and looked up in open invitation. There weren't many men Stef trusted enough to fuck his mouth, but for some reason he trusted Cass. Cass studied him for a few seconds as if to be sure what was on offer, then blew him a kiss and cradled his jaw gently in both hands to keep his head still. They stared at each other for a second or two longer before Cass tried out a few gentle thrusts. Stef nodded encouragement, and Cass quickly built to deep, long drives, eyes laser focused on where he slid in and out of Stef's mouth, glancing up at times to check his expression, then back down.

If Stef gagged, Cass paused until Stef urged him on again. Saliva dripped from his mouth, tears welled in his eyes, and he loved every fucking minute of it. Cass groaned and shuddered above him, incoherent with pleasure, until Stef was pretty sure the only thing keeping Cass on his feet were Stef's hands wrapped around Cass's thighs.

It was so fucking hot, and unable to stand it a second longer, Stef reached for his own aching cock, too far gone to care about being fucked, just desperate to get off, but as soon as he grabbed hold, Cass pulled out and backed off, squeezing his own dick to stave off orgasm.

"Goddammit, get back here," Stef grumbled.

"Not on your life," Cass barked. He was already halfway out of his clothes, his shirt on the ground and acres of lean muscle and ivory skin on display.

And yeah, well, Stef wasn't gonna argue with that. Cass was toned and real-world muscled, a generous helping of blond hair covering his chest to track down a firm stomach and into a gorgeous treasure trail that Stef wanted to bury his nose in and follow to its conclusion. The man might be a wet dream, but watching him hop around trying to get his second boot off with his jeans still around his knees was hilarious.

"You've got me wound so damn tight I'm about to go off like a rocket. My fingers won't work, and my brain can't focus on anything except you sitting there naked," Cass grumbled, still working on his clothes. "So, if you think I'm turning down the opportunity to feel what it's like to be all up inside that heat, you need serious fucking help." He finally got the second boot off, kicked his jeans and briefs to the side, and grabbed the condom and lube. "Now, turn over on that hay bale and get that world-class arse in the air. I just... I can't... ugh... just do it, will you? Words can come later."

A soft nicker floated over from the pen, and Stef glanced up to find four pairs of horsey eyes looking their way. *Well, shit.* "Um, Cass? I think we have company."

Cass spun and then laughed. "Fuck off, you lot. This isn't a free show."

Stef frowned, feeling himself droop just a little. "Um... I'm not sure I can do it with"—he nodded to where Arwen was studying him intently, a thick swatch of hay hanging out her mouth—"you know..."

Cass's smile turned wicked. He approached and knelt on the large haybale next to Stef, taking Stef's flagging cock in hand. "You sure about that?" He gave it a couple of firm strokes, running his fingers over the piercings while he nibbled on the curve of Stef's shoulder, sending flutters of arousal all the way to Stef's toes, and... *hello there...* things were looking up. Then Cass ran his tongue up Stef's throat, pulled his earlobe into his mouth, and *oh God*, everything south of Stef's waist that had any questions left, lit up like a bloody Christmas tree.

And just like that, Stef was back in the game. *What horses?*

"Well, I... um... fucking hell." Stef turned his head to lock lips with Cass, plunging his tongue down the man's throat before shoving him away. "It appears I might have"—he hauled Cass in for another assault on his lips while rubbing his body the length of the other man's, because... damn—"overstated the whole stage fright thing."

More kisses, more tongue, and a lot more... lubrication. "I may in fact have discovered exhibitionist tendencies hitherto unknown. Not to mention the context possibly fits, with the fact that you're, um... hung like a fucking horse, so yeah... there's that."

Cass choked out a laugh, stepped back, and slapped Stef's arse. "Brat. Hands and knees, gorgeous."

"You, um, need a hand with that?" Stef eyed the condom in Cass's hand with a cheeky smile, which earned him a sexy-as-fuck growl in reply and—*holy shit*—he was lucky he didn't come from that sound alone.

Cass's silence spoke volumes, and Stef's mouth may or may not have run dry.

He cleared his throat. "No? Good. I, um... have somewhere I need to be."

Cass arched a brow.

"Hadn't you heard?" Stef grinned mischievously. "I'm getting fucked... apparently."

Cass went to grab him, but Stef leapt on to the bale and scrambled to get in position. He wasn't sure he'd ever had a guy so keen to fuck him in his life—or if he'd ever felt so keen to *be* fucked, for that matter. Warning bells sounded all through his head that this man wasn't going to be easy to walk away from, but he didn't give a goddamn. Nothing was stopping this from happening. Nothing.

Cass wasn't convinced he *could*, in fact, fuck Stef. Not since that would involve moving, which was currently a problem, seeing as how he'd yet to get even his eyes to shift from Stef's naked body splayed over the blanket on his hands and knees like a fucking banquet, all for Cass. Nope. Cass was pretty sure he could stand here and have the most explosive orgasm of his life just watching and thinking about what he could do to the other man, with his sassy mouth, sexy piercings, and cheeky fucking smile—an immaculate ejaculation all over that gloriously curved arse.

There was a late-summer olive to Stef's skin, his body lean and tight with shapely thighs and a spray of freckles over his right shoulder that begged to be kissed. His cock was equally pretty—not thick, but long and uncut, with an intriguing tapestry of veins and a slight curve to the right... and all those fucking piercings. Nothing about this was a good idea. Nothing about this man was gonna be simple to forget.

As if to underline that very notion, Stef turned and looked at Cass over his shoulder and gave a slow sexy smile. He licked his lips, reached a hand back, and ran a finger over his tightly furled hole before sliding it in, and then another, prepping himself as Cass watched, hand on his suited and slicked-up cock, stroking himself, totally enthralled. It was the hottest damn thing he'd ever seen—and a guaranteed menace to his heart.

This funny, snarky, super-smart guy was sex on a fucking stick, plain and simple—and miracle of miracles, he wanted Cass. Cass had lived long enough to know complex men like Stef didn't come along very often. Stef ticked boxes Cass didn't even know he had, and for that reason alone he was everything Cass should've stayed away from. But Cass was now too far gone to fight the temptation and to be honest, he no longer wanted to. He'd simply enjoy the moment, commit it to memory, and tend the bruises later.

"You waiting for an engraved invitation?" Stef pulled his fingers free and wiggled his hips.

Jesus Christ. Cass had crossed the distance between them before he even realised he'd moved, running both hands over Stef's arse, up to his neck and back down. Stef shivered under his touch, and Cass relished the ability to draw that response from the sexy man. He draped himself over Stef's back, his cock nudging Stef's crease, and thrust his hips lightly, earning a needy groan from the man under him.

Cool night air fluttered across his back, and the corrugated iron on the lean-to rattled as a breath of autumn wind picked up. But Stef's skin was electric hot beneath him, and where they touched, Cass sizzled. He nuzzled into Stef's neck and bit down lightly on the curve of that long, lean shoulder. Stef arched and spread his cheeks so Cass's cock could plunge gently through the crease, slicking Stef's hole as Cass's lips peppered Stef's back with tiny kisses and drew forth an endless stream of incoherent mumblings.

He worked his way down Stef's spine with licks and nibbles until he got to those two dimples in the small of Stef's back. He paused and kissed each one, added some more lube to his fingers, then spread Stef's cheeks and ran a flat tongue up from his balls to his hole.

"Oh my f-fuuuucking G-God." Stef dropped his forehead to the blanket, which pushed his arse even higher and opened him right up to Cass, who took a second to appreciate the view and grin to himself. *Achievement unlocked.* He slid a slicked finger into Stef's hole and added his tongue to the mix, fucking Stef with both until the man was a drooling puddle of desire on the hay beneath him. Then Cass pulled up, wiped his mouth, and slapped Stef's arse.

"Turn over. I want to see your face when you come," he said thickly, then stood back as Stef rolled, hiked his knees high, and put himself on full display, dick leaking like a damn faucet.

Good grief. The sight stole Cass's breath, not least of all the piercings he couldn't rip his eyes from. The need to touch and kiss them took over.

"God, look at you. You are the sexiest damn thing I've ever seen." He gave himself a couple of strokes, then crawled up between Stef's legs, sat back on his heels, and fingered the run of three rings on the front of Stef's scrotum. Stef's cock twitched, and he shuddered as they jingled and sang, but when Cass dropped his head and drew one whole sac into his mouth and tongued the rings, Stef moaned and arched up, his fingers tugging at Cass's hair to take more.

Cass lingered a few seconds, savouring the way Stef arranged him just where he wanted him, and then he pulled off, pushed Stef's leaking cock aside, and brushed his lips over that tempting bar sitting front and centre at its base. Then he moved across to the hip bar and placed a firm kiss over that before licking a trail up Stef's firm, flat stomach to the bar in his clavicle, which Cass took gently between his teeth and tugged, before letting it go. By the time Cass was done, he was trembling with need.

He never thought he'd be into piercings, but he couldn't get Stef's out of his head: the feel and straight-up sexiness of them. They weren't in-your-face, look-how-cool-I-am ostentatious like the way some guys talked about theirs. These were jewellery, like track lights to your favourite work of art, and they turned Cass's crank in a totally unexpected way. Though whether it was the piercings alone, the sexy man who wore them, or the whole package, Cass had no idea—not that it mattered.

Stef's eyes had followed Cass the whole way, rapt, pupils huge, his body releasing little shudders of appreciation. When Cass was done, Stef forked his fingers through his hair and pulled him up till they were face to face.

"You know I'm never gonna be able to see a hay bale again without popping a boner, don't you?" He licked Cass's lips, his short stubble grazing Cass's jaw, before plunging his tongue inside. When he'd had his fill, he pulled back and rubbed their noses together. "You're a wicked, wicked man, Cassidy Martin. Who knew you had such a filthy mouth and could rim like a fucking trooper. Lucky me."

Then he winked and shoved Cass back. "Now, fuck me like you mean it. I want your dick so far inside me I can feel your slit on the back of my tongue."

Holy crap. Cass snorted. "Great. No pressure, then."

He scrambled to stand at the end of the bale, shoved his bundled coat under Stef's arse, and watched as Stef hooked his arms under his thighs and lifted them high. Cass stepped forward and tapped his cock on Stef's crease a couple of times before glancing up to find Stef's eyes locked on his.

"Nice and slow, maestro." Stef flashed those dimples. "I can take you, no problem, but let's not run before we can walk, yeah?"

Cass felt his mouth quirk and nodded. "You got it. But just so you know, I don't need to have this. I fucking love that you want to, but I'll take you any way you say. There isn't a thing we could do together at this moment that would be disappointing, understand?"

Stef's bright eyes twinkled. "Thanks for the out, but I think I'll be just fine."

"You need a safe word?" Cass arched an amused brow.

"How about 'stop'?" Stef answered with a cocky smirk.

"How about I give that mouth of yours something else to think about?" Cass cradled Stef's face and leaned forward to cover his mouth while his cock nudged at Stef's hole.

Stef melted against him, wriggling to try and take him in, but Cass had meant everything he said. He never took it for granted that his male partners would bottom for him. More than one had taken a single look at his generous proportions and opted for door number two instead. Size sounded good in porn, but the reality could be daunting and not so fun. Cass loved sex in all its forms, but unnecessary discomfort wasn't on his list of favourite things to inflict on his bed mates. There were lots of ways to have fun, and he wasn't averse to a single one of them. The fact Stef wanted him inside so badly was just bonus points in Cass's books. Speaking of which—

Stef pushed him off with a frustrated growl. "Not that I don't love your lips, but..." He took purchase on the blanket, blew out a big breath, and eyed Cass pointedly. "Enough messing around. I need to feel you inside me. Ready, set, go."

Jesus, this man. A huge grin split Cass's face as he nudged at Stef's slick hole and slowly pushed at the resistance, sliding, centimetre by tantalising centimetre, into the smooth furnace that was Stef. His eyes locked on Stef's face, watching every twitch, every expression. That he didn't blow his load at the pop of the first ring of muscle had to be down to divine intervention alone, as he walked the slimmest of knife-edges, his orgasm less than a badly timed twitch away.

Stef's eyes remained closed at first, and he breathed deeply, slowly, his body tense as he adjusted. He kept a hand on Cass's wrist, a quick squeeze to still his progress and another to push him on. Seconds, days, weeks later, Cass was seated fully and so close to falling apart it wasn't funny.

Stef's eyes popped open, pupils huge, a big grin on his face. "Holy shit. That was intense."

Cass searched Stef's expression. "You okay?"

Stef winked "Just fucking dandy. You don't even need to move. My prostate's so squished already, it's like a full-court press down there. One little twist and it could all be over." He grabbed his slightly flagging cock and stroked himself back to the full enchilada. "I am so fucking down for this."

The porn-worthy sight of Stef pleasuring himself added to the strain of trying to keep himself in check. "Don't try that twist thing just yet, yeah? I'm about to give the land speed record a run for its money as it is."

Stef's expression turned seductive, and he slowly circled his hips. "You mean this twist?"

Goddammit. Cass hit defcon one, grabbed his dick at the base, and squeezed hard. "Gah... yes... stop that, goddammit."

Stef grabbed his own dick and froze. "Okay, yeah, maybe that wasn't such a good idea."

Cass narrowed his gaze. "Serves you right. You ready?"

Stef's arse clenched around him. "Hit it."

Cass eased back, then rocked forward in a series of small thrusts until he was sure Stef was managing, but a pair of hands behind his thighs tugging him harder answered that, and he finally let go, snapping his hips and angling his drag over Stef's prostate till the man was moaning beneath him. Teetering at the edge, Cass wrapped his hand around Stef's swollen cock, his arousal rocketing as he contacted the metal rings at its base with each stroke.

It didn't take long. A dozen strokes at the most till Stef arched up under him, head thrown back and neck corded as he came apart in spectacular form, with a grunt and a string of obscenities, his come spilling between them from stomach to chin as Cass watched. He followed a few strokes later, falling forward on his elbows and caging Stef in as the waves of pleasure crashed through them both. He buried his face in Stef's neck till the aftershocks calmed and things grew quiet, their bodies slick with sweat and come, neither making any move to pull apart.

The hoot of a morepork and the soft huffs of heavy breathing were the only sounds to break the silence as Cass waited for any tell-tale tension of regret to rise in Stef's body—the push away, the apology, the quick move to clean up and leave. But it didn't happen, and he was shocked by the level of relief that surged through him. It would've hurt, sure, but it would've made things easier. He'd relied on Stef to be the sensible one, to keep Cass as a convenient fuck, nothing more.

But that wasn't what this felt like. He glanced down to find a smiling Stef staring at him. The slightly surprised look he wore likely mirrored Cass's own. He lifted his chest to allow Stef to slip out from under his weight, his own cock sliding free of Stef, and that felt all kinds of wrong. But instead of getting up to retrieve his clothes, dress, and leave—which would have provided a painful but necessary balance to Cass's heart—Stef gently removed the condom from Cass, tied it off and dropped it to the ground, and then turned on his side and curled up in Cass's arms, folding the loose edge of the blanket over the top of them. His fingers played with the thick blond hair on Cass's chest, and his breathing slowed to a contented, peaceful cadence, as if he'd always belonged there and they fucked like that every night. *Shit.*

And with that, everything changed. Cass *should* move. If Stef couldn't, Cass should. But instead his arm circled around Stef's waist, his heart already spilling into his head and muddying his thinking. And all because of... *this. This,* he missed. *This,* he craved. *This,* the thing he'd known would happen with Stef. This simple and so utterly complicated connection.

The thing he pretended not to need, not to want, not to regret, not to hope for. This... possibility. Apart from Tricia, no one had caught Cass's interest like this, man or woman. And even if there had been, that was no guarantee that person could live in this isolated place. Tricia had loved him, and still she couldn't stay. Cass wasn't naive; he wasn't kidding himself. He barely knew the man in his arms, but he knew what he felt was more than just off-the-charts sexual chemistry. And it scared the shit out of him. Stef might just be cosy and appreciative and caught in the afterglow of some great sex, and a million miles from wanting anything more than a one-time thing, but Cass was already grieving the ache in his soul from losing him.

Stef wasn't country. And Cass's soul couldn't survive without it.

Stef wriggled in Cass's arms and tried to hook more of the blanket from under them. "Do you think they heard?" He nodded towards the hut.

Cass shook his head free of his ridiculousness and shrugged. "Do you care?"

Stef glanced up with a warm smile. "Not in the slightest. But I thought you might."

Cass frowned. Did he? He considered that for a moment. He *should*. What they'd done was a million miles from professional, but... "No." He pressed a soft kiss to Stef's swollen lips. "I had a good time, a great time. You're amazing. I expected no less, but still amazing."

Stef tucked his chin and his gaze slid shyly away, and Cass was reminded of the haunting gap between sassy, en pointe Stef and this softer side that pulsed just beneath the prickly surface. But it didn't pay to think too hard on that, because that way lay heartache and a whole lot of trouble Cass couldn't afford to go through again, even though a part of him was already screaming that it was too late.

"Well, you were pretty damn good yourself," Stef mumbled against his chest. "So, definitely bent as fuck."

Cass laughed. "Definitely. Bi, to be precise."

Stef licked at Cass's nipple. "Mmm, figured as much. But it was fucking hot, right?"

Cass nuzzled Stef's hair and slid his hand down all that bare skin to rest in his crease. "The best." *With anyone.* But who wanted to go there?

Stef's head shot up. "Really?" He looked delighted.

Cass's heart squeezed. "Really."

"Huh." Stef grunted approvingly and nestled back into Cass's armpit. "Thank fuck. I thought it was just me. Thirty-seven years to hit the jackpot, but who's counting?"

His words froze Cass in place. He couldn't mean them. Could he?

With Stef plastered head to toe alongside Cass, sucking every bit of heat he had to offer, Cass wasn't moving a muscle. The wind whipped up and blew knots of prickly tussock into the lean-to, raising more than a few goosebumps between them, and still neither moved. If Cass wanted to be silly about it, he might let himself believe that Stef was as reluctant as he was to end their stolen time together.

Stef shivered and snuggled even closer.

"Hey." Cass kissed the top of his head. "You should go in and get some sleep. Another big day tomorrow." He reached for Stef's clothes and lifted the blanket for him, admiring the smooth line of the man's shoulders all the way down to his curvy arse. "You'll freeze out here. There's some weather blowing in that shouldn't be."

Stef hesitated a few seconds, clearly reluctant to go, which warmed Cass's heart, but eventually he accepted his clothes and crawled out into the cold. A flash of metal in his groin caught Cass's eye, and he had to will his dick to behave.

"Thought it wasn't supposed to rain till tomorrow night." Stef quickly pulled on his T-shirt and glanced up at the clouds now blocking out the stars.

Cass shrugged and searched the skies. "It's not. But this isn't the southerly flow we were expecting either, so who knows? Besides, this is Southland. It rains any damn time it wants down here—up to six metres a year. Weather patterns can be a bit freakish. This might pass us by... or not. Either way, you need some rest."

Stef finished buttoning his jeans, teeth chattering. "What about you?"

Cass got to his feet and held the blanket open. "Come here." He enfolded Stef in its warmth and held him tight, tucking his head against Cass's shoulder.

"Mmm, I like this version too." Stef licked a swathe across Cass's chest. "You naked, me dressed. You sure I can't tempt you to stay a little longer?"

Cass chuckled and slid a hand down to cup Stef's half-hard dick. "If you're around, I'll always be tempted. But I suspect we've pushed our luck enough for one night. I'll be in after I check the horses."

They turned as one to look at the pen, where all four horses were dozing on their feet.

Stef chuckled. "I think that's horse for, 'Don't give up your day job,'" he mused. "I don't think we have a future in equine porn."

Cass snorted. "A fact I somehow find... comforting."

Arwen chose that moment to open her eyes and send them her best withering look.

Stef looked thoughtful. "We could always try again, see if we can improve our performance."

Cass leaned in and nipped his bottom lip. "I think your arse has had enough for one day, what with me *and* the saddle."

Stef winced. "You might have a point, though who said anything about *my* arse being involved?"

And just like that, Cass was hard again.

Stef wriggled against him, fanning the flames. "I can see I struck a chord. Good to know. So, I'll be expecting a rain check on that second round sometime tomorrow, Mister"—he lifted his head for a kiss, which Cass supplied, tongue included—"so make sure you eat a good breakfast."

He freed himself from the rug and Cass's embrace, turned, and sashayed back towards the hut, carrying his socks in his hand and

enough attitude in that curvy arse to have Cass rethinking his decision. He blew out a long sigh and tried to check the burgeoning
emotion in his chest. There was no point in wishful thinking.

Arwen nickered from behind the fence to catch his attention. He
sent her a rueful look. "I know, alright. You don't need to remind me.
He's just so... unexpected."

Cass made his way over to the mare, needing some time to calm
the fuck down before he had even the slimmest chance of sleeping in
the cot alongside Stef without needing to haul the sexy man outside
for that promised round number two. He doubted their luck would
hold twice, and all he needed was Andrew fucking Murchison to
come looking for them.

CHAPTER EIGHT

STEF JOLTED AWAKE AND NEARLY FELL OFF HIS COT. "HOLY SHIT, what was that?"

"Thunder." The sharp reply came from the far side of the hut amid a scrabbling of boots.

In the shadows, Stef could just make out the shape of Andrew pulling his coat on, while overhead the hut's corrugated roof creaked ominously as a gust of wind did its damnedest to strip it clean off.

"Tomas, wake up." Andrew slapped his brother on the thigh.

"Okay, okay, give me a sec." Tomas grumbled his way from under the sleeping bag and reached for his oilskin as a frightened whinny split the night.

Arwen. Stef turned to face Cass's cot, but it was empty—if he'd even gone to bed to start with. Stef had fallen into a deep sleep when he'd returned from their romp in the hay bales and hadn't heard a thing from then on. He reached a hand across and felt a lingering warmth on Cass's sheets. Okay, so he had been there at some point in the not-too-distant past. He checked his watch: five a.m. Did no one sleep in this bloody place?

A flash of lightning jerked his gaze to the window, just in time for another crashing roll of thunder to pass overhead. He flung his sleeping bag aside and shivered as he dropped his feet to the floor and stretched under the bed for his boots. "Fuck, it's cold."

"Stay here," Andrew ordered. "Cass will be out settling the horses, and he won't want you under his feet."

Stef sent him a withering glare. "Like fuck. If Cass needs help, I'm coming too." He shoved his arms into the hellishly ugly calf-length oilskin coat that looked waterproof enough for Noah to have given the damn thing a five-star rating. "Don't be such a prick."

Andrew stared at him for a moment, then shrugged. "It's your funeral. Just don't get in the way if the horses are spooked. You'll be of no fucking use."

Tomas flashed Stef an apologetic look. "He's not entirely wrong. If the horses have the wind up them, it'll be dangerous getting close." He patted Stef on the shoulder and followed his brother out. "Just think about it."

Stef wavered for a second, not wanting to add to Cass's problems. Then he recalled their earlier conversation about Stef needing to back himself more, and determination kicked in. *Fuck 'em.* "Hey."

Tomas turned with his hand on the door of the hut.

Stef drilled him with a steely-eyed glare. "I'm coming to help, so you two can just get over yourselves."

Tomas's lips twitched. "Fine. Just watch yourself." Then he was gone.

"I will," Stef said to the empty hut, and finished lacing his boots. "And while I'm doing that, I'll try and understand why the fuck I just volunteered to go out in a fucking thunderstorm to calm huge, fuck-ing-terrified animals when I've been given the perfect excuse to stay safe and fucking warm inside." *What the hell is wrong with me?* Another panicked whinny sped him out the door and into—chaos.

Holy fuck.

He needed a second to orient himself. The fire was dead, ashes blown all to hell in the fierce, whipping wind that nearly knocked him sideways. The ground was dry, but Stef could feel the rain threatening—he could smell it in the air, the dampness hitting his lungs with every gulping breath the wind drove into him. As if to slam the idea home, another spear of lightning cut across the black sky, the accompanying thunder close on its heels.

Stef dragged the hood of his oilskin over his head and aimed for the broken snippets of conversation coming from somewhere in the gloom to his right. Jesus and Mary, the place was like a war zone. He could barely see beyond his outstretched arm—the sky, thick with cloud, leaving a dense black curtain of night. Branches and leaves kicked up around him. One snagged his cheek. He flinched but kept going.

Somewhere ahead, Cass shouted, half his words lost to the howling wind. "She's... in between... railings...you'll need... twist it... or... it off."

"On it..." Tomas shouted back. "Andrew, get... from the... tie off."

If Andrew answered, Stef couldn't hear it. He fought his way toward the voices he could hear, relieved to finally spy Cass's tall figure inside the pen. *And holy shit.* As Stef got even closer and the gloom broke apart, the reason behind all those urgent, half heard instructions became all too clear. Cass had his hands full, battling to calm a wild-eyed, panicked Arwen, who'd somehow managed to get her right rear leg below the hock, through the small gap between the middle two fence railings, and was now caught fast—able to stand straddling the fence from the hock down, but unable to move or get it out without major contortions.

Gandalf stood patiently alongside his stablemate, his silver tail almost horizontal in the gale, while Bilbo and Eowyn raced circles inside the fence, only adding to Arwen's stress. Gimli stood off to one side, snorting and pawing at the ground, his eyes white-rimmed with fear.

Holy shit. Stef was way, way out of his depth, like light years out.

He could just make out Andrew on the far side, trying to steer the two careering horses into the smaller pen while Tomas battled his way back to Cass with what looked like a tyre iron and disappeared over the fence on the other side of Arwen—to pry the railing off, Stef guessed.

"What can I do?" he yelled to Cass, grabbing on to the fence to steady himself as another blast of wind shoved him sideways.

Cass started and jerked his head to face Stef with a puzzled frown. Then he grinned.

It was so out of place with the melee happening all around them that Stef couldn't help but smile back.

"You sure?" Cass yelled.

In answer, Stef climbed the fence and edged his way over to where Cass fought to keep Arwen under control. She was lathered in sweat, shaking with terror, her eyes rolled back in panic. Stef trod a wary path around Cass's back to avoid all that struggling horseflesh and spoke into his ear. "Putting myself out there, right?"

Cass laughed. "You sure pick your moments." He battled with the mare's halter to keep her still as Bilbo and Eowyn flew past on another circuit of the pen.

Stef slid a hand around Cass's waist and leaned in. "You okay?"

Cass nodded. "Just. If those other two would calm the fuck down I could maybe get her settled. How's Tomas doing?"

Stef stepped closer to the fence and peered around Arwen to check on Tomas, who was still trying to work the railing free. Arwen's leg was caught fast. One wrong move and the bone could snap.

"He's still working on it." Stef stepped back. "How the fuck'd she manage that?"

"She hates lightning," Cass explained, hauling on the halter to stop the mare rearing up as another flash of lightning bit through the night. "Goddammit."

Stef had a sudden idea. He dug in his pocket for the leftover doughnut pieces he'd saved for Arwen and showed Cass. "What do you think?"

Cass's eyes lit up. "Worth a try." He motioned Stef beside him. "Just watch her front hooves. If she breaks free, you get back over that fence, understand? I can look after myself."

Stef nodded, held out his hand, and aimed for a calm voice. "Hey there, gorgeous. You want a treat?"

Greedy as she was, Arwen caught the scent of the doughnut almost immediately and thrust her nose forward, her lead rope going temporarily slack.

"Thank Christ." Cass rolled his shoulders for a second to find some relief before it tightened again. "How much have you got?"

Stef angled his head closer to Cass. "Not much, but I'll try and eke it out. How long have you been out here?"

"Twenty minutes, give or take. The wind woke me, and then I heard her squeal. I found her like this and then couldn't leave in case she broke her leg. I've been yelling ever since, hoping one of you would hear me."

Stef shook his head. "We didn't hear a thing. It was the thunder that woke us."

Muffled curses streamed from behind Arwen as Tomas continued to work on the railing. Then Arwen tugged at her leg, the fence rattled, and Tomas jumped back as the whole thing threatened to go.

Cass white-knuckled the rope and held firm. "Hey, hey, hey, shh, girl, let him get you free. It's okay."

Stef tentatively reached a hand forward to pat the horse's neck while he offered another sprinkle of crumbs. A few fat splats of rain hit him in the face. "Fuck. Just what we need."

Cass looked up. "Yeah. Let's hope it's not going to be much—" Arwen threw up her head. "Hey, hey, it's okay, girl. Watch your feet."

Stef jumped just in time to avoid Arwen's front hoof landing on his toes.

Gandalf gave a nicker of concern and pushed his nose into Arwen's flank as if to check she was okay. As the alpha of the little group, he was helping her keep calm, Stef guessed.

She turned her head towards the gelding, eyes wild. Stef shoved another few crumbs under her nose to distract her, and it worked. She found his hand once again and wolfed them down.

"Tomas, how long?" Cass yelled.

"They're fucking screws," Tomas shouted back. "But I'm almost there."

The drops turned to steady, then insistent rain, and in seconds Stef could hardly see past Arwen's head. A few more seconds and his head was soaked to the skin.

Cass leaned into him. "You can head back if you want."

Stef summoned his best glare. "Like shit. I'm fine. Quit worrying."

"The other two will—"

"I said, I'm fine..." He was about to say more when he locked on to Cass's hands—his gloveless hands. *Holy shit.* The skin on both was red and torn from rope burns, and for the first time, Stef noticed how Cass grimaced in pain every time Arwen pulled back.

"Jesus Christ. Your hands are a fucking mess. Here." Stef yanked off his gloves. "Give her to me for a second, and put these on."

Cass shook his head. "You won't be able to—"

Stef shoved the gloves into the other man's pocket. "Just fucking do it, will you? I can hold her." He fed Arwen another tiny piece of doughnut and grabbed her rope just above where Cass held it.

Cass hesitated for a second, then nodded. "Okay, lean your weight back to keep her steady." He let Stef take the rope and quickly pulled on the gloves before taking the lead back. "Thanks."

Stef let go and nodded with a smile. "You're welcome. Good to know you can take instruction as well as give it." He winked and fed another titbit of doughnut to the mare. But Arwen scuttled on her front hooves and whipped her head around to where Gandalf stood. He nudged her reassuringly, but Stef could see she was starting to lose it again.

He searched his pocket for more doughnut but came away with only a few morsels. "Last bit," he warned Cass, who planted his feet in anticipation.

Arwen hoovered the crumbs in a second, then pushed at Stef's coat pocket for more just as a broken branch flew through the air and bounced off her flank. She startled, her eyes running white at the edges, nearly pulling Cass's arms out of their sockets.

Remembering the state of Cass's hands, Stef grabbed on to the rope, adding his weight to haul her back.

"Get ready," Tomas called from the other side of the fence.

Andrew ran up beside them. "I got Eowyn in, but I can't get near Bilbo."

"Here it comes," Tomas shouted.

Arwen was still fighting both of them as they tried to hold her in place.

Andrew pushed at Stef. "Get out of the way. Let me."

Like hell. Stef knew if he let go, Cass would be yanked forward in an instant. "I'm fine," he shouted. "We've got her."

But Andrew thrust himself between them and made a failed grab for the rope, sending Stef stumbling sideways and leaving Cass on his own.

Cass spun. "What the fuck are you—"

The railing snapped loose with a crack. Arwen careened forward, and the sudden loss of tension on the rope sent Cass flying backwards. He kept his feet somehow, frantically gathering up the rope as she danced a circle on the end of it. A sheet of lightning broke the sky, with an ear-shattering clap of thunder hot on its heels.

The combination sent Arwen into a state of frenzy, and she raced backwards, yanking Cass with her as he desperately tried to hold on.

"Let her go," Andrew shouted.

"No!" Cass answered. "I have to check her leg. She might have damaged it."

Stef could do nothing but watch, terrified, as Cass fought to calm the mare and get her back under control. Then Andrew made a grab to release the lead's clip on Arwen's halter, and everything went to shit.

"Don't!" Stef tugged Andrew's jacket.

Andrew pulled free. "He has to let her go."

The mare was getting more and more spooked.

Cass shouldered Andrew aside. "Get back. You're frightening her—"

But it was too late. With one upward jerk of her head, Arwen yanked herself free and Cass fell backwards to the ground. Her nose caught Andrew a solid hit under his jaw as she went up on her hind legs, and he stumbled, nearly barrelling into Stef in the process.

Stef caught Andrew with a grunt and then shoved him away. "You fucking arsehole." Then he ran over to Cass and had managed to drag him halfway to his feet when another rumble of thunder shook the mountain. He spun back to see Arwen come down on her front hooves and then leap backwards.

She might have continued that direction unchecked and out of harm's way if not for Bilbo racing at her from behind. Unable to stop in time, he veered into her rear end, and the impact shot her forward once again. Stef found himself yanked to the side by Andrew as Arwen crashed into Cass and sent him flying back to the ground while she buckled at her knees next to him.

"Cass!" Stef lunged, but Andrew hauled him back just in time to avoid Bilbo's skitter over the tangle of legs and bodies.

"Get inside," Andrew growled.

"Fuck off." Stef shoved him aside and turned to help Cass, but there was nothing he could do other than watch as Arwen scrambled to her feet and, having nowhere else to go, barrelled straight over the top of Cass who was still on his knees. It seemed like she did everything she could not to trample him, but gravity and balance were against her, and one heavy hoof connected with Cass's temple and another with his loin before she could jump free. He lurched and dropped like a stone, face-first into the mud.

"No!" Stef jerked his arm free of Andrew's hold and ran to where Cass lay ominously still. He dropped to his knees in the sludge. "Cass! Cass!" He used his shirt to wipe Cass's face clear of hair clotted with mud as the rain bucketed on their backs. The hood on his oilskin had long since given in to the howling wind, and his head was saturated, rivers running down his collar and back. He angled his body to protect Cass from the worst of it.

"Cass, are you okay? Cass, open your eyes."

Andrew fell to his knees on the other side of Cass. "Get those fucking horses in the corral. They'll likely follow Gandalf in now," he ordered Tomas, who immediately took off. Then he turned to Stef. "Is he breathing?"

Ignoring the urge to punch Andrew in the mouth, Stef tore open Cass's oilskin to watch his chest and dropped his ear to Cass's mouth, and... thank God. "Yes, he's breathing. We need to get him into recovery." Stef mentally thanked Tanner for bullying him into that first aid course all those years ago.

They manhandled Cass on to his side and Stef tried not to panic. Cass was like a fucking rag doll in their hands, and although he was breathing, it didn't sound normal—more like a snore. He swept a finger through Cass's slack mouth to check it was clear. It was. Small fucking mercies. He pinched the guy's arm, hard. Nothing. No reaction at all.

Andrew shook Cass by the shoulder. "Cass!"

Stef shoved Andrew's hands out of the way. "Don't you fucking touch him. Are you happy now? He didn't need your fucking help. He knows his horses. What the hell did you think you were doing? Goddammit. We need to get him inside and warm him up."

A shout from Tomas drew both their attention, and Stef turned to find all but one horse now safely corralled. Arwen was still giving Tomas the runaround, but Tomas was rattling some feed pellets in a bucket and she was beginning to look interested. She wasn't limping, so maybe her leg was okay after all.

"He needed to let her go. It was too dangerous," Andrew pressed.

"He needed you to let him do his fucking job," Stef snapped back. "Who the hell do you think you are? All you had to do was leave us alone. We had her."

"You know nothing about it. You're a fucking city boy. You had no business—" Andrew broke off and blinked slowly. "Look, it doesn't matter. Is it okay to move him, do you think?"

Stef's eyes widened. "How the fuck should I know? But we can't leave him out here in the rain, in the dark, can we? Have you got your phone on you?"

Andrew's lip curled, and he rolled his eyes. "Yes, but there's no—"

"The flashlight, dipshit." He rubbed Cass's shoulder and checked his breathing again while Andrew dug his phone out of his inside pocket.

"Good. Hold it under your jacket and shine it this way—let's see what damage she's done." Stef loosened Cass's shirt from his jeans and pulled it free, exposing a nasty red mark on his right side just under his ribs—roughly the shape of Arwen's hoof. Not to mention a five-centimetre gash, likely from the horseshoe. The blow had missed Cass's ribs, but Lord knew what internal damage might have resulted.

"Shit. That's gonna hurt." Andrew winced.

Stef prodded gently at Cass's ribs, not sure what he was looking for, but he guessed if there was a crunch or wiggle, that wouldn't be a good thing. There wasn't, so he counted that as a win. He wiped Cass's brow and leaned in close. "Come on, Cass. How about you wake up and tell us what hurts? Give us some help here."

But there was nothing in reply—nothing but that weird snoring breathing.

Stef scowled up at Andrew and took a deep breath to stamp down the urge to fucking slap the man. "We'll have to be careful moving him. Go grab one of those sleeping bags. Then we can just roll him on and carry him in."

"What?" Andrew's brows pinched, clearly unhappy about being given instructions. "But—"

"Just do it." Stef wasn't about to debate with him. "And make it quick. I'm done with this fucking rain."

For a second, Andrew looked ready to argue. But he must've thought better of it and ran to the hut instead.

"They're all in," Tomas called from the corral. "Is Cass alright?"

"He's unconscious," Stef called back. "We're gonna get him inside."

"Fuck. Hang on, I'll be there in a minute. At least the rain's easing. We must've caught the edge of the system. All piss and vinegar for five minutes and then gone."

Tomas was right. The rain was already down to a light drizzle, and a weak dawn light was beginning to spill over the land. Stef wiped more grime from Cass's face and took stock. His colour wasn't looking crash hot—more grey than pink—but his breathing seemed quieter. Was that good or not? Stef didn't have a fucking clue.

He leaned close and whispered in Cass's ear. "Hey, sweetheart. I need you to wake up, please. I've exhausted all the first aid I know, so now would be a good time for you to rally and take shit over again— all that manly stuff you're so good at. I mean, you have to know more than me, right? I'm sure you don't get to do this tour guide shit without training in some of this stuff. So, how about rescuing the city boy?"

"Is he awake?" Andrew reappeared, and he set about laying out the sleeping bag on the other side of Cass.

"No. I thought if I prattled on enough, he might come to just to shut me up."

Andrew snorted. "Would've worked for me."

Stef was saved from coming up with a suitably snarky response by Tomas's arrival. He got Tomas to kneel alongside him so the two of them could roll Cass on his side towards them while Andrew, under Stef's direction, pushed the sleeping bag right up against Cass's back. Then they rolled Cass towards Andrew over the lump of sleeping bag, flattened it out, and eased him back on to it. Now all they had to do was lift him on it like a cot before the thing absorbed the puddle of water it was sitting in.

"When did you learn how to do this?" Tomas marvelled as they worked.

Stef shrugged. "My brother has Down's syndrome. When he was younger, he needed surgery for a tethered spinal cord. I remember watching the nurses turn him like this when they had to change the sheets. I figured if we had to move Cass, we could at least try not to make things worse."

Tomas regarded Stef with interest. "You're not just a pretty face, are you?"

Stef rolled his eyes. "Don't get your hopes up. Right now, I doubt I'm even that."

"Oh, for fuck's sake." Andrew got to his feet and brushed himself off. "Let's get him moved while it's not pissing down, yeah?"

Tomas dropped his gaze to Cass and frowned. "He's been out a while. That's not normal, right?"

Stef joined Andrew and shrugged. "I don't know how the fuck it works. I just want him to wake up. But I'll settle for getting him inside."

Tomas blew out a sigh and stood. "Okay, so what do you need us to do?"

Stef's horrified gaze jerked between the two brothers. "Did you miss the part where I said I have no fucking idea what I'm doing?" Andrew wouldn't meet his eyes, and Tomas just looked... lost. *Awesome.*

A gust of wind blew the corner of the sleeping bag over Cass's face, and Stef bent to lift it aside. Cass looked so vulnerable. Nothing like the sexy, confident guy who'd fucked Stef's brains out only a few hours before. Jesus, he needed to get a grip.

"Well, you clearly know more than us," Tomas said. "And if we have to wait for professional help, God knows how long that'll take. A while, to be sure."

Goddammit. Stef's heart sank. "Define a while."

Tomas glanced at his brother, who muttered, "Tonight.

Tomorrow if we're unlucky, which... yeah... let's say I wouldn't count on luck at this point."

Stef dragged a hand down his mucky face. "Fuck."

A low groan fell from Cass's lips, and his head gave a sudden jerk. But before Stef could get excited, the man stilled again without any sign of waking.

Tomas rubbed Stef's shoulder. "Come on. I trust your instincts on this."

Stef gaped at him. "Then you're batshit." He glanced to where Cass lay limp and unresponsive, sighed, and scrunched his eyes. "Goddammit." He opened them again. "Okay, you two jocks take his upper half—one either side. Roll the sleeping bag right up close to his body before you lift so it doesn't sag too much. I'll carry his feet."

Andrew sent him a sour look, mumbling something spiteful about taking orders from a woofter, but moved into position nonetheless.

Stef ignored him. "When we get inside, we'll put him on the cot closest to the potbelly fire that *you're* gonna start, Tomas, okay? We need to get him dry."

Tomas nodded. "Got it."

Andrew glared at his brother, but whatever he might have thought about saying regarding Tomas's deference... he didn't.

Jesus Christ, how had Stef ended up team leader to the fucking goon show?

"Watch his neck," he added tartly. "I don't think he landed on it, but... be careful."

CHAPTER NINE

THEY CARRIED CASS INTO THE HUT AND GOT HIM SAFELY ON TO the cot. Stef checked his breathing, then pulled Cass's boots off and flung them in the corner under the saddles.

Tomas hovered nervously, chewing at his non-existent thumbnail. "He still okay?"

How the hell would I know? Still, Stef nodded, if for no other reason than that Tomas looked about to lose his shit completely. "I think so, but we need to get him out of these wet clothes." He unzipped Cass's jeans. "It'll warm up soon, but we can't wait. How about you get that fire going? Andrew, I'm going to need your help."

Tomas went into action, and Andrew approached warily.

"You sure he'd want you to do that"—Andrew watched Stef start to pull down Cass's jeans—"with you being... you know?"

Stef snorted. "I'm gonna ignore what you just implied, dickhead. Now grab his jean legs by the ends and pull. And you can stop with all the homophobic bullshit. I don't give a fuck what you think about me, but unless you want to take over making decisions about Cass, shut the fuck up."

Andrew mumbled something Stef ignored but then did as he was told. All the manhandling prompted a couple of rumbling protests from Cass but no real sign of waking. When they were done undressing him, they rolled him from side to side to get the sodden sleeping bag free, then put him back in recovery. Stef arranged a dry sleeping bag over top and tucked it in, then brushed the back of his hand across Cass's icy cheek. "There. You can rest now."

"I'm gonna check the horses," Andrew muttered, and left the hut.

"Good riddance," Stef said under his breath and took a seat next to Cass. It didn't take more than a second's thought to reach for Cass's hand and enfold it in his own. *Fuck 'em.*

"Sorry about Andrew." Tomas fanned the kindling into flames in the potbelly stove he'd just filled. "He's a jerk sometimes."

"No kidding." Stef studied the younger man. "He giving you a hard time? I, um, saw you arguing yesterday."

Tomas's head shot up, he took in the joined hands, and his ears tinged pink. "No." He looked away again. "Well, not really. He just has these... ideas, you know?" His glance flicked to the hut door and back to Stef. "He's kind of old-fashioned."

Stef shook his head and rubbed his thumb over the back of Cass's hand. "Old-fashioned, huh? So that's what they're calling it these days. In my time it was just good old redneck homophobia."

Tomas winced. "Yeah, well, that too, I guess."

The man looked like a scared rabbit about to bolt, and Stef didn't know whether to push or not. *Fuck it.* It wasn't like any of them had anywhere to run to, right? "I take it he doesn't know... about you, I mean?"

The immediate panic that lodged in Tomas's eyes was the only answer Stef needed.

"Don't worry, I'm not going to say anything, but I'm guessing that's what the argument was about. You gay? You don't have to answer."

Tomas sighed and prodded at the fire, adding a log which sent sparks crackling to the hearth. "Bi. Not that anyone knows. I don't—I mean, I've never... Ugh. Andrew told me to stop talking to you so much—stop looking at you like I wanted to suck your dick." His cheeks flamed. "Said that I was embarrassing him. That I'd give you the wrong idea or something." He huffed sardonically. "Holy fuck. If only he knew. It was exactly the *right* idea I was aiming to give you..." He glanced to their joined hands again and sighed. "Guess I wasn't the only one, right?"

Stef chuckled. "Yeah, I bet your brother never picked Cass as the one he needed to watch out for, right?"

Tomas laughed. "Never in a million years. He's, um... hot, though."

Stef ran his eye over Cass's face and pulled the sleeping bag a little higher under his chin. "Yeah, he is."

"How'd you know... about him?"

Stef winked at Tomas. "The way he looked at me when you guys weren't watching. Like he could eat me alive."

Tomas seemed to consider that. "Huh. What about me? How'd you guess?" His blush turned beetroot.

The guy was too adorable for words. "Same thing, plus you were too comfortable around me. I'm hardly a shrinking violet, and most straight guys throw me at least a second look before they get too close, but not you. I'm guessing your brother saw it too, though he probably didn't recognise it for what it was. Still, a few more times and you're not going to be able to keep your secret."

His face fell. "I know. I just... don't know what to do about it. I've known I was bi for... a long time, but I've um... never acted on it. I thought I could take the safe road, right? I mean, I figured if there's a choice, why make it hard on myself, especially with"—his eyes strayed to the hut door again, then back—"well, you know."

Stef snorted. "Yeah, how's that working out for you?"

Tomas laughed. "Guess you don't really get to choose who interests you, right? Lesson learned."

Stef roughed Tomas's hair. "Hey, I'm flattered you like me. But you're right. You'll need to decide if you're going to be open to that love in whatever form when it comes."

Tomas blinked slowly and picked at some imaginary lint on his T-shirt. "I hear you, and if it weren't for Andrew..." He stared wistfully at the fire. "But we run a business together, so it's not that easy to come out. He's gonna flip his nut, and I don't know if we'll survive—the business... or even as brothers. So, yeah..." He threw two more logs on the now-raging fire and clanged the door shut before sitting cross-legged on the floor at Stef's feet.

"So, you two... um..." Tomas glanced meaningfully between Stef and Cass.

Stef tapped his nose. "Nice girls don't kiss and tell."

Tomas blushed red again and looked away.

Something gurgled in Cass's throat, and pink-tinged saliva bubbled from his mouth. Stef jumped to his feet with Tomas right next to him.

"Shit, what was that?" Tomas grabbed Stef's arm and stared down at Cass with wide eyes.

"How the hell should I know?" Stef snapped. "Get me a clean cloth and a water bottle, will you?"

Tomas did as instructed while Stef pried Cass's mouth open to take a look. There was a cut on the inside of his bottom lip, which Stef hoped to hell was the cause of the blood, because other than that he had no fucking clue. When Tomas handed him the damp cloth, he set about cleaning Cass's face properly while taking inventory of the man. It kept his hands busy and made him feel like he was doing something.

He checked his watch. Cass had been out nearly thirty minutes. Why the hell wasn't he waking up? His breathing had settled—it was regular and calm, all that choking snoring gone. But he was cold and pale, too pale—almost white—and Stef wasn't happy about it, not one little bit. Fuck. What should they do? They couldn't leave him like this. They needed to get him some help.

Tomas stood over Stef as he worked, and Stef could feel the panic coming off him in waves. "What are we going to do, Stef? Why isn't he waking up?"

"Do you think I have any more answers than you?" Stef bit back. God, he was being a dick. "Sorry." He glanced up at Tomas. "He's freezing, that's all I know. And I don't have any fucking idea what I'm doing, so stop asking me questions as if I do. Please?" He scanned the room. "There must be a first aid box in here somewhere, or something in his saddlebags. Can you take a look?"

Tomas was on it in a flash.

An idea sprang to Stef's mind. "What about his satphone? He had it in his oilskin earlier. Check that."

Tomas grabbed Cass's coat, running his hands through the pockets. "*Fuck.*" He pulled out the broken remains of a phone.

Stef's heart sank. "Jesus Christ." He needed to have words with that damn horse. "Can we not catch a break here? What about your phone? Still no reception?"

Tomas turned from rifling through the storage boxes on the shelves to stare at him. "Do you really need to ask?"

"Fuck." Stef was never. Camping. Again.

"Found it!" Tomas slid a plastic container with a red cross on top from under a stack of five others and handed it down to Stef, who could've kissed him.

"Let's see what's in it, and I'll need another bottle of clean water. We'll need to put him on his back, so you watch his breathing, okay?"

Tomas nodded. Stef was still unloading the first aid box on to the cot when Andrew returned and slammed the door before tracking half the corral's mud through the small hut. He stank like a wet carpet, and that was being generous.

"Horses are fine. Arwen's leg's a little swollen and boggy but not broken." He took a seat by the fire and frowned. "What are you doing?" There was more than a grain of accusation in the tone.

Stef didn't bother to look up. "Since he's not waking up, I figured we needed to take a closer look. Clean him up and dress those wounds. Why? You want to take over?"

Andrew held up both hands. "I was just asking."

"Well, don't." Stef had reached his limit. The cut on Cass's stomach wasn't deep, but it had bled... a lot. He'd dabbed the worst of it clean, not wanting to fiddle too much in case he disturbed a clot and set the whole thing off again.

"How's your jaw?" Tomas distracted his brother, earning Stef's gratitude.

He glanced up to see the shadow of a decent bruise taking shape under Andrew's jaw. Good fucking job.

Andrew gingerly pressed his fingertips to the site. "Nothing's broken, but I can't open it fully."

Stef made a mental note to buy Arwen a whole fucking bag of cherry doughnuts.

"Shit. Is this what I think it is?" Andrew ran his fingers through the remains of the satphone.

Tomas nodded.

"Fuck." Andrew kicked the table leg.

Stef grabbed a pack of gauze swabs and set about dressing the wound on Cass's abdomen, the bruising already turning a deep angry red. "Yeah, well, bitching isn't going to help things. We need a plan, so get thinking."

Silence, bar a shuffling of feet.

Awesome.

When he was done with the stomach wound, Stef grabbed more gauze and tended to the gaping laceration on Cass's forehead. It was a struggle to clear all the mud and gunk from the slicing injury, and he winced, thankful Cass appeared impervious to the pain Stef had to be causing him. The man would be sporting a golf-ball-sized swelling before too long, and no doubt a headache to match.

"What's the weather doing?" Stef pressed, handing the filthy gauze to Tomas. "Give me a fresh one, will you?"

Andrew grunted. "Skies are clear, except down south where that rain's supposed to come from. Let's hope it doesn't arrive early."

Fuck. That's all they needed.

Andrew continued, "There wasn't enough rain in that squall to cause any real problems at the river crossing, but without a bloody phone someone's gonna need to ride for help, and we shouldn't leave it too long—the wind is still punching hard out there, and if that rain arrives..."

Andrew might be a royal pain in the arse, but Stef hadn't missed the edge of concern in the man's voice. He wanted his brother safe. Goddammit, the guy had a heart after all.

"Well, Cass is going nowhere," Stef said flatly. "I might know zip about head injuries, but I'm guessing you don't move a guy who's still unconscious any more than you have to, especially not on a horse. Not to mention he can't tell us what else might be wrong with him. He could have a broken pelvis for all we know."

As if he wanted to add his two cents to the pot, a long, gurgling moan spilled from Cass's. Stef's hands jerked away, and everyone gaped.

Andrew's face blanched like he'd seen a ghost, and Tomas's eyes blew wide. "Jesus George, that was creepy as fuck."

Stef couldn't disagree. He was about done with the unholy grunts and groans coming out of Cass's mouth—it was weirding him out, and he fought the sudden urge to just shake the man's tree until he woke up. Instead he stroked his fingers over Cass's forehead and cupped his jaw. "Do that again, Cowboy, and I'll pee my damn pants."

When he was sure Cass wasn't gonna give an encore, Stef set about covering the freshly cleaned wound while sending up a silent prayer to anyone who might be listening to keep Cass safe until they could get help. All that mud and shit—literally—from Arwen's hoof— Cass was a sitting duck for an infection. What if it got into his brain? Stef sucked in a truckload of air, then breathed himself down. No. There was bone between the skin and the brain... unless there was a fracture. *Shit.* Still, there was nothing he could do about any of that now.

Andrew helped with the tape and scissors, somewhat to Stef's surprise, so he thanked him. Didn't mean the man wasn't still an arsehole. Andrew grunted and went on to pack the first aid box away while Tomas bagged the rubbish, then they all grabbed seats around Cass, Stef staying closest, one hand on Cass's arm. "Right, spill," he said, eyeballing Andrew. "I know you've got a plan stewing in that head."

Andrew's gaze slid to Cass and then down to where Stef's hand covered Cass's arm. His brows pinched in a scowl, and his lip curled.

"Don't." Stef beat Andrew to whatever offensive comment the man was about to make. "There's no one to impress here, and you don't know half of what you think you do."

Andrew drilled him with a glare and chewed on his lip, but he said nothing.

"Andrew, come on." Tomas's foot connected with his brother.

Andrew nodded and sat back. "I'll ride back to the farm where we saw Beorn's house, just across the river. I can handle the crossing even with a bit of extra volume. It won't be more than that, not yet. It'll take me a few hours max, hopefully only two if the ground's hard enough to canter on the far side. We barely moved at a snail's pace yesterday." He eyed Stef pointedly.

It wasn't worth the energy to respond. Besides... "You're right," Stef grumbled. "Without me you could probably halve the time, maybe get someone back by this afternoon. Plus there's the mountain rescue helicopter, right? If Cass is too bad to move."

Tomas nodded. "And there's the old mining access track this side of the river. It starts at the downstream bridge. Cass said it was his alternative if the river flooded. But it's not maintained and would take a lot longer. And I don't know whether anything more than a horse could travel it, let alone a quad with a cot. I think it's best if we try and get across the river the same way we did yesterday, if we can."

It didn't seem like they had a choice. "Sounds like a—fuck—" Stef snatched his hand away as Cass's body arched up and jerked in a series of spasms, his head thrown back, neck corded, jaw clenched against the hiss of air trying to make it down his throat.

Stef shot to his feet. "Son of a goddamn bitch. Get that pillow out from under his head," he ordered Tomas, who had it on the floor in seconds while Andrew stood at the end of the bed, mouth opening and closing like a damn goldfish. "Andrew, get his legs over so he stays on his side," Stef instructed.

"Wh-what?" Andrew turned, looking stunned.

"His legs. Get the top one over in front of the other, now."

"Oh, right." Andrew did as he was asked while Cass spasmed in Stef's hold. Bubbles of pink saliva streamed from between his lips, then broke and ran down his shuddering chin. *Fuck, fuck, fuck. Come on, Cass. Don't do this to me. Stop it. Come on, man.*

Andrew watched with a horrified expression. "Shit. Is that blood? Should we put something between his teeth?"

Stef shook his head. "No. You don't do that. He'll be okay on his side. He's got a cut on the inside of his lip is all."

"Jesus." Andrew looked like his head was going to explode. "What should we do? Why is he doing this?"

As if Stef had any fucking answers? "How the hell should I know?" His own voice trembled with the force of Cass's convulsions. "And would you stop asking me shit like that? I. Don't. Know. Okay?"

"Here." Tomas shoved a rolled-up blanket behind Cass's back to help support him on his side.

Saliva poured from Cass's mouth as his rigid body shuddered, and all Stef could do was pray. Goddammit, the guy was gonna owe him big time if he got through this okay—which he would. A fucking date, at least. *Shit.* Stef really, really didn't want to acknowledge how good that idea sounded. It was so not the time.

He bent his head. "You will," he whispered close to Cass's ear. "I don't care if we have to go to fucking Oamaru so no one recognises you, but you are taking me out on a damn date, understand?"

Cass shook violently, and Stef thought he might fucking cry. He was out of answers. *Fuck.* He didn't even have the right questions. It was only his determination not to give Andrew the satisfaction that kept him from howling in frustration. He sucked it back and swallowed hard.

"I'm gonna take that as a yes," he told the man vibrating in his hands. "And it's not gonna be some cheap-arse place either. Oh no, Mr you're-more-capable-than-you-think-you-are Martin. I'm gonna wring your wallet dry for putting me through this. What the hell did you think you were doing, going out there on your own?" Stef was vaguely aware of the other two men staring at him, and he paused to check—nope, not a single fuck to give. "I want steak, Mister, and lots of it. And those potatoes in cream and cheese, you know, that French dish, what's it called—"

"Potato gratin," Tomas answered.

Stef looked up. "Thank you." He glanced at Andrew, who was staring at him like he couldn't decide whether he wanted to hit him or lock him away. *What the fuck ever.*

He got down on his knees so he could look into Cass's unseeing eyes. "And then we're going dancing—you are so taking me dancing. And none of that country line-dancing shit, we're gonna bump and grind in a club till we're all sweaty, and then... well, then we'll take it really slow, maybe stay till the last dance and just sway close together, right? But you need to stop this, Cass. Please? Stop and wake up."

And then, as abruptly as it had started, Cass sank back against Stef's hands and went still. *Holy fuck.* He'd like to think Cass had heard him, but... yeah. Tears pricked at Stef's eyes, but goddammit, he was not gonna cry. He eased Cass gently back on to the cot mattress, still on his side, while Tomas retrieved the pillow, and then he tucked Cass's hair behind his ears and wiped his slack mouth.

"Fucking hell, Cass. You can't do that to me." He leaned forward, resting their foreheads together.

A hand landed on his back. Tomas. "Hey, you did great. Better than I would've, I can tell you that."

Stef wasn't so sure. He hadn't done anything, not really. He blew out a shaky sigh. "Thanks. But in case we didn't already know it, we really need to get help, soon. We can't stick him on a horse like this." He cast a worried glance at Cass. The man was pale but breathing easily. "And we're gonna need to swap mattresses."

Tomas followed his gaze. "Oh, right."

Stef shrugged. "No big deal. It's part of what happens, I think."

Tomas frowned. "But it's..."

"Pink? Yeah. Not much we can do about that."

They changed the damp mattress for Stef's one as Andrew gathered his riding gear.

"I'll leave now," he said.

Tomas jerked his head around. "What do you mean? You can't go alone. What if something happens? The river will be high—maybe not flooding, but it'll be a lot higher than yesterday. You're gonna need roping to cross."

"I'm a good rider. I'll be fine."

"What if it's not fine? We'd never know if something happened. We could be waiting for days. Stef will be okay with Cass. The most important thing is to get help as soon as possible, and the best way to ensure that happens is for us both to go. You can't cross that river alone."

"No!" Andrew turned on his brother. "You're staying here. Stef might need your help—"

"*You'll* need my help."

"He's right," Stef interrupted, and then wondered who the hell had taken over his brain. "Tomas needs to go with you, Andrew. I'll be fine." Nope, nope, he wouldn't. "He knows even less than I do—apparently you both do. And if something were to happen with Cass, we could only do so much anyway. There's nothing more anyone can do until we get help, so just go and get there safely. I'll... fuck. I'll manage, whatever, just go."

Andrew stared at Stef for a long minute as if weighing his options. But Stef already knew there were none.

"Okay, we'll both go." Andrew kept his eyes on Stef. "But we'll be back before tonight. You just need to watch him for a few hours."

Stef swallowed. "Right." He could barely look at the other man, worried Andrew would see the terror in his eyes.

Tomas's hand landed on Stef's arm. "Cass will be fine, I'm sure of it. You've done an amazing job already, Stef."

He met Tomas's gaze with a brief nod of thanks and hoped the day had room for one more miracle.

CHAPTER TEN

STEF CHECKED HIS WATCH. EIGHT A.M. TOMAS AND ANDREW had been gone an hour—one hour and he was already climbing the fucking walls, not helped by the endless groans coming from Cass, punctuated by the odd licking of lips and grinding of teeth. His eyes had flickered open a few times and even appeared to look around the room... once. But there was no light behind them, no one home, and each time they'd quickly shuttered closed again and Stef was simply left to hope it meant *something*. Better than lying there like a damn lump of jelly. Maybe.

All Stef knew was it had been over two hours since Cass had been hit in the head and he still hadn't come around. That couldn't be good. Trust the cowboy to do it all in his own good time. They'd be having a conversation about that. Plus Stef was too scared to move far in case Cass convulsed again, which left him boiling in the heat of the cabin now the sun had come up, and the horses were stomping their feet in the corral—*hooves*, they were stomping their *hooves*... ugh.

Tomas and Andrew had taken Gimli with them, so as not to leave too many horses this side of the river. That left Arwen and Gandalf, and Stef really needed to check on them—maybe let them out into the larger pen to stretch their legs? Did horses need to stretch their legs? Who the hell knew? What if they went nuts again? *Fuck.*

He paced a triangle between the door, the cot, and the window. The hut was now a few ticks short of maxi-grill, so he damped the fire and opened the window, standing in the cool current of air for a few seconds to try to clear his head and still the panic that hadn't left his chest since he'd seen Cass under Arwen's hooves. He couldn't align the jolting memories of Cass fucking him senseless in the lean-to with the man now sprawled unconscious on a cot.

Stef fanned himself with his shirt, and a thought suddenly hit him. *Shit.* Keep head injuries cool, right? Hadn't he read that somewhere or seen it on television? He thought so. Maybe? *Ugh.* He didn't fucking know, but he'd have to go with his gut. Now that Cass had dried off and warmed to above freezing, Stef needed to make sure he didn't cook him. *Jesus Christ.*

He rested a hand on Cass's brow. The man was sweating. *Fuck, fuck, fuck.* He shoved the empty cots back against the wall and hauled Cass over to the open door and into the breeze. He yanked the sleeping bag off and froze for a half second—God, Cass was a gorgeous creature. But he didn't need Stef perving on him while he was knocked out. What kind of creep did that?

Stef grabbed his old T-shirt from the day before and threw it over Cass's groin to give him some privacy as the cool air ran over his body. He couldn't help his grin at the "Brokeback Since Way Back" lettering strategically on display as he remembered Cass's comment.

"Bent as fuck, huh?" Stef stared down at Cass, still on his side with a pillow at his back to keep him there and seemingly sound asleep. "Well, sugar, I need you to get through this nightmare so we can discuss that in greater detail. And since I'm not done with you yet, we need to talk about that whole not-coming-out-locally strategy you got going on, 'cause I have to tell you, it's not working for me right now."

Cass groaned and mumbled something, and Stef took his hand. "Hey, sweetheart. You waking up?"

But Cass didn't move. Just another rumbling moan, and that was it. Stef wiped Cass's slack face with a cloth and then dabbed the dampness from his own eyes. *Dammit to hell.* He sniffed, then banged himself on the forehead with the palm of his hand. He wasn't fucking going to do this. He wasn't going to fall apart. A part of him wondered what Paul would say if he could see Stef now, and the thought steeled his determination to keep his shit together.

"Fuck you," he said to the silent room. "Seems to me I would've rocked a refugee camp."

He threaded his fingers through Cass's hair and let out a breath. "You know, I'm getting damn tired of holding up the conversation, buster. This is a fucking piss-poor first date, and if you're not careful I'll swipe you so far left you'll be skating off the side of my iPhone into my *holy shit* file—and yes, I have one of those. Why, I hear you ask? Well, because... have you seen this arse? *Hmmph.* Do I need to say more? Sufficient to say that I have, on occasion, be known to attract a guy a sandwich short of a picnic, if you get my drift.

"Tanner says it's because I need more filters on my attraction index than just *hot* and *available.* I prefer to think it's because as an indoor sport, sex is the only athletic endeavour I have a better-than-average skill set for. In the bedroom I'm a fucking triathlete. So, yeah, there's that.

"Hence the file. Not that all my *holy shit* encounters were necessarily failures, I'll have you know, at least on the sex side. But the file is there for those special boys with whom it wouldn't be prudent to risk a second round without law enforcement supervision.

"You, of course, don't fit into that category. Your attention to detail on my arse was spectacularly dextrous and warrants further consideration, at my leisure, which is why you need to wake. The. Fuck. Up."

He rested the back of a hand on Cass's forehead, his shoulder, and then his chest, relieved to find his skin cooler. There was more colour in his cheeks, and his breathing was quiet. Stef blew out a sigh.

"Come on, Cass, tell me to shut up—something, anything. Open those gorgeous green eyes and tell me to shut my trap. Everyone does. It's what I do. Eventually people get sick of me. It's my superpower. Come on. You're ruining my rep here, man."

Nothing.

Stef blew out a sigh and collapsed on the floor against the door frame. "Okay, well, you asked for it. About this proper date we're gonna have. I need somewhere there's good wine... no, great wine. I'm a bit of a wine snob, which I bet you'd never have guessed."

Stef paused as a thought hit him, and his eyes sprang wide.

"Oh no. Don't tell me. I bet you're a beer man. All cowboys are, right? Oh. My. God." He hissed in mock outrage. "You probably drink out of one of those disgusting cans that makes everything taste like metal, in a place with sawdust and peanut shells on the floor. Does Queenstown even have one of those places? If it does, I'm sure you're a life member. You listen to country music, for fuck's sake. I literally know no one who does that."

He opened the soft clench of Cass's fist, straightening his fingers on the cot and then patting them gently. "Yeah, I thought so. Damn. How the hell am I gonna get a decent Manhattan in a place like that? Wait. You did not just tell me to order a beer. *Pfft*. It's like you don't even know me. What's that? No, well, I guess you don't."

He threaded his fingers through Cass's and squeezed gently. "But you could, you know? *Get* to know me. If you wanted, that is. I mean, I wouldn't be averse to the idea. Hell, look at me. I had a beer last night around a campfire and talked shit with three testosterone-fuelled cowboys, then slept on a damn cot under a minus-a-thousand-thread-count sleeping bag. I've got fucking green shoots of new psychological growth coming out my damn arse. Who'd have figured that in a million years?"

He snorted. "Well, admittedly two of said cowboys turned out to be about as straight as a banana and probably wouldn't look out of place in pink jockstraps and chaps in a pride parade, but still, you know... could've knocked me over with a feather."

A lonesome whinny had Stef on his feet and out the door in an instant, only to find the two remaining horses staring forlornly at the hut. Arwen took one look at him and snorted her disapproval. Gandalf just stared with a decidedly *what she said* look in his eyes.

Stef threw out his arms. "What? Use your words. How the hell do I know what you want? You've seen me. I'm about as country as a Kardashian."

Arwen's ears flicked back and forth. If Stef didn't know any better, he'd say she was considering her response and how to keep it seemly. God, he really was losing his mind.

She sauntered to their water trough with a coquettish swish of her tail, a sashay in all but name, and Stef had to laugh. Even Gandalf turned to watch her butt, and Stef shook his head at the gelding. "Why, you dirty dog. She's far too young for you... I think. Actually, I have no idea, so go for it. More power to you. She looks like she needs a daddy."

Arwen threw him a withering glare and stomped her front hoof against the trough, and it finally sank in. "Oh, shit. Are you guys thirsty?"

Stef was damn sure that was an eye-roll. "Okay, okay... let me think."

He spun to find Cass unmoved, eyed the door, and did a bit of mental calculation. Yeah, it should work. With some difficulty, he manoeuvred the cot through the door and out on to the shaded deck where he could keep an eye on Cass while he... *shit*... how the hell did he fill the trough? He couldn't see a tap.

"Don't go anywhere." He patted Cass's shoulder and headed for the corral.

"Be nice to me," he said to the two horses as he squeezed through the railings and into the corral, heading for the trough. "Any hanky-panky and there'll be no more doughnuts for either of you."

Arwen followed and nudged her nose into his jeans pocket from behind, rudely shoving him when she found it was empty.

"Stop that." He turned and eyeballed her. "If you'd behaved last night, there'd be plenty left."

In answer, she lifted her soft muzzle to Stef's face. Her whiskers tickled his nose, and he smiled—then froze, suddenly and terrifyingly aware he was face to face with a set of very large teeth. *Fuck.*

She nickered, and a wash of warm breath fanned by flickering whiskers caressed his skin, and—*holy crap*—she kept going, nosing around his face, blowing air up his nostrils—the inside of her velvet upper lip leaving a trail of slightly rank slobber over his cheek and through his hair while he tried to calm his stuttering heart and the deep desire to turn tail and run the fuck away.

When she was finally done, Arwen dropped her head in front of his chest and nudged him for a scratch. He blew out the breath he'd been holding and rubbed his trembling hand up and down her nose while trying to suck in another lungful to replace it. Not. Working.

"Okay." He blinked slowly. "That was... intense. How about we not do that again, sweetheart. It's all very quick, you know. I'm really not that kind of girl."

Arwen nickered again and batted his hand for another scratch.

He chuckled. "Yeah, okay, so I am totally that kind of girl, but let's keep that between us. And just so you know, we could've done with this level of affection about four hours ago when you were doing your panic dance. Anyway, about this water..."

It took a little time to get the trough figured, but in the end, Stef surprised himself. There was piping from the trough into the ground that he guessed came from some kind of holding tank, though fucked if he could see any sign of it. Eventually, after scrabbling in the dirt and other unmentionable biodegradable material, he found a lever by the shelter attached to piping that looked similar, and when he turned it on—hey, presto, water flowed into the trough. No sound of a pump, so maybe it was gravity fed. Look at him, all technical and shit.

Arwen and Gandalf immediately bumped noses in the trough and drank their fill while Stef went to grab some hay from his and Cass's little love nest from the night before. He tried not to think about what they'd got up to in there only hours ago, but the evidence was all around him, especially the hay bale with its top flattened from the force of Cass pounding the living daylights out of Stef. Holy shit, the man knew how to fuck.

He grabbed an armful of hay and threw it into the corral to keep the two horses happy, and when he was done he wiped his... *Oh. My. God...* filthy hands down the front of his jeans. Lifting them cautiously to his nose, he took a short whiff and nearly choked. *Son of a goddamn bitch.* Horse shit. He had fucking horse shit under his fingernails. He flicked some water from the trough over his hands and cleaned them as best he could, then stood back and felt a surge of something like pride. *Hell yeah.* He could do this cowboy shit.

Arwen jerked her head up and eyed him accusingly.

"Don't even with me." He scowled at her. "You got a problem, write to your mayor... get it, mayor... mare... *ugh*, whatever. Tough crowd. And you need to improve your toilet etiquette." He held up his dripping hand. "Has no one ever taught you to wipe your arse—"

"I'd pay good money to hear her answer to that."

Cass! Stef spun to find the man swaying and holding on like grim death to a roof support while holding Stef's T-shirt in front of his groin with the other and choking on a laugh.

Stef bolted from the corral and stormed on to the deck. "What the hell do you think you're doing? Get your arse back in that cot." He grabbed Cass around the waist and guided him back to the bed, where he eased him down gently.

"Now stay there." Stef stood back, hands on hips, and summoned his best glare.

Cass returned a sheepish smile, then winced and dropped his head.

Stef immediately fell at his side. "What's wrong?" He tipped Cass's chin up till their eyes met and took stock of him. He was pale, but other than that, his pupils appeared to be normal size—whatever the hell that meant, although it had to be an improvement on the dinner plates they'd resembled an hour ago—and he looked... better. At least a little.

Cass's hand limped to his forehead. "Fuck, my head feels like a tractor ran over it."

"Lie down." Stef helped swing his legs up on to the thin mattress. "Arwen's hoof, not a tractor. Caught you right above your brow." He touched the dressing on Cass's forehead, then quickly dropped his hand.

Cass grabbed Stef's wrist. "I need to piss. That's where I was heading."

Stef stopped in his tracks. "Oh, right. Um. Hang on." He grabbed a bucket from inside the hut, emptied it, and held it out. "All yours."

Cass stared at it, then back up to Stef. He opened his mouth to say something, caught the look on Stef's face, and closed it again.

Stef grinned. "Excellent decision." He stood waiting.

"Um, can you..." Cass spun his fingers in a circle.

Stef jolted. "Oh, of course. Sorry." He spun around to give Cass some privacy, mentally smacking himself sideways for looking like a complete weirdo as the dull thud of a pee stream hit the plastic. It went on... forever. "Jesus Christ, how did you hold all that inside?"

"One of many talents. Anyway, I'm done."

Stef spun back and took the bucket.

A deep crease formed between Cass's brows. "It's, um..."

Stef looked and shrugged. "Oh. Yeah. It was like that earlier when you, um... I mean, when I had to change..."

Cass looked beyond horrified. "I pissed myself? Jesus..." He closed his eyes.

Stef leapt to reassure him. "No. Or, at least, not how you mean. Look, let me chuck this, and then I'll fill you in on whatever you don't remember."

Cass held his gaze for a long minute. "Okay, but I want to know *everything*." He searched their surroundings. "And where are the others?"

Stef held the bucket aloft. "First things first. Now, don't fucking move this time."

Cass saluted, and Stef's heart squeezed. His throat clenched and

his eyes misted and he couldn't move a goddamn muscle. "You... you
—I thought you—"

Cass reached for his hand. "Hey, it's okay. Shh. Come here."

Stef almost did, then violently shook his head. "Nuh-uh. No. I
am not having this conversation with a bucket of your bloody piss in
my hands. I'll be back in minute."

By the end of Stef's explanation, Cass's head was teetering in no
man's land. The relentless, pinched ache across his forehead he'd
woken with had now entrenched itself in his neck and shoulders as
well, his eyelids sagging under the weight of what felt like an entire
solar system. Not to mention his right side burnt like someone had
poured Agent Orange on it, the bruising on his stomach a nasty
tapestry of reds, blues and greens. It wasn't rocket science to work out
why he was pissing blood, but he couldn't afford to worry about that
now. Not much he could do about any of it stuck up this damn
mountain.

At least it wasn't raining... yet. The sun was out in all its finery,
but menacing clouds gathered to the south and the relentless wind
had taken squatter's rights in the valley. At least the deck offered
some shelter. He hoped to God Andrew and Tomas had got down
safely and help was on its way. Stef had played down his role, but
Cass guessed there was more to it. He couldn't imagine Stef letting
either of the other men take responsibility for Cass's care, not after
what he and Stef had shared. The thought did funny things to his
heart.

Stef fussed over him like he was a damn toddler, re-dressing
Cass's wounds as Cass lay on the cot under the deck roof. It was...
cute. Not to mention really, really nice. He felt like crap, but Stef had
threatened him with all kinds of creative bodily harm if he didn't
drink some water, at least. And so he had, enjoying the whole feisty
mother-hen thing Stef had going on. Not that he'd say that to Stef's

face, or anywhere near him for that matter. The guy had eyes and ears like an apex predator.

Cass had nearly hit the deck both times he'd tried to stand, and the tongue-lashing he'd received had been enough to put paid to any further attempt. A riled-up Stef was a sight to behold. He'd put a Tasmanian devil to shame, and was it wrong that Cass had... thoughts... about how else that might manifest?

He couldn't even summon the energy to be embarrassed about waking naked as a jaybird or the fact Stef had needed to clean him up after he'd apparently had a seizure—something Cass very definitely did *not* want to think about too hard. But it had only happened once... that had to be a good sign, right?

Cass had no memory of anything after he'd finally taken himself off to bed, other than the amount of time it had taken him to get to sleep. He'd been too busy studying Stef in the cot next to him. Relaxed in sleep and with a rare softness to his mouth, the prickly man looked like a damned angel—a million miles from the sassy, cut-you-like-slicing-a-peach, smart-mouthed attitude he wore like a second skin the rest of the time.

Both versions were intriguing. Both got Cass hot under the collar. He loved sparring with high-spirited Stef, but he also loved the quiet, reflective side that had briefly showed its face in the forest, and again when it was just the two of them by the fire. Cass would take a bet not too many saw that particular side. Stef kept his guard up, and Cass didn't blame him. He'd been hurt, and Cass knew what that felt like.

Stef had also made no mention of their lovemaking, and Cass didn't know whether that was because he regretted it or because he was being cautious. Either way, Cass didn't have the energy to raise it himself. Not yet. But he would. He hadn't experienced anything like the connection they'd briefly shared in... well, ever, if he was honest. It was unsettling, to say the least. Terrifying was closer to the mark. He hadn't wanted to know a man, a person, like this in a long, long time, and he didn't know what to do with that.

After changing Cass's dressing, Stef helped Cass into clean briefs and his jeans, which had dried by the fire. But Cass's T-shirt was beyond redemption, filthy and ripped. He had no option but to borrow a clean one from Stef—the man had brought his entire wardrobe, it seemed. It was a little too tight and a whole lot too gay, with "*Coffee THEN Cowboys*" written across the chest in rainbow letters.

"You're sure this is the only one you have?" Cass narrowed his gaze.

Stef bit back a smile. "Well, I do have a couple of others." His gaze raked Cass with unapologetic approval. "But they're a lot worse, believe me."

Cass sighed. The man was incorrigible. "I don't even want to know. Just tell me why?"

Stef beamed. "Because Tanner would've died when I made him wear them, that's why. Pretty much like you. You look... sweet." He bit back a smile.

Cass's eyebrow twitched. "I look fucking gay is what I look. And no one knows I'm bi, remember?"

"Mmm, about that. Just so you know, it's a discussion yet to be finished." Stef gave Cass a calculating sideways glance, which Cass pretended not to see.

The man was a terrier. A five-foot-ten terrier with green nail polish. "I'm pretty sure it's finished."

"Nope, it—"

"Oh, shit..." Cass's stomach lurched into his throat, and he flailed wildly for the bucket.

Stef jammed it into his hands just in time for Cass to hurl most of the water he'd drunk and a good deal of acid bile along with it. He continued to retch, the pain firing a trail across his gut, and all the while Stef's hand remained lightly pressed to his back, running in soothing circles. When Cass was done, Stef handed him a cloth.

"Thanks." He wiped the sour taste from his lips and took a deep breath.

"You're gonna have to replace that fluid." Stef took the bucket from him.

"In a minute. Just... give me a minute."

Stef placed a water bottle in his hands. "Little and often, when you can. I'll be checking."

Of course he would. A pushover, Stef was not.

Cass scooted gingerly on to his back and tried not to focus on the cramps darting across his belly like thin, sharp knives. "What's the time?"

Stef glanced over. "Eleven. They should be across the river and almost at that farm by now, right? They thought they could be back by two-ish, with a bit of luck."

Cass wasn't so sure. "Depends on how high it's running. From what you said, it didn't rain for long, so... maybe. But it'll take some time to get a team organised and up here." His gaze shifted to the dark southern skies. "And then there's that."

Stef followed his gaze, his lips set in a thin line. "Well, you can't ride out of here. Hell, you can barely sit upright without passing out, and we have no idea what's under all that bruising on your stomach. They have to get you out of here. There's always the helicopter, right?"

Not unless the wind drops. But Cass didn't share the thought. Stef didn't need the added grief. "I'm pretty sure I haven't broken anything."

"Maybe so—but what about your kidneys, or your liver? They're right where she stood, aren't they?"

Cass arched a brow. "How'd you know that?"

"Hey, I watch television." Stef waggled his brows. "I know stuff."

Cass laughed and grabbed his side. "Ow, ow, ow. Don't make me laugh."

Stef's brows knotted. "Anyway, Andrew said they should be able to get a four-wheel-drive ambulance thing right up to the crossing, then just take a quad over. So it's only the last bit they'll have to navigate with a stretcher when they take you down, and that's plenty wide enough."

"Sounds like a plan." But with one eye on the sky, Cass wasn't going to take that bet.

All the signs were there. The rain predicted for later that evening had been given a boot up the arse by the electrical storm and its funnelling winds. Thick grey clouds hovered south of Lake Wakatipu, and if he had to guess, Cass would say the rain was going to hit them in an hour, two at the most—long before help could possibly get to the hut.

It didn't take much wet in these sheer-faced ranges to put the river valleys in flood—a steady hour would do it. After that, no one would be crossing that river, not for a day or two at the least. Cass swallowed hard and decided to say nothing.

He kept his eyes on the skies, sipped at his water, and tried to stuff the nausea down while Stef ran around like an Energizer bunny, tidying the hut and stuffing all their belongings into their bags so they'd be ready to go when help arrived. Yeah, right. It kept him busy, Cass figured, and just kept quiet.

When Stef finally ran out of steam, he collapsed on the deck beside Cass with an exhausted groan. "It's one. They won't be long now, right?" He handed Cass a slice of plain buttered bread keeping one for himself. "Eat."

Cass pushed it away. "I can't— "

"Eat." Stef glared and shoved it back under his nose.

Cass returned the glare but took the bread anyway. "Did anyone ever tell you you're a bossy little shit?"

"It may have been said once or twice." Stef flashed him an amused smile, ate his bread, then frowned and dabbed at Cass's temple with a piece of gauze. "You're bleeding again."

"Oh." Cass's hand went to his brow, his fingers coming away slick with blood. *Shit.* Still, he shrugged. "It's nothing."

Stef stared at him. "If that's how you want to play it. Anyway, eat up. It's good carbs, and you need something in your stomach or you'll feel like crap when they take you down."

Cass's gaze slid away. "Fine." He took a bite and pushed it around his mouth. It tasted like cardboard and sat like a lump of glue on his tongue for about two minutes until he finally managed to squeeze it down past the Everest-sized lump in his throat. There was no chance to spit it out with Stef staring at him like a Halloween version of Mother Teresa.

"Good boy." Stef patted his hand.

Cass arched a brow. "You gonna spank me if I don't finish?"

Stef looked up with heat in his eyes. "Do you want me to?"

Yes. Yes, he did. And where the hell did that come from? Cass snorted. "Not with this headache, sweetheart."

They locked gazes for a few seconds longer, and Stef looked about to say something more when a few splats of rain hit the edge of deck and grabbed his attention.

"Shit." He ran to the step and peered south. "It's black as Hades over Glenorchy. I thought it wasn't supposed to rain till tonight." He turned back, caught Cass's guilty expression, and narrowed his gaze. "You knew. You knew the rain would be early." There was enough acid in the comment for Cass to flinch. "You knew they might not get back in time."

He hesitated, then nodded. "It's the wind."

Stef's eyes flashed. "What the hell? Why didn't you say anything? If it rains too much before they get to the river..." His forehead puckered.

"They won't be able to cross," Cass finished for him. "I know. I just... I guess I didn't want you to panic."

Stef's hands clenched at his sides. "Panic? Did it seem like I was panicking? You let me pack everything without a single word. I... Jesus, Cass, I feel like a fucking fool—"

Dammit. "I didn't mean—"

"I may not have your whole woo-woo mountain man skills, but

I'm not a fucking child. You could've warned me. I could have got my head around it."

"You were a bit anxious and jumpy—"

"No!" Stef held his hand out, fury etched into every inch of his face. "No. You do not get to say that shit to me. I don't need to be jollied along and wrapped in fucking cotton wool. Do I need to remind you who was the one unconscious for three fucking hours, and who was the one who looked after your sorry arse, kept a fire going, fed and watered the damn horses, dressed your wounds, held you while you fitted, cleaned up your piss—all the while terrified about how badly injured you might be? So how in holy hell do you have the nerve to think I wouldn't handle knowing we might be stuck here a little longer than I hoped. Anxious? Jumpy? Hell yeah, I'm jumpy. But I'd say that was a fairly understandable reaction, all things considered. Didn't stop me handling shit. And I think you'd be *anxious and jumpy* too if I was lying there—you just might hide it a little better."

Fuck. He was right. Cass had done to Stef exactly what everybody else did... what his ex had done. He stumbled through an apology. "I'm sorry. I didn't—"

"Save it." Stef's gaze steeled. The rain spots behind him turned to a slow drizzle and then into heavy sheets as the skies opened, the corrugated roof above the deck thundering with the onslaught. Stef turned and grumbled, "It appears we'll have plenty of time to discuss this later." His gaze found the horses, their backs turned into the lashing, and softened. "There's not much shelter in the corral. Should I let them into the other run where they can get under those trees?"

Cass should've thought of that. "Um, yeah, good idea." It was a brave thing to offer.

A flicker of nerves crossed Stef's face. "They won't lose their shit again, will they? I mean, I'm not sure I could... on my own..."

Cass's heart cracked open just a little more. "No, they'll be fine," he said. "That was just the lightning and thunder. They're used to bucketing rain. Six metres a year, remember?"

Stef hesitated a second, then turned to go, but Cass grabbed his arm. "And I really am sorry. You're right, I treated you like a child. It was an arsehole thing to do. You've got more balls than me. I'm not sure I would've managed so well if it had been you."

They locked eyes for a minute before Stef gave a sharp nod, grabbed his oilskin, and headed for the horses. Cass watched him clamber a little less than artfully over the railings, losing his hood in the process. It wasn't long before those unruly chestnut waves were plastered to his head and whipped across his face, and Cass's fingers itched to set them right. He remembered the way those silken locks felt the night before when Stef's mouth had been around him and Cass's hands had been fisted in his hair... and yeah, that had gone nuclear fast.

Cass sucked on his water bottle and watched Stef work, admiring the line of his lean body and the way he danced around the rapidly growing mud puddles rather than walking through them. He chatted away to the horses like he'd been doing it all his life, discussing some inanity Cass could only imagine. The guy couldn't seem to do anything without a conversation, giving a loud laugh as Arwen nuzzled his pockets looking for those damn doughnut crumbs. The sound drifted over Cass like a warm wash of air.

An image flashed into Cass's mind of Stef standing beside him, keeping Arwen focused with doughnut crumbs while he struggled to hold her. *Fuck.* It had been a courageous thing to do. Yesterday Stef had barely managed to feed Arwen a carrot without having a full-on panic attack. Yeah, Cass had a slice or three of humble pie to eat.

When Stef finally got the animals through the gate into the larger run, he threw them a couple more handfuls of hay and the two horses delighted in their relative freedom, running the inside length of the fence before making for the shelter of the two stunted beech trees— just tall enough for them to push under and scratch their backs up against. It was a two-for-one deal, and they nickered contentedly.

Cass grabbed the towel Stef had left on his cot and waited.

"Jesus, it's pissing down like a water-sports dream out there." Stef ran up on to the deck with his hair sodden, rain streaming down his face, beads of water suspended from those outrageously long lashes, and that ridiculous T-shirt plastered to his lithe body and highlighting the piercing in his clavicle.

Cass nearly choked on his tongue. "Um, nice imagery, thanks."

Stef shrugged out of his oilskin, hung it over the door to drip, and shook his hair over the edge of the deck.

"Take that drenched T-shirt off and come here." Cass shifted to the edge of the cot and indicated the floor between his feet. "Facing me."

Stef stopped mid-shake and stared at him through a curtain of wet hair. It was one of the sexiest fucking things Cass had ever seen.

After a second's hesitation, Stef sat warily between his legs, and Cass lifted the towel, wincing as the movement pulled at his stomach.

Stef grabbed his wrist, eyebrow arched. "Really?"

Cass flashed him an amused smile. "Really." He pulled free of Stef's grasp and began gently drying his hair. Stef grumbled something but didn't fight it, and eventually he relaxed.

When he was satisfied he'd dried the worst of it, Cass caught Stef's eye. "I'm sorry I was a dick."

Stef's mouth quirked up in a soft smile. "You really were."

Cass snorted and brushed a corner of the towel down Stef's nose to catch a few drips. "You looked after the horses, you looked after me. For a born-and-bred city boy, it's kind of amazing."

Stef's gaze slid away, his cheeks bright. "It was noth—" He stopped himself and worried his lip for a second. "Nah, you know what? It *was* fucking amazing." He laughed, and his whole face lit up. "Holy shit, who'd have guessed? Move your arse over, Bear Grylls."

Cass snorted. "You're kind of cute, you know that?"

Stef glared at him.

Cass swallowed another smile. "So, prissy city boy, how about you close your eyes and let me finish?" He held the towel out, and Stef stared at it, the crease between his brows deepening for just a second. Then he closed his eyes, and Cass wiped them one at a time —slowly.

When he opened them again, Cass's gaze dropped to Stef's mouth, and the air between them thickened with unspoken memories of the night before. "You, um... you're still wet... there." He pointed to Stef's mouth.

Stef licked his lips, sending a shiver through Cass, and then he frowned. "You shouldn't. Your head. You need to rest."

"I'm fine."

"Oh... well..." Stef drew a shaky breath and tilted his chin up. "Have at it, then... if you're sure."

And so Cass did, that and more, beginning a leisurely and thorough drying of every square centimetre of skin he could reach on Stef's body.

He went slowly over the clavicle piercing—the wet bar gleaming in the light, the golden leaf stuck to Stef's damp skin and slightly off-centre. Cass lifted the leaf and studied it again, feeling the weight of Stef's eyes on him. He took his time to drink in the man's full and intimate presence as the rain hammered on the iron roof—the noise and the curtain of water off the deck creating a bubble of time and space that locked them out from the world. "On your knees and lift your arms... please."

Stef did as he was asked, eyes laser focused like white-hot needles slicing right though Cass's brain, whipping up his desire. Cass did his best to ignore it, letting the towel follow the fluid lines of Stef's slender arms, shoulders to fingertips, then down both sides of that tight torso to the soft, dusty brown smattering of hair in his treasure trail, and then further, to the waistband of his jeans.

That done, Cass returned to Stef's chest and ran the rough towel over the nubs of his stiff nipples, taking a second to blow on each one, relishing how Stef squirmed under the attention—his sharp intakes of breath, the growing bulge in those soft jeans.

"Turn around... please." His rough voice cut a scorching path between them.

Stef didn't even open his eyes, shuffling around without question to present his smooth, tanned back for Cass's indulgence.

Holy hell. Cass's breath caught in his throat, his gaze roaming those acres of skin. Memories stormed his mind from the night before. The feel of Stef beneath him, urging him on—laughing, demanding, soothing, arching in desire.

Cass massaged as he towelled, revelling in the small grunts of pleasure that made their way to his ears. And when Stef rolled his shoulders in approval, killer headache or no, Cass wanted nothing more than to fold himself over that body and kiss every inch, finishing the job with his lips and tongue before running his hands over those tight shoulders and all the way down to the swell of the heavenly arse all tucked up in those soft-as-butter jeans. Then he'd reach around and drag Stef's zip down and—

"You okay back there?" Stef chuckled softly.

Cass cleared his throat and sucked in a shaky breath. "Yep." He lifted the towel and brushed long, unhurried swathes from Stef's shoulders to his hips, and down both arms. "There, all done." He sat back, barely recognising his own voice.

Stef didn't miss it either. He turned and rested his hands on Cass's thighs before locking eyes with him—deep hazel pools, more brown than green in the dull light, piercing Cass with questions he had zero answers for.

"So, um... have fun?"

Cass raked his gaze over Stef and threw the towel aside. With their gazes locked, he ran the fingers of one hand lightly from Stef's temple to his jaw, down his neck, and over that damn piercing. He hesitated just a second to absorb the tantalising feel of it, then continued over one taut nipple and down those tight abs to Stef's jeans.

Stef shivered, and his eyelids fluttered closed.

Cass withdrew his hand and breathed out a sigh. "You are so fucking beautiful."

A blush formed at the base of Stef's throat and worked its way up to meet a shy smile. It was... unexpected. His eyes blinked open, and he wore a slightly dazed expression. "Jesus, Cass. What the hell was that?"

Another question Cass had no answer for.

"I feel like I've had an exhausting, dirty long weekend away with all the optional extras, and you haven't even kissed me."

Cass grinned. "I think perhaps I need to remedy that. Come here."

Stef arched a brow. "I think that bang on your head did more damage than we thought." He cut a quick glace away, then back, uncertainty clouding his eyes. "I, um, I wasn't sure if you regretted last night. I didn't, just so you know. It was kind of... spectacular, to be honest. But I get if it's uncomfortable for you. You don't have to—"

"Shut up and come closer."

Stef shuffled forward, one hand reaching to cup Cass's cheek. "You sure?"

"No. You?"

Stef grinned. "Not a bit."

"Good. Now that we've cleared that up..." Cass reached for the back of Stef's neck, leaned in, and pressed their lips together, trembling at the first brush of skin, much as he'd done the night before. He ignored the edge of the cot digging into him and the sting of the wound on his belly. They could wait.

The slight chill of the rain on Stef's mouth danced across Cass's heated skin like a cooling balm. The kiss was chaste and sweet. Just a soft *Here I am*, and *Mmm,* and *Finally*, and a whole world of doubt was soothed and put to bed.

He pressed a little harder, the tip of his tongue dipping in and out for a quick taste—the tang of rain, a hint of bubble gum, and the earthy edge of damp horse. He grinned against Stef's mouth and then pulled back and eyed him. "You've been kissing my horse."

Stef flushed to his hairline and ducked his head.

Cass tipped Stef's head back up with a finger to his chin.

Stef bit back a smile. "Well, she does have the most tempting velvet lips."

Cass ran his finger over the seam of Stef's mouth. "So do you."

He pulled Stef's mouth back to his, and this time Stef melted against him, opening to the first slip of Cass's tongue, sucking it into his mouth to play alongside his own as he tasted in return and humming with the delight of it.

A rumbling groan filled Cass's throat as he wrapped his arms around Stef, wincing as the bruising on his stomach protested the awkward position. It could protest all it damn well liked. This. This feeling. This startling man. This need—it fired a hunger in Cass that incinerated all other thought. They kissed, licked, nipped and fed on each other until the simple need to fill their lungs forced them apart, panting, foreheads pressed together, unwilling to break the connection.

"Holy moly, Cassidy." Stef straightened his back and rested on his heels, eyeing Cass like he might pounce and devour him at any moment.

A great fucking idea, actually. A stab of pain sliced through Cass's temple. *Or maybe not.*

Stef inclined his head and fired him a wicked grin, then reached up to brush a few stray locks of hair from Cass's face.

He leaned into the touch and closed his eyes as the rain continued to lash at the iron roof. He felt... fuzzy. Like someone had taken his brain and dropped it in a bucket of water. Things felt... distant. Dull.

Stef blew on his lids till he opened them again. "Hey, you don't look so hot. Lie back."

Cass did, or rather collapsed, and Stef lifted his legs for him before taking a seat on the deck and wrapping the towel around his shoulders.

"That's better," Cass said. It wasn't.

"Mmm." Stef looked sceptical but didn't push. "So, I take it you're not out—or at least not fully, since Ethan assured Tanner you were straight. Told me you'd been married to a woman."

Cass stiffened, jolted by the question that wrenched him back into his life, one where Stef had no future. As those walls began to slide back into place, he considered letting them do their thing, then rejected the idea. Stef deserved more, deserved better. He took Stef's hand instead and brought his palm to his lips. "I'm not out *here*. I was out at university and when we lived in Wellington after that. Tricia always knew."

Stef arched a brow. "She was your wife?"

Cass nodded.

"Must be hard, living two lives like that. I never had to come out, not really." Stef swept a hand dramatically over himself. "Shocker, right?"

Cass laughed and traced the line of Stef's lips with his fingers. "I like that about you. I—"

But he never finished, interrupted by a white-hot poker being shoved into his right eyeball, or at least that's what it felt like. He cried out and rolled into a ball on his side.

Stef reacted in an instant. "You okay? Cass, what's going on?"

Cass answered without opening his eyes. "Fucking pain... in my head. It's going away now. I just... uh..." He blew out a breath and slowly opened his eyes. "God, that's better. I think I'm just really fucking tired. I might, um... try and catch some sleep."

"Okay. Hang on a minute." Stef disappeared inside the hut, and Cass must have fallen asleep then and there because he was woken by a hand on his chest. He opened his eyes to find Stef with an oilskin in one hand and his sketchbook in the other, and dressed in a fresh T-shirt.

Cass squinted to read the caption and laughed. *Don't flatter yourself, Cowboy, I was looking at your horse.*

Stef waggled his eyebrows, dropped the sketchbook and oilskin on the cot and then went back inside to bring out a second cot which he placed sideways at the bottom of the other. "Come on, let's get you sat up so you can scoot down," he said.

He helped Cass sit with a hand around Cass's shoulder, the heat from his touch soothing all manner of anxieties bubbling in Cass's head. Cass knew things weren't right up there, he just didn't know what he could do about it.

With Cass far enough down the cot, Stef squeezed in behind, resting his back against the wall of the hut, cradling Cass between his open legs. Then he put the pillow in his lap and settled Cass's head on top. He pulled the sleeping bag over them both to shield against the wind, tucked it in around Cass's shoulders, and threw the oilskin over top to keep any rain off. "There. Sleep."

Cass grumbled, "You won't be comfortable—"

"I'll be fine. I'm gonna use the time to draw some ideas that have been circling my brain. Now, go to sleep."

"Bossy little fucker."

Stef stroked Cass's forehead gently. "You don't know the half of it."

He brushed Cass's hair aside, and in seconds Cass's world closed its doors to all but the soothing slide of Stef's cool fingers on his brow, until even that disappeared into a dreamless sleep.

CHAPTER ELEVEN

IT RAINED FOR HOURS—RAINED UNTIL STEF WANTED TO SCREAM at the fucking clouds to piss off back to Antarctica and leave them the hell alone.

He sketched until he damn near filled the notebook—designs pouring from him like rain from the sky. All kinds of designs—piercing jewellery, cuffs, leather neck straps with silver beading that looked suspiciously like a cowboy's neck tie, rings, bracelets and... *ugh*... belt buckles—big western belt buckles. He sketched till he wore a blister on his finger, then threw the pad aside, exhausted. And still it rained.

It rained until he did the only thing left he could to pass the time and fell asleep himself, his arms draped over Cass's warm shoulders, fingering that ridiculous T-shirt—he really shouldn't find Cass wearing his clothes as sexy as he did—while the man in question slept like the dead, a turn of phrase Stef was by no means happy with, but at least he slept.

As did Stef, deeply, before peeling his eyes open to sunshine and the smell of damp, steaming earth. A quick glance at his watch showed it was five p.m. A rainbow cut across the sky, and although the wind was still blustery, the temperature had picked up. A hand to Cass's bare shoulder found it reassuringly warm, his chest rising and falling in quiet sleep.

Relief settled in Stef's chest. He threaded his fingers through Cass's hair, noted no fresh bleeding from the wound on Cass's head, and sent a prayer of thanks to wherever people sent those. Cass stirred briefly at his touch but didn't wake.

A glance at the pen found Arwen resting on three feet under the trees, nodding in sleep. Gandalf stood quietly at her side, snorting softly and swishing his coarse silver tail at the few bugs that had ventured forth to see what delicacies the rain might have tempted out. The low-lying bush was magically still bar a few bird calls, but everywhere Stef looked was wet, so fucking wet. He grimaced. The river would be in flood. There was no way help was coming up that track any time soon.

He raked his gaze over Cass, sprawled between his legs, and took stock, loving the weight and feel of his head in his lap. That kiss. Holy shit, *that kiss*. Stef loved kissing, and he frequently lamented with his friends how so many of his casual hookups didn't. It was intimate, and he knew lots of guys avoided it for that very reason, not wanting to cross that line with someone who didn't really matter. But Stef didn't get it. Regardless of whether it was for a night or a year, he loved to kiss. And Cass was a master. Which was kind of a surprise— and a big fucking bonus.

Stef wanted to know a lot more about why Cass hadn't come out in his home town. He wanted to know about the woman he'd married, why they'd split, and why he'd lived in Wellington. Truthfully, that had shocked him. The way Cass talked, his heart and soul were rooted in the land of Glenorchy, in his horses, in his passion for the history and spirit of the place. He couldn't imagine him anywhere else—and he'd tried. But even picturing the guy coming to Auckland for a visit to try to nurse along this thing they had going had died a quick death. Never. Gonna. Happen. Stef didn't need to talk to Cass to recognise any idea of moving as a hard limit. He just didn't know what to do with that information.

Cass stirred unexpected feelings in him—familiar, scary emotions. Emotions he didn't want. Emotions he didn't know how to process but which were inescapable nonetheless. And all this in one day. He didn't believe in that sort of nonsense. And yet...

He ran his fingers through Cass's thick hair, luxuriating in the intimacy of the act.

Did this connection they seemed to share really mean anything? Or was it as simple as Stef being so far out of his comfort zone that he'd opened to Cass, exposing a weak spot in his hard-won armour, and then unexpectedly Cass had needed Stef's help in return—and now here they were, sharing a bond of something more than friendship. It was nice, but contextual. Nothing to build anything solid on—or was it?

It was hard to see it. They were so different, as different as any two men could be in terms of careers, and lifestyle, and interests, not to mention where they called home. Could it ever be more than a crush? *Should* it ever be more than that?

A delicious wriggle between his legs sent Stef's thoughts sailing in an entirely different direction, which was just as well considering he had zero answers to the first. Cass was waking. They needed to eat, and Stef needed to get some decent fluids into the other man if they were going to have to wait out their rescue for another day. The fresh supplies were almost gone, but there was some leftover bread and a good choice of canned and dried goods from the cupboards.

"If you think any louder, I'm going to have to take your battery out." Cass plumped the pillow in Stef's lap, which did a ton of unmentionable stuff to elements of Stef's southern geography.

"What's up?" Cass turned to his back and stared up at the sky. "Hey, it's stopped raining."

"Food is what's up." Stef bent over and pressed a soft kiss to Cass's forehead. "And yes, it's stopped raining, but only just. It pissed down most of time you were asleep. It's nearly six."

Cass squirmed. "Fuck. That means the river will be flooding for sure, and the wind's still up. Jesus, I slept the whole afternoon. Nothing to eat, please. Stomach's still dodgy. Did you get some sketching done?"

Stef bristled. For a practical guy, Cass had zero common sense. "Yes, lots. And let me rephrase that. You'll eat because you need to and because I tell you to. Nothing big, just enough to absorb the acid and give you some strength. But more importantly, you'll drink."

Cass batted his lashes at Stef. "Is this another one of those trick questions? Like if I say no, you'll punish me, so I should go ahead and do that anyway?"

Stef rolled his eyes. "No, it's one of those 'If you don't do what I say, the next time we have sex, I'll edge you till your eyes cross and then leave you hanging' kind of things."

"Can I see your sketches?"

"No. And that's the worst pick up line ever, by the way."

Cass pouted, and Stef wanted to kiss the man senseless. "Maybe later, if you eat something. Now, do you feel any better?"

Cass tipped his head from side to side and grimaced. "Headache's still there. A bit better, maybe. Stomach wound's a bitch, though—I think I'm stiffening up." He blew out a sigh. "I guess I could drink a little water... if it'll keep you happy. But I'm not guaranteeing the food will stay down."

"Just try. And yes, it *will* make me happy." Stef pulled the blanket back to reveal the patchwork of reds, blues, and gathering greens fanned out over Cass's taut stomach. "Ouch."

Cass prodded the area and winced. "Yep." He kept poking. "At least it's soft. I think that's a good sign. Means hopefully, I'm not still bleeding."

Stef wasn't convinced. "Yeah, well, much though I'd like to trust your clinical expertise, *Dr Martin*, forgive me if I wait for an actual medical professional before I get all excited."

Cass caught his eye. "Sourpuss."

"And stop poking at it." Stef swatted Cass's fingers away. "Now,

I'm gonna get us some food, and then you're going to pee and let me change those dressings. Lean forward. I'm kind of pinned in here."

Cass levered himself up on his elbows, allowing Stef to wriggle free and get to his feet. Cass grabbed his hand. "Maybe I like you pinned under me."

Stef rolled his eyes. "How's that head injury going? How many Stefs do you see?"

Cass bit back a smile. "At least three, if I'm lucky."

Stef snorted and ruffled Cass's hair. "Then you're short two dicks. Sorry, champ. Wait here."

Everything took a lot longer than Stef anticipated. Cass was unsteady as all hell on his feet, needing Stef at his side as he did the whole pee-in-a-bucket thing and then freshened up with the towelettes that everyone had mocked Stef for. Stef smiled at the irony and made sure to point it out to Cass, who merely rolled his eyes.

He helped Cass into warmer clothes for the night and then back on to the cot so he could change his dressings. Both wounds seemed to have clotted well and were looking okay, although what the fuck they were supposed to look like Stef had no idea. Not bleeding was at least a good start, he figured.

Dinner consisted of tinned-spaghetti toasted sandwiches, all done in a skillet on the top of the wood burner inside the hut. Getting the charcoal barbeque going was a bridge too far in Stef's Camping 101 practicum if they wanted to eat sometime before the next millennium, but the potbelly he could manage, thanks to a crappy flat with a similar contraption he'd shared for three years. Look at him—making fire and not even in the bedroom.

Cass managed a whole sandwich, much to Stef's delight, and so far it hadn't made a reappearance. More importantly, he'd swallowed close to a litre of water and was looking a lot better. Stef was doing his best to keep a lid on his anxiety, after tearing strips off Cass for questioning him about it earlier. He kind of felt bad about that now, seeing as how he was two eye twitches away from completely losing his shit about getting through another night before help could get to them.

With the light fading, he checked on the horses and under Cass's instructions from the deck, he managed to get them into the smaller corral for the night with some hay and fresh water. Arwen cornered him as he was about to climb the fence to leave and rubbed her long, bony nose up and down his back, squishing him against the palings and leaving a snot-and-saliva trail from hip to shoulder on his —*goddammit*—formerly clean T-shirt. He maybe had one left in his bag.

Two days earlier, he would've reeled from fear and disgust. Which only made the laugh that bubbled from his mouth at her antics more shocking. He turned and cupped her enormous jaw in both his hands and pressed a kiss to that ridiculously long schnozzle, stared into those limpid, kind eyes, and smiled. A tender shoot of affection for the massive animals and the land they walked on had taken root in Stef's soul, and he couldn't ignore it.

He also couldn't fathom it. He'd never lacked for inspiration in his work—always had more ideas than he knew what to do with—but this was different. Edgy, hip, and sassy were his trademarks. City was his soul, or it had been. These new flashes and patterns reminded him more of Benny's leaf: swirls and colours, explosions and layers, nature. Out of all of it, one thing he understood—he needed to keep this new side fed and watered when he returned to the city. You ignored creative insight at your peril.

The thought wasn't as comforting as it should've been. City ran in his blood, it was easy and familiar, but Stef wasn't at all sure the more tamed version of nature within his reach back home would do the job.

Arwen dropped her head to rub up Stef's thigh and hip. He laughed and pushed her away before she caught his balls, telling her she really needed to work on her game, although her grinding had potential with the whole nose-bone thing she had going on.

The comment drew a low chuckle from the deck and the man who had squirmed his way into Stef's heart in such a short time. He wrapped his arms around Arwen's neck and she nickered, resting her snotty nose on his hips.

Paul wouldn't believe his eyes.

Well, fuck Paul.

Stef climbed the fence with Arwen's help in the form of an unwelcome nose to his butt. Then he brushed his jeans off, banged his boots on the railing to dislodge all the mud, and wandered back to the hut, thinking all the while.

Paul had never really believed in him, something Stef was only just beginning to understand. He was also coming to understand how it had likely suited Paul for Stef to be a little... helpless, and that he'd even encouraged it. When they hung out with Paul's friends, he'd often teased Stef about his prima-donna ways—his aversion to dirt, how he needed someone like Paul to look after him—all of them laughing. Stef as well, more often than not.

It might have pissed Stef off a little, but he'd always assumed it was in good fun, and he'd gone so far as to play it up for the audience. But now he wondered if they'd been laughing at him, not with him. After all, Paul was never like that in front of Tanner. And now Stef thought about it, if Paul had tried anything like that, Tanner would've nailed his balls to the wall. Tanner never for a second believed in Stef's prissy, self-deprecating bullshitting around. He knew Stef was strong and capable—expected it. *Huh.* How had he not realised any of this earlier?

And as it turned out, Stef's so-called helplessness had given Paul the out he needed. Maybe that had always been the plan. Stef's head spun. The idea stung, but he couldn't dismiss it. He rolled it around in his brain, letting it fester. Had Paul never intended to stay? Had he let Stef fall in love with him knowing he was leaving? Because he sure as fuck did nothing to discourage it, returning the words at the drop of a hat. What if he'd never meant them? Because you didn't do that, right? You didn't love someone, all the while planning to leave them.

"No, you don't."

Stef's gaze jerked to Cass. "Shit. I said that aloud, huh?"

Cass gave a half smile. "You did."

"Yeah, well, more fool me, right?" He grabbed his sweatshirt and one of the spare sleeping bags and, after scooting Cass down the cot again, climbed in behind so Cass was once again lying between his legs, resting back on Stef's chest.

Cass was quiet for a moment. "More fool him, actually. You wanna talk about it?"

Stef swallowed the sudden lump in his throat and resisted the urge to kiss the man senseless, because *damn*, Cassidy Martin was gonna be the death of him. If nothing else, he was going to ruin Stef for other men.

Yeah, like that ship hadn't sailed already. Flirting, arrogance, and snark were the bread and butter of Stef's dating life. Those he could handle. Niceness, honesty, and support? *Fuck*. Those suckers were flaying him alive. "Maybe later."

Cass didn't push it, and Stef was thankful to him for that.

Things between them went comfortably quiet as darkness settled over the landscape. The chill of the altitude had Stef dragging the oilskin over top of the sleeping bag that covered them both. He couldn't see Cass's face, but he could feel the tension building in his shoulders and wondered about it.

"Maybe we should get inside before you turn into a Popsicle." He tucked the coat around Cass's shoulders.

Cass remained quiet, eyes facing the flickering shadows in the inky bush line. From behind the hut, the wind continued its relentless hammering, buffeting the surrounding foliage into a constant background rustle and raising goosebumps on Stef's arms even with his sweatshirt for protection. But it had also blown the remnants of any clouds far off to the west, leaving a starlit canopy above their small slice of the Southern Alps and opening the door to a bit of glacial air.

"Cass?" Stef leaned forward to make sure the man's eyes were open. They were.

"Sorry." Cass flicked Stef a thoughtful glance, then nestled back. "Just thinking."

The warmth of Cass's weight on his chest undid all Stef's good intentions to be careful about growing anything more between them. He hesitated just a second before wrapping his arms around Cass's shoulders and holding him close.

Cass sighed and rested a hand over Stef's. "So, I'm bi."

Stef snorted. "Yeah, I think I got the part where you weren't exactly straight, back when you had that gorgeous dick of yours lodged firmly up my arse."

Cass chuckled and elbowed him gently in the stomach. "Brat. But yeah, I guess that was a bit of a giveaway."

His tone was joking, but Stef caught the uncertainty there. "You don't have to talk—"

"I do. Or I want to."

Stef pressed a kiss to the back of Cass's head. "Well, I can't say I'm not curious." Understatement of the year. Like burning-a-hole-in-Stef's-damn-chest curious.

Cass swung an arm back and patted Stef's cheek. "I figured. I've pretty much known I'm bi my whole life. High school consisted of this endless dance, like a damn tennis match. Look to the left, *Mmm, she's pretty.* Look to the right, *Wow, his arse is spectacular.*"

Stef chuckled. "In my case it was *Oh God, not in a million years* to door number one, versus *Well, hello* and *Goddammit, YES* to door number two. But you said you never came out around here. Was it just easier or safer to go with the het option in school? No judgement from me."

Stef waited out the pause before Cas answered.

"No? Yes? Maybe. But I didn't only stick with girls. I'm not saying all that didn't come into it, but to be honest we were a small high school, and the whole dating thing was pretty intense anyway. Everyone knew everybody else, but I... managed."

"So you experimented with both?" That surprised Stef.

"A couple of guys. On the quiet. Not because *I* wanted to stay in the closet, but because they did. As I said, small school, small community, only a couple of gay students. Although Queenstown itself is pretty cosmopolitan, these small farming valleys can be a little less... open-minded. And since I dated girls as well, no one really thought of me as anything but straight, I don't think."

Stef threaded his fingers through Cass's hair. "I can understand that."

"It's funny, but because everyone thought I was straight, I was also a good bet for the other gays. They could hang around me without suspicion. Being bi doesn't always make things easier, you know. Sometimes it's a big, fat complication. I went back and forth in my head about whether to come out to my parents or not. Being able to slide by as straight can be seen as an advantage, but it can also put a hefty doorstop on that closet.

"It can cost you community down the track, because some of those important friendships never get made. And when you're older, it's even harder to come out, especially if you marry someone of the opposite sex. You live in a straight world when you're not straight, and no one wants to know about it. But on the other hand, the queer world often doesn't accept you either."

Stef squeezed his shoulder. "Yeah, I've heard those comments. I don't agree with them, by the way. People have a fucking cheek if you ask me. There's a ton of ways to be queer. Anyway, you got married."

Cass sank back against Stef a little more, and Stef dropped his hands to Cass's shoulders and dug into those tense muscles as Cass continued to talk.

"I did. That was the other reason I never really came out to my family, or around here. We met in high school when we were sixteen and then went to university together in Wellington. We married in our second year. I... loved her. It was real—"

Stef squeezed his shoulder. "That's good."

"She knew about me, and I was out to all our friends in Wellington. It was such a different life, and in that way, I loved it..."

"But..."

Cass slumped. "Yeah, a big *but*. The Wellington gig was only supposed to be for a few years. Get our degrees and then come back here. Tricia's parents live in Te Anau, and she was going to try and get a teaching job in the primary school either down there or up this way. I'd use my accountancy degree along with her income to keep us afloat as I built up some business around horses, training or trekking or... something."

Stef had a good sense where all this was leading. "I'm guessing she didn't want to stick to the plan?"

Cass shuffled around till he was more on one hip and Stef could see his face. He looked... conflicted. Maybe even remorseful. "Once we were back down here, it all went to shit. Tricia loved Wellington—loved the city and wanted to go back. I... didn't. I'd enjoyed my time there, but I could never live there forever. My plans were always around horses and this place. I fucking love these mountains..." His words dried up, and he swallowed hard.

Stef ran the back of his hand down Cass's cheek. "Anyone can see you belong here."

Cass flashed him a grateful smile. "To be fair, Tricia saw that too. And it's not like she didn't try. She got a job, stayed for four years, but it was never gonna last. She hated being cooped up here, tucked away in this little corner of New Zealand. She'd had a taste of the big city and was completely sold—couldn't go back." He grimaced. "You'd understand that, right?"

Stef nodded, even though his answer was in fact less straightforward than Cass would have expected and the throwaway comment stung a little. He did understand. Or, at least, he had. His gaze lifted to the shadow of Mount Aurum in the distance and the razor-tooth cut of the ranges that flanked it.

There was a staggering, overwhelming, and untamed beauty in

this place, and the itch to grab his notebook again and flesh out the lines and forms that were streaming in and clogging up his brain was almost overpowering. And with all that wild splendour came a challenge to everything Stef thought he knew about himself. He felt more... rounded in its clutches, and oddly, more known. Maybe freer was a better word. Some of it was about Cass, and didn't that throw Stef for a loop. Cass had a calm presence and a fluid, quirky take on life that seemed to smooth all Stef's sharp edges.

He didn't know what to do with his feelings or how to put all that change into words that might make sense to Cass, so he said nothing.

Cass's gaze fell away as if Stef's nod had answered everything. "She's a lot like you, actually. Too bright, too much energy to try and hold in your hands, too much of... everything... for this place, for me. The wedge between us grew until we were so far apart it just didn't make sense any more. We floated warily around each other like guests in our own house, sharing meals and a bed but so far out of sync we might have been strangers. Then one weekend she went to visit a friend in Wellington for a couple of weeks and... never came back."

Stef's mouth fell open. "As in, *never*?"

Cass shrugged but didn't meet Stef's eyes. "She called at the end of the first week, and we talked honestly for perhaps the first time in over a year. We agreed to stop hurting each other. I packed up her stuff, dropped it at her parents', and said my goodbyes to them. We were renting in Glenorchy, so there was no house to sell, and that was pretty much it."

Holy shit. Stef knew it couldn't have been as simple as Cass made it sound, and he was beginning to understand how the wariness in the man's eyes got there. "How old were you?"

"Twenty-eight. We were married six years."

"Do you guys still see each other?"

The line between Cass's brows deepened. "We met for coffee a couple of years back while she was down visiting her parents. It was... hard. She's married again—has a couple of kids. To tell the truth, I was a bit envious. I looked at how happy she was and wondered if she looked at me and just felt... relieved."

Stef turned Cass's head with a light touch to his jaw and was immediately lost in the depths of those green eyes, sparkling in the reflected glow of the lantern at their side. "Would you have changed your decision?"

Cass held his gaze. "No. I'd have withered in the city as much as she did down here. It was the right thing to do, for both of us. But I miss what we had. We had a lot of fun together. I love it down here, I love my life, but it can get..."

"Lonely?"

Cass nodded. "Ridiculous, right?"

"Nah. Understandable, really. Turn back around." And Stef recommenced his mission to iron out the knots in Cass's shoulders.

"The city can be a fucking lonely place too." Stef's fingers dug beneath Cass's shoulder blade, eliciting a groan of approval that put a smile on Stef's face. "There's nothing like being in a crowd of over two million to realise just how bloody lonely you are. At least down here you have all this beauty to distract you."

"Maybe," Cass mumbled. "But you'd get sick of it soon enough, just like she did."

Stef wanted to protest but didn't. This thing between them was too fragile to push, and in all honesty, Cass was probably right. Until twenty-four hours ago Stef would've agreed with him in a heartbeat— he was city to his core. Gas fumes flowed in his veins. Galleries, clubs, and shopping, the stuff of his dreams. Finding a new restaurant or a quirky boutique craftsperson filled him with ridiculous joy, and dancing in clubs nourished his soul.

And yet...

He cast a quick glance to where Arwen stood asleep on her feet, her head dropped to her knees, and he couldn't help the smile that broke over his face. He doubled down on the knots around Cass's spine and pushed his own doubts aside.

"You never came out when she left?"

"Goddamn, your fingers are little pockets of magic, you know that, right?" Cass dropped his head further to his chest.

Stef chuckled. "Stop trying to distract me, and answer the question."

"So fucking bossy. But no, I didn't. It wasn't a deliberate decision, as such. When Tricia left, I was pretty much done relationship-wise, full stop. I moved back to the farm, got my shit sorted. Got the trekking business up and running, some accounting clients under my belt, and if I needed some relief with an actual, living person—I got the job done."

Stef laughed. "Any men?" He was jumping out of his skin with curiosity.

Cass turned and slid him a sly, sexy smile that almost melted Stef's briefs right off his hips.

"You angling for some dirt there, city boy?"

Stef returned the heated gaze. "Damn right I am. Teenage fumblings aside, there's been no mention of any other man-on-man extracurricular activity. And yet you knew your way around me last night like a pro—"

Cass raised a brow.

Stef flushed hot. "Well, not exactly a *pro* pro, if you know what I mean."

"Aha."

Amusement danced in Cass's eyes, and their gazes locked for long enough Stef thought Cass might actually kiss him. But he flashed a brilliant smile and turned to face away again instead.

"Well, you needn't worry that pretty little head of yours about that," he answered drily, dropping his head to his chest once again. "I've had plenty of hookups over the last few years, men and women —the film industry provides more than just cash for the locals, you know."

"Oh. My. God." Stef slapped at his shoulder. "You have *so* fucked a guy up behind that barn of yours. Any actors? Anyone I'd know? If you tell me a hobbit, I'll be so fucking disappointed. You need to raise the bar to an elf, at least. Some of those guys were seriously hot."

Cass chuckled. "I refuse to answer that." He shuffled out from under Stef's hands and turned gingerly to face him, straddling the cot and taking a few moments to work himself into a comfortable position. Then he found Stef's gaze and locked on. "Now, I believe I would benefit from the application of your lips to mine. How about it?"

Stef snorted. "Is that right? I'm not at all sure that would be medically advised," he said primly, brushing at a speck of dust on his sweatshirt.

Cass tilted his head. "I'm waiting."

Stef cracked a smile. "The magic word?"

Cass ran a hand around the back of Stef's neck and pulled him forward till Stef felt the heat of Cass's breath on his lips.

"Now," Cass whispered.

Stef smirked. "Good guess."

Their tongues tangled straight away, the fierce kiss lingering just this side of get-those-damn-clothes-off-now hot. Cass held Stef in place as he feasted on his mouth, then nibbled along Stef's jaw to his ear before letting him go, his hand trailing over Stef's cheek as he did.

"The stubble looks good on you," he said hoarsely. "And you taste like damn sunshine. Dangerous stuff."

Stef's brows bumped together. "Well, you taste like summer rain. Equally disconcerting, I'll have you know."

They stared for a second, then dissolved into laughter.

"Jesus Christ, we're a fucking embarrassment to good kiwi blokes everywhere." Cass wiped at his eyes then winced and leaned back on his hands.

The man was struggling.

Stef arched a brow. "Yeah, well, I was never gonna feature high on their favourites list anyway. I'll take the embarrassment if it means I get to hear you say shit like that."

Cass stilled. "Shit. I didn't mean—"

"I know you didn't." Stef patted his chest. "Come on. Turn around and lie back on me again. You look like you're gonna puke."

"I'm fine."

"You're not. Just do it and quit arguing with me."

Cass glared at him for a second before his shoulders slumped in surrender. He dragged his legs back up onto the cot, grunted with the effort, and then collapsed back between Stef's legs. When he was finally settled to Stef's liking, Stef squeezed Cass's shoulder. "Take a look at that fucking sky, will you? When did that happen? Are those the Southern Lights?"

Cass lifted his gaze with a soft gasp. "Hell yeah. That's exactly what they are."

Stef frowned. "But they're pink, kind of. Aren't they meant to be green?"

Cass shrugged and ran his hand down Stef's calf, sending little shivers of delight up Stef's spine. "It happens," he said quietly, eyes glued above them, more than a little awe in his words. "Depends on what's floating around in the atmosphere and a bunch of other stuff I know nothing about. But I've never seen them quite this colour. Must be that storm. God, look at them."

No problem there. Stef couldn't take his damned eyes off them.

The sky was lit from east to west in bands of shaded colour—wide, deep pink at the top fading into thinner blue, and finally a slice of greenish yellow near the horizon. They moved like rainbow ribbons through treacle, and before he knew what he was doing, Stef was up against Cass's back, his chin on Cass's shoulder, his lips pressing a series of soft kisses on the man's neck, jaw, and face.

Cass angled his head, bringing their cheeks less than a breath apart, and returned the kisses with a sigh, a hum, and a hand in Stef's hair. They nibbled and brushed their lips over each other's, barely touching. Whispered nothings floated between them, noses gently pressed and cheeks gliding past. Pleasure wedged tight in Stef's throat while a warm and inviting sensation of a very different kind squeezed his chest. *God almighty.* The other kiss might have been sizzling, but this exchange was devastating—an intimate, rule-crush-ing, game-changing temptation—and Stef had to pull back before it choked him.

Cass looked equally shaken and quickly turned his gaze back to the sky. *Way to go. Scare the man off. That's why you don't do shit like that.* Stef cleared his throat. But he didn't sit back.

"You're, um, so lucky to get to see this whenever you want," he whispered against Cass's cheek, every nerve in his body vibrating. "It's like some mystical dragon's breath, floating over the forests of Lothlórien. It's so fucking beautiful."

Cass froze for a second, then turned and pressed a kiss to the corner of Stef's mouth, and Stef almost jumped from the shock. Maybe he hadn't scared Cass as badly as he thought.

"No, *you're* the beautiful one." Cass cleared his throat. "'The moon waxed round in the night sky, and put to flight all the lesser stars'." He pressed another kiss in place on Stef's lips. "Except for you. And I'm just the lucky guy who gets to share that light, if only for tonight. "

Stef's heart squeezed. He cocked a brow. "Did you just quote *Lord of the Rings* to me?"

Cass's cheeks pinked, and all Stef wanted to do was pinch them and kiss him senseless. "Maybe," Cass offered softly. "Doesn't make it any less true."

Cass smiled, and Stef's heart spilled with a depth of feeling he wasn't prepared for. At a loss for words, he returned the kiss instead, and Cass deepened it for a minute.

When they finally pulled apart, the words bubbled from Stef's mouth with no filter. He was done pretending about this shit.

"At the risk of sending you running for the hills," he said, "just what the hell are we doing here, Cass? This has pain written all over it, in fucking mile-high lettering."

Cass traced Stef's lips with his finger, and his smile slipped. "You think I don't know that? Do you"—those green eyes clouded—"do you think we should stop?"

Stef snorted. "Stop what? We've hardly done anything. Yes, we fucked—and don't get me wrong, that was primo outstanding—but this is way, way more complicated than that. We'd have to stop talking altogether, or stop looking at each other, because all this"—he waved a hand between them—"whatever this is, is the product of not much more than that."

Cass rolled his eyes and went to look away, but Stef cradled his face. "Nuh-uh. Don't do that. Don't pretend you don't know what I'm talking about. You felt it, before. I saw it in your eyes. We... fuck, I don't even know what we are. We fit, or something. I like you. Fuck. I like you, more than I should for all of the three bloody seconds we've been together. But there, I've said it."

Cass held his gaze as if he were searching for the truth in Stef's words. "I like you too."

Stef threw his hands in the air. "Oh, great. Well, that clears things up nicely. Especially since we have about a day left together. *And* you're injured. So, what do you suggest we do about whatever this is when that time's over?"

Cass's lips tightened, and he dragged a hand across his mouth. Then he sighed, and Stef heard the footsteps of a man running scared in the soft rush of air.

"Honestly? I don't know."

"Wonderful," Stef grumbled. "It's been a pleasure, I'm sure. Maybe you can friend me on Facebook. We can share pictures of our grandchildren down the track."

Cass watched in amused silence. "How about we get down off this damn mountain first?"

Step pouted. "Always with the sensible plan."

"Not always. For instance, I'm thinking there's a lot of time between now and when we get help." He arched a brow Stef's way.

Stef pretended to think about it. "That's very true. And I'll bet you have another one of those sensible suggestions for how we can fill that time."

Cass waggled his eyebrows. "Not so much. But I *was* thinking you could start with kissing me again."

Stef rolled his eyes so hard he was surprised they didn't rattle. "Like that's a hardship. But it's not gonna help with the whole confusion bit, is it?"

Cass shrugged. "Call it data gathering."

Stef snorted.

"After that, I suggest we watch this light show for a bit"—Cass's eyes flicked to the sky—"and then go inside and push two of these ridiculously uncomfortable cots together so you can hold me in your arms, just to make sure I don't fall off, and then we sleep." He waggled his eyebrows. "Too exciting for words, right?"

If only he knew. Stef tipped Cass's chin up and locked on to those green eyes, now almost black in the dim light. "Best damn pickup line I've heard in years."

CHAPTER TWELVE

"Cass, wake up! Come on, sweetheart, please, open your damn eyes!"

Someone shoved at Cass's shoulders and a brutal tide of icy air lapped at his skin, but he was tired, so damn tired. He didn't have the strength to open his eyes, let alone yell at the voice to leave him the fuck alone.

The voice... shit. Stef. That sweet, tempting ball of trouble and green-painted-fingernail frustration. Who the fuck painted their fingernails green? Cass should've taken that shit for the warning it was, especially seeing as how he couldn't take his eyes off them, or the man who wielded them like a peacock's tail, from the first minute they'd met.

But not even the lure of Stef could lift the anvils from Cass's eyelids. Nope. In fact, he decided in the murky depths of his porridge-like thoughts, the best option was to hunker down and pretend he didn't exist. Then the equally annoying and intriguing man might just disappear and leave Cass to his business—his very successful, rewarding, and heart-achingly lonely business. It was a good plan, a great plan. He tucked his head and drifted.

Another jolt on his shoulder. "Cass, you need to wake up. There's a chopper coming up the valley. Jesus, how can you not hear it? The noise is damn near vibrating the roof off. I about fell off my cot. Cass, goddamn you, open your fucking eyes!"

Something cold and wet landed on Cass's face, fragrant with a dodgy, yeasty odour that he wanted nothing to do with. He jerked his head sideways and flailed an arm. The wetness fell away, and he could breathe again. But it had done its job. He was awake.

"Ow, what the hell?" Cass peeled open his eyes to find his wrist pinioned in Stef's hand. "What the fuck was that on my face?"

The beginning of a smile dangled at the corner of the other man's lips. "Thank Christ. I thought you were unconscious." Stef glanced to where the cloth had landed. "It was just a cloth—the closest thing I could reach. Worked, didn't it?"

"If I survive whatever's been incubating in it." Cass made an effort to lift his head, but a sharp bolt of pain froze him in place. "Holy son of a bitch."

Stef shot forward in his seat. "What? What's wrong?"

Cass grimaced and eased himself back down on the cot, the *thwump-thwump* of the helicopter blades breaking into his thoughts for the first time. "Go. You need to get out there. I'm... not going anywhere... just yet." His eyes screwed shut. "I need... a few... goddammit... a few minutes. Feels like my head's... got a nail gun inside, firing shots out my eyeballs... and my neck's... stiff as concrete."

"But what do I do? What do I tell them?"

Cass tried to breathe himself down from the pain shrieking through his head and the wash of bile rolling up his throat. "Just... argh... just go out there. See what they do."

Stef's tone turned slightly panicky. "But—"

"You'll... be fine. Watch the horses... with the noise... give them some hay. Go. I can hear it coming... over the ridge."

There was a moment's pause, then Cass heard Stef take a deep breath. "Fuck it. Okay." Another, shorter pause. "Don't go anywhere."

Cass made a wordless noise.

"Don't get smart with me," Stef said, and then Cass heard him leaving.

When the pain eased, Cass cranked his eyelids open again and took a dispirited look around. Even with the clamour of the chopper, there was no mistaking the howling wind still banging away at the back of the hut. No pilot worth their salt would land on a mountainside in this. They were well and truly fucked.

He'd slept, a little, waking time and again to find Stef's lithe form at his back, legs tanged between Cass's and one arm thrown over his chest. The man was like a damn furnace, and Cass was positive an imprint of his body was seared into Cass's back. Not that he was complaining. He was still damned tired, but that didn't explain why he couldn't seem to get two words aligned, or keep his eyelids from crashing together, or hold on to more than one thought at a time. Nor why his head felt like it was circling the drain at a far greater rate of knots than it had the night before.

He'd expected to feel better. He'd been talking last night, alert-ish and doing okay. But now? Now the very idea of getting on his feet felt like it presented more hurdles than Cass had answers for. And his vision was foggy—like he was looking through a gauze curtain—while his head pulsed ominously.

He lifted his hand to the dressing on his forehead and winced. There was a lot more swelling, and his fingers came away slick with blood. *Dammit.* Could it account for his sluggish brain? Maybe. Infection could too, though it was a bit early to be noticing the effects of that. But if the swelling was *inside* Cass's skull, then absolutely that could explain things... but Cass really didn't want to go there. And it certainly didn't paint a rosy picture for being of any help to Stef.

He gripped the edges of the cot as the hut lurched on its foundations with the wash from the helicopter. Cass had been on a few search-and-rescue missions in the valley. The world-famous Route-burn Track started not far from where he lived, and a combination of tourists, poor kit, hellish weather, and unforeseen injuries saw at least a half-dozen rescues a year. The locals all did their bit.

The building rattled and shook as engines roared, and shouts rang out between Stef and whoever was in the helicopter. Then the noise of the blades suddenly receded, and Cass almost heard the hut's sigh of relief as it settled on its bed once again. The door slammed to the wall and Stef stepped inside, cheeks flushed, dark hair whipped across his face. He looked wild-eyed and... stunning.

He stalked straight over and held out a satphone.

"That's all?"

"And another first aid box. It's on the deck. You better talk to them. It came with instructions and a number to call."

Cass pushed the phone away. "You'll have to. My head's a little clearer, but I... might forget something."

Stef immediately fell to his side and levelled him with a concerned gaze. "Shit. You're bleeding again. Has your head settled? Is it worse than yesterday?"

Cass gave a half-shrug. "A little."

Stef narrowed his eyes. "Don't lie to me. We do this together or not at all, okay?"

He was right. Cass couldn't shield him. "Sorry. Yeah, the pain's worse. A lot worse. But I'm thinking better than I did when I woke up."

Stef lifted the cover to check the other dressing. He grunted. "At least that looks okay." He took a seat and picked up the phone, his lips set in a grim line. "Okay, what do I do?"

With Cass's direction and the instructions that came with the phone, Stef was quickly connected to the rescue centre. Cass listened in as Stef relayed everything the operator said. He was direct, succinct, and controlled, giving a solid breakdown of Cass's injuries and symptoms, asking pertinent questions and checking for clarity. Cass's heart swelled with pride. As Cass thought, the wind was too strong for the helicopter to land or to drop a cot, and it wasn't set to ease for a few more days. The alternative route from the road up their side of the river was a washout for all but horses. There was no chance of getting a quad with a cot up that way. Besides, it would add hours to the trip—hours Cass would never manage on a horse, and too long to leave an unspecified head injury.

According to the rescue team, since Cass was now awake, the best plan was to get him back down to the river crossing, where they could use the flying fox to rig up a secure cot transport across to a four-wheel-drive ambulance on the other side. It wasn't without risk, but it was his only chance to get to a hospital any time soon. A neighbour's son, Hoff someone, had offered to make the trek up the alternate long route to stay with the horses and bring them down when the river dropped, and Dee had rung Tanner and brought him up to date on the delay. He and Ethan would be waiting at Martin's Stables.

To be honest, Cass didn't love the plan—the thought of getting down that track in the state he was in fucking sucked. But one glance at Stef after he'd ended the call and Cass knew his own concerns were nothing compared to what was going on in the other man's head, at least if that expression of sheer, unadulterated horror was anything to go by.

Stef's mouth opened and closed several times before any sound came out. "But you can't... I mean, look at you... you wouldn't make it... how do they expect me to... Holy shit, Cass. What the fuck are they thinking?"

"It'll be fine."

Stef pinned him with a glare that could've stripped paint from the walls. "It will *not* be fucking fine. It will be anything *but* fucking fine. I have no idea what I'm doing, and you"—he waved a hand towards Cass—"you're barely sitting, let alone walking, not to mention there's a nervous look in your eye that can only mean you don't like the idea either. Why can't they airlift you off?"

"You know why."

Stef pursed his lips. "I can't do it. I can't get you down there safely. I'll screw it up. What if you can't walk—"

"I'm not going to walk."

Stef's eyes widened. "What do you mean, you're not going to walk? You can't fucking ride..."

Cass stared in silence as realisation hit Stef.

Red flared on his cheeks. "They never said—"

"It's what they meant, Stef. When they said you were to take me down, that's what they meant. How else—"

"No!" Stef shot to his feet and paced the small room. "Cass, you can't do that to me. I can't ride to save myself, let alone watch out for you. For fuck's sake, Arwen only had to break into the slowest trot known to humanity and I was a hot mess on her back. And you even had her on a lead! It's not possible."

"It is."

Fury blazed in his eyes. "I'm telling you—"

Cass grabbed his arm as he passed. "Sit down and listen, will you? I can't—" He closed his eyes as a jolt of pain travelled behind them.

Stef immediately slid alongside and rested a cool hand on Cass's brow. It felt... God, it felt amazing, and Cass wanted nothing more than to sink into the touch and slip away to where he didn't have to think at all.

"I'm sorry." Stef brushed his lips over Cass's, a warm, dry breath of connection that instantly grounded Cass. "I'm just... well, fucking terrified isn't putting too great a slant on it. You're worse than yesterday, and I couldn't live with myself if—"

"Nothing's going to happen. You've got this, right?" Cass locked on to those hazel eyes and watched them slowly steel. It felt good to be able to create that certainty, help Stef see in himself what Cass saw so clearly. He might not have experience, but he had determination. Stef knew more than he thought he did, and to his own surprise, Cass realised he felt safe in other man's hands.

Stef straightened and gave a curt nod. "Okay. So, what's the plan?"

Cass took his hand and squeezed it. "And there he is. I have no doubt at all that you can do this."

Stef's cheeks brightened. "Says the man with a head injury."

Cass pressed a kiss to the inside of Stef's wrist and felt him shiver. They locked eyes for a second before he pressed on. "So, the plan is this. You're gonna tie me to Arwen so I can't fall off, and then you're gonna lead her on foot down the track. She's the quieter of the two, and Gandalf won't mind being left, whereas she might."

Stef's fingernail found his mouth, but Cass removed it and kissed the finger instead.

"So I don't ride?" Stef checked.

"No. In that you were right. It wouldn't be safe. But Arwen is sure-footed and reliable—thunderstorms aside." He gave a wry smile. "We'll be okay. All you have to do is keep hold of the lead rope, walk alongside, and keep her on track. She knows the trail. She'll do the rest."

Stef rolled his eyes. "Oh, goody. That's all I have to do. For a minute there I was worried I might have to, I don't know, get a barely conscious man on a horse down a mountain and across a river. *Pfft*. Piece of cake."

Cass cradled Stef's face. "I trust you." The incredulity in Stef's expression made him laugh, which was a miracle considering how he felt.

"Then you're missing some vital information about my serious lack of skills," Stef said in complete seriousness.

Cass held his face steady so he couldn't look away. "No, I'm not. You have more than enough, and I'm an excellent judge of character. Now come here."

Stef bit back a smile and eyed him sideways. "I'm thinking that would be a bad idea."

Cass shot him a heated look. "Absolutely. Now get those sweet lips of yours down here." He pulled Stef down and covered his mouth with his own, teasing the seam until Stef opened and Cass could sweep inside for a quick taste. It seemed he lost all common sense around Stef, but he was too tired and fucked up to fight it any more. He kept Stef close until the other man finally relaxed into the kiss, and they made out for a bit, until the flashing lights and jolts of pain behind Cass's eyes couldn't be ignored any longer. He pulled off and fell back on to the cot with a groan.

Stef's brows crunched together. "Goddammit, Cass, you can't be kissing me when you feel like crap." He peered closer. "Why are you looking at me like that?"

Cass grimaced. "There's, um, more than one of you."

"How many?"

"Two."

Stef glanced quickly away, but not before Cass caught his stricken expression. "Huh," he said way too casually. "Well, you better send the second one packing. I can't be worrying about any more shit, understand? I told you kissing was a bad idea. You don't get enough oxygen sucking on my tongue."

Cass smiled and closed his eyes against the light. There was clearly a box in Stef's head for all that *shit that we can't do anything about until we get down this mountain.* "I'll be fine. You're pretty potent stuff. I need to build my immunity slowly."

Stef poked him with a finger. "Good luck with that. Better men than you have tried and failed." He forced a bright smile. "Anyway, I need to get us organised. They want us down there by lunchtime, and God knows how long it's going to take me just to get you roped on Arwen. I'm going to have to do the whole saddle-and-bridle thing on my own, aren't I?" He side-eyed Cass. "I'm pretty sure that was never part of the disclaimer you made us all sign. I'm gonna be needing a refund."

Cass chuckled and took Stef's chin in his hand. "I'll talk you through it. And, uh, maybe we could come to some kind of... agreement... about the refund thing?" *What the hell am I doing?*

Stef slowly raked his gaze over Cass, head to toe. "Let's make sure you're not broken first, before you make any rash promises. Then we'll see. I'm not mending no Humpty Dumpty just to have him crack apart in my arms."

Cass rolled his eyes. "Fucking hilarious."

Stef popped a hip. "And don't you forget it."

The one-and-a-half-hour haul back down to the river was worse than Cass could possibly have imagined, and he felt sorry for Arwen, having to carry his groaning, teetering arse all the way. Stef had done a good job of getting her ready, saddling, bridling, and following instructions to a T.

The only hiccup was a slight snafu with Arwen taking the bit, when Stef's fingers disappeared into her mouth—to the man's total horror. He'd yelped in panic, startling Arwen sideways, and she'd stood on his foot. Cass had managed to suppress a laugh, which in retrospect he figured was the only thing that saved him from his balls being unceremoniously removed and shoved down his throat. That's if the angry look on Stef's face as he hopped around the pen on one foot, cursing at the top of his voice, was anything to go by.

Getting Stef's hand back around the mare's mouth, and her allowing it, took a bit of encouragement for them both and a stodgy wad of bread and peanut butter for Arwen, but they got there. Cass was so fucking proud of how Stef had handled what had to be a massive learning curve—not to mention overcoming his own personal fear—and he'd told him precisely that.

The compliment earned him an epic blush and a sizzling few minutes of making out on the deck. Fucking adorable, and a win-win any way you looked at it. Cass tucked it all into his bulging file of Stef-related spank-bank material for when the man was gone—his feelings on which he refused to look at too closely.

Gandalf barely raised an eye at being left behind, content with an oversized mound of hay and a trough of clean water. Arwen had been a little more fidgety, constantly looking behind for her friend and leader. Stef had needed to tug sharply on her lead a few times to get her attention and avoid Cass being thrown around like a sack of potatoes as they headed off down the soggy track.

That was another thing. The heavy rain had filled the water table to the brim, and nothing was draining fast. The track, which had been dry and hard as nails two days ago, was now a quagmire of sucking mud on the more level sections and a slippery slide of death on the others. Keeping Arwen true to her path was no easy feat, even with her mountain-sure feet.

Stef was managing, just. However, Cass saw the tension mounting in his shoulders and the white-knuckled grip he had on the rope as Arwen slipped all over the show trying to maintain her footing. On Cass's instructions, he'd let her lead play out so she could self-correct without sliding into him or burying his feet under hers. But it meant more rocking from side to side for Cass, and he was struggling to keep up a brave face. He was barely holding his seat to begin with.

If he hadn't been roped to the saddle, he wouldn't have lasted the first twenty metres. But although the rig made it difficult for him to fall, it wasn't impossible, which made the whole thing even more risky. If Cass did tip over, he wouldn't fall free. He would drag the saddle with him and potentially get caught sideways or under Arwen, which might spook her to bolt—and Cass wasn't even going to consider the ramifications of that particular disaster. But Stef simply wasn't a good enough rider to sit behind him, hold him, and get them both down safely. So, it was tied to the saddle or nothing.

But the constant rocking and sliding, and the tension playing out in his body from the need to focus so as not to fall or pass out, had every single fucking nerve on high alert. Bands of pain pinched around Cass's head, down his neck, and all the way to the base of his spine. And he was constantly wiping fresh blood from his eyes—so much that his sleeve was saturated. He didn't even want to look. The few times he'd caught Stef staring at it, Stef had said nothing, but

Cass had seen the furrows in his brow dip all the way to fucking China.

What's more, Cass's reserves of energy—meagre to begin with— were dwindling fast. Stef had fed him a little breakfast and forced more fluids into him before they left, but Cass was paying the price. Twice already he'd lost the contents of his stomach on the side of the trail, hanging as far as he could off Arwen to avoid blowback on her. Stef hadn't been so lucky, catching the second effort on his jeans and shoes as he'd rushed to stop Cass tipping too far over and losing his seat. The man deserved a bloody medal.

Thank Christ they were nearly there. Fifteen minutes, give or take. Cass focused on the centre of Stef's back, as he had all the way down, using it as a point of balance for his body and his heart. Stef was light on his feet, handling the boggy terrain with a dancer's flair: tip-toeing around the edges, picking his way through the patchwork of smaller puddles and leaping over the larger ones. Stef would shine in the city clubs, shine like a fucking summer's sun, and Cass ached at the knowledge he wouldn't be the one watching... or dancing with him. Dear Lord, the image of dancing with a wound-up ball of bouncing, sexy Stef in his arms nearly undid Cass there and then.

Men would be drawn to that lithe body and all that sinuous, seductive rhythm—how could they not? And once in Stef's orbit, they'd be held captive by his sheer energy and sass. Stef fitted that scene like satin hot pants on a go-go boy. And here was Cass, still mourning the death of line dancing in his favourite Queenstown bar. The last time Cass had been in an actual gay club, he'd nearly suffocated in the swarming tide of half-naked bodies. If Stef was a pair of hot pants, Cass was a pair of fucking gumboots—as out of place in Stef's world as it was possible to get.

It would be better for them both, less heartache, if they simply parted at the river. It was the perfect out, regardless of their vague murmurings about a special spark between them. Cass was headed to the hospital, and Stef was headed back to his friends. Cass should leave it at that.

As much fun as it sounded, what they had would never go beyond a few more hot encounters anyway; they were simply too different. Stef was apparently a fan of music from the German club scene, for fuck's sake. Hell, Cass didn't even know what that was. If he couldn't find a good country song to get down to, he pouted. And those were the least of their differences. Liking each other wasn't enough. If anyone knew the truth of that, Cass did.

Damn Stefan Hamilton and his bright smile, wicked sense of humour, sexy looks, and sly hazel eyes tinged with mischief. The man tasted of coconut and metal and had green fucking fingernails, for Christ's sake. And he'd thrown not just a spanner but a whole fucking toolbox into the smoothly running engine that had been Cass's life.

Cass had liked that life, goddammit. Maybe not all of it, sure, but he could live with loneliness. *Liar.* He didn't need a fancy, high-maintenance city boy sashaying in and fucking with his head. *Double liar.* In his experience, those stripes didn't change, and it never ended well. If he shouted it to himself often enough, maybe he'd begin to believe it.

"Hey, this is it. We're here." Stef pulled Arwen to a halt. "Cass, you okay?"

Cass, who'd been lost in his ridiculous head, jerked wide awake and stared around him. The relief on Stef's face when he saw that Cass was still conscious, struck Cass hard. He owed this amazing man more than he could say.

Stef had gone so far past the extra mile to get Cass safe down the mountain, Cass could never repay him. Every metre of it was carved in deep worry lines around Stef's mouth and eyes. He'd clearly ridden every painful step of the journey down with Cass, and if Cass was exhausted, Stef was equally so. If Cass was scared, Stef was terrified for both of them. He couldn't have offered Cass any more of himself, and Cass wanted the chance to bury himself so deep inside Stef he'd leave an echo of his gratitude there forever. *Goddammit.* He was acing that whole *leave him at the river* plan.

"Sorry, I'm fine." Cass struggled for a smile to reassure Stef that he wasn't feeling quite as godawful as he actually felt. Then the roar of the river caught his attention, and he turned in shock instead. *Holy shit.* The look on his face must have said it all.

"Uh, yeah." Stef blew out a horrified sigh. "I think someone stole our river and replaced it with the washing machine from hell."

He wasn't wrong, and Cass suddenly got why Stef had pulled them up still in the bush, well short of their usual approach. The churning maelstrom of muddy water, thick with branches and a pick 'n' mix of other treacherous debris, had tripled in both width and height, and its thunderous passage was deafening to Cass's ears.

He glanced upriver at the flying fox, and his heart sank. The attachment trees on both sides were surrounded by turbulent water running vortexes around their base. In the state Cass was in, without help, it would be a mission for Stef to get him *to* the flying fox, let alone up and across it. He hoped SAR had some muscle and a good plan.

Stef followed his gaze and gasped, and Cass could feel the man's horror mount. A flash of yellow and a wave grabbed Cass's attention from the other side of the river, where two of the rescue team had caught sight of them. They yelled something that he couldn't hear above the raging water.

Stef waved back, then rested his hand on Cass's thigh and looked up. "This is gonna be bad, isn't it?"

CHAPTER THIRTEEN

STEF'S HEART WAS BANGING OUT OF HIS CHEST. HOW THE FUCK were they meant to get across that? Jesus, it had been bad enough imagining them being winched across while they were still safe back at the hut. Now, witnessing the full destructive power of the raging torrent and the impossible mission for them to even reach the damn flying fox, Stef was calling bullshit. They'd never make it. He'd exhausted all his miracles for the day, and no one, *no one* was going to convince him that he could get himself, let alone a barely walking Cass, on to that thing and across to the other side safely.

"Someone call an Uber?"

Stef nearly jumped out of his skin as a bearded apparition pushed through the bush next to him wearing an orange-and-black Land SAR coat and a big, toothy grin. Search and rescue—thank Christ.

"Fucking hell, warn a guy next time." He sucked in a couple of breaths and tried to knuckle down his heart rate to a little south of explosive. His eyes flicked to the flying fox and back to the man, whose grin Stef felt an urgent need to slap off his face. None of this was funny.

"How did you... where's the..." He sucked in a breath and

eyeballed the man. "Don't tell me you came across on that thing through... that." He flicked his head to indicate the half-submerged trees anchoring the flying fox.

"Stef..." Cass's hand landed on his shoulder.

The SAR man gave a sympathetic half smile. "I know it looks bad, but it's the only way."

"Bad?" Stef's eyes popped. "It looks fucking suicidal."

"Stef, please..."

Stef's gaze jerked up to find Cass ashen grey and fighting a losing battle to keep his eyes open. He swayed ominously, his head falling forward on his chest. *Shit.* Stef's hands grabbed Cass's hips to hold him steady in the saddle, and Arwen flicked her head around, sensing the sudden tension.

"Cass, what's wrong?" Stef peered up into Cass's downturned face, receiving only a grunt in reply.

The SAR man whipped around to the other side of Arwen and began working at the knots to free Cass from the saddle. "Let's get him down so I can take a look. I'm Kevin, by the way, and I'm one of the search-and-rescue doctors."

Oh, thank God.

Before long they were able to slide Cass sideways and ease him to the soggy ground. It wasn't easy, or graceful. Cass had over six inches on both of them, and many more kilos, but they managed it. Then Kevin got one of Cass's arms out of its oilskin sleeve while Stef secured Arwen to a tree.

"Is he okay?" Stef hovered as the doctor checked Cass out, his boots sinking in the sucking mud.

"Has he been doing this?" Kevin flicked a flashlight over each of Cass's pupils. "Just dropped out like this?" He pulled a blood pressure monitor from his pocket.

Stef shook his head and worried his left index nail between his teeth. The thing was down to the quick. "Not like this." He tried to keep his voice even. "He took hours to wake up after he was knocked out, and then yesterday he had a seizure"

Kev's gaze flicked up briefly.

Stef continued, "Then this morning he was hard to wake, and he's been a bit spacey, seeing double at times—but he's been conscious."

Cass's eyes fluttered open and Stef almost sank to his knees with relief, but it was short-lived.

"Fuck... my head... what happened..." Every word was slurred like Cass was talking through treacle. He tried to lift his head, then sank back again. "I... shit... I can't remember... Stef?" He reached a hand out.

Stef grabbed it. "I'm here, babe."

Kevin slid him a curious glance, then got to his feet. "Stay with him." He pulled a satphone from his jacket and took a few steps towards the river.

Stef cradled Cass's face and kept talking, senseless shit, anything to try to keep him awake. He got the odd mumbling reply and a whole lot of silence. Behind him, Kevin spoke urgently into the phone—something about a blown pupil, high blood pressure, and needing help. Stef wanted details, but he wanted Cass to open his eyes more.

Kevin finished his call, and together they got Cass back into his oilskin. Then the doctor laid a hand on Stef's shoulder. "I take it you two are... close, so I'm not going to sugar-coat it, okay?"

Stef swallowed hard but said nothing.

"I can't say for sure what's going on with him, but that was a heavy blow Cass took to his head, and he might have a haematoma sitting under the bone, a build-up of blood from the knock, understand?"

Every scrap of air sucked out of Stef's chest and his throat closed over, but he managed a nod.

Kevin's expression softened. "Good. That means he needs help now, as soon as we can."

Another nod as a wave of fear ran through him.

"Okay. Now, I've got two more men coming across on the flying fox, and then we're going to get your guy back the same way, safe and sound."

My guy. It felt... right. But hell no, Stef wasn't letting them stick Cass on that thing. He went to say just that when Kevin's hand locked around his wrist.

"There's no other option, Stef. And I'm not asking, I'm telling you what's going to happen, so you need to listen. At the moment Cass is breathing fine, so we need to do this now in case that changes—"

Changes? Oh, fuck. His hand flew to his mouth.

"You're going to have to trust us on this. I know it looks bad, but the trees are solid. They're not gonna fall any time soon. We'll transfer Cass to the rescue stretcher right here, and then we've got a plan to get him over to that flying fox wire and across, okay? Working together, with everyone safely roped this side and the rescue cradle secured to the wire, we'll winch him into place and he'll be safe across the other side in no time."

Stef nodded blankly. "Just... don't drop him, okay?"

Kevin's mouth twitched. "We won't. And once he's safely across, we'll come back for you, unless you want to stay and come down with the horses tomorrow."

Like hell. "No. I um, I want to stay with him. But what about Arwen? We can't leave her tied up."

"One of the guys offered to stay and help Hoff with the horses when he rides up via the other track later today. It'll all be good."

Stef blew out a sigh. "Okay, I guess." He gave the river a horrified glance. *Fuck. Fuck. Fuck.* "Just so we're clear—I'm way past terrified."

Kevin's hand squeezed Stef's arm. "Just don't do anything except what we tell you to. No independent thinking, okay? I take it you want to see Cass into the ambulance, right?"

Stef gulped in a breath and nodded away like a fucking car toy. "Right. Yeah, okay, I want that."

Kevin smiled reassuringly. "Good. It'll be fine."

It wasn't fine. In no fucking way was it *fine*. In fact, if Stef was to be searingly honest, the whole transfer shitshow was so far from fine, that sucker needed life support just to get it back to acceptably *terrifying*.

His fear for Cass's well-being kept at bay any alarm as to how they were getting *Stef* to the other side... until it was his turn. After that, all bets were off, and Stef was pretty sure that halfway across he'd offered one of the men the best blowjob of his life if only he'd let Stef off that stretcher so he could walk home instead. He couldn't be certain, but he thought—hoped—there'd been laughter involved in the man's response. Whatever. Stef was a million clicks beyond giving a fuck by that point, and he was only half joking with the offer anyway.

To their credit, the SAR guys kept their promise, and all Stef had to do was lie back and relax. *Yeah, right.* He still couldn't believe he'd actually done it without losing his shit entirely. But he had, praying his heart out as the stretcher lurched and groaned its way across, pummelled by the wind and the updraft of the storming river in the longest ten minutes of Stef's entire life. If Cass thought he was getting away with just a single date in recompense, the man had no idea what was going to hit him.

As soon as Kevin unstrapped the stretcher, Stef leapt to his feet, slid past a hovering medic wanting to check him over, and tore over to the ambulance, where Cass was being bundled up for transport.

He rapped lightly on the open door, his gaze fixed on Cass, who was lying ominously still on the stretcher. Two paramedics worked on him, intravenous fluids hanging from the ceiling and plastic bags littering the floor.

"How is he?"

The quick concerned look he got was less than reassuring. "You family?"

Shit. "No... a friend. I was up there... with him."

One of the medics shrugged apologetically. "Sorry. Rules."

"But—"

"We're taking him now." A third medic motioned for Stef to stand back so he could close the ambulance door. "You can follow to the hospital once they've cleared you, but it'll be a while till they'll let you see him, just warning you."

Goddammit. Every molecule in Stef's body demanded he stay with Cass. The fact he was being shunted aside, that he had no say, that he was being dismissed like some fucking nobody, tore at his heart. He stood back while they got ready to leave, his blood pounding in his ears. It wasn't just the fact that Cass was injured that made Stef want to stay by his side. He was also terrified that if he didn't keep one hand on the man, Cass would find a way to push Stef away and retreat to his carefully contained life. And Stef needed at least the chance to let Cass know that he wanted to give things a try between them.

But Cass was gone. Stef was about ready to tear someone a new one when a hand landed on his shoulder, and he turned to find Kevin standing beside him with sympathetic eyes. "He's in good hands, Stef. How about you get yourself checked out and cleaned up, then head up to the hospital to see what's what. You've got time. He's gonna be a while. He'll need scans and a whole lot of other tests. Possibly even surgery, if it is a haematoma."

Stef started. "Surgery?"

"If they have to relieve the pressure."

"Oh. Right. Fuck."

A familiar face drifted into view. "I'll look after him." Dee slipped a hand through Stef's arm. "Come on, Stef, the medics and SAR want to have a quick chat, then we'll get you back to the farm. Your friends are waiting there. Cass's dad is on his way down from a big muster in the high country and won't get here till tomorrow. I'm gonna try and get word up to him that we at least got Cass back down safe. His mother is in Melbourne ready to fly back if needed, so it's just me at the moment. Under the circumstances, his dad gave the hospital permission to deal with me. They'll ring me once he arrives."

A thought suddenly occurred to Stef. "Tomas and Andrew—?"

"Safe and sound. Got across before the rain. Tomas said he'd call tomorrow. He wanted your number, but I said I'd have to check with you—"

"He can have it."

Dee nodded. "And before you ask, Arwen and Gandalf will be fine. Hoff knows what he's doing. He's a fine horseman."

Not like Cass though. Stef stared after the ambulance. "Good. They won't know what's going on. Look, I, um, I really need to know how Cass... I mean, he—we—dammit." Stef sighed in frustration. "We became friends, and I'd, uh, like to see him... if that's okay."

She eyed him curiously but didn't press. After a few seconds, she nodded. "Yeah, okay. I'm fine with that." She stood in front of him to get his full attention "You did good, Stef, really good. Hell, for an inexperienced rider, you were amazing. I want to make sure you understand that." She squeezed his arm. "So let's get this interview over and then go get you cleaned up. If you want, you can come with me when the hospital gives us the all-clear. I could do with the company."

"Really?" Stef let out the breath he didn't know he'd been holding and gave Dee a grateful nod. "Thanks. I, um... really mean that."

She gave him a considered look and seemed about to say something when the SAR guy called his name again. He sighed and let Dee lead him over to the second ambulance, his thoughts pinned on a pair of laughing green eyes, the cowboy they belonged to, and the ache in his chest from being too damn far away from him.

CHAPTER FOURTEEN

"Hey," Tanner brushed the dirt off the back step of the farmhouse deck and took a seat beside Stef.

A clatter of plates could be heard from inside where Ethan had clearly been left to clean up the remains of Dee's lunch on his own. She'd insisted on preparing them something before heading out to check on the animals—like Stef could eat a thing. His stomach was tied up in gnarly knots, his mouth a pit of sawdust. He'd forced a bite of banana and half a sandwich down with a few sips of surprisingly good coffee that Ethan had made for them in Cass's trendy and expensive machine. The cowboy was a coffee snob, go figure.

The hospital had called Dee twice. The first time to say Cass had arrived safely but they had a lot of testing to do and no one would be able to see him for a while. The second was to tell her that Cass was headed for surgery—getting a burr hole drilled into his skull to relieve the pressure on his brain. From there he'd be going to ICU and it would still be some time before she could see him.

Apparently, Kevin had been spot on. The CT scan revealed a small subdural haematoma—a clot lodged between Cass's skull and his brain. But the burr hole surgery wasn't without risk. Moreover, if it didn't work, they'd have to do a craniotomy—lift off a whole section of skull to remove the clot. Stef panicked at the thought of either option, but Cass's haematoma was small and the surgeons had been very positive with Dee.

Stef had wanted to head to the hospital straight way but Dee wanted to make sure all the sheep and farm animals were fed and cared for first, not knowing when she would get back. Plus the hospital would ring if Cass came out early.

It made sense but Stef didn't have to like it. He wasn't even sure they'd let him in to see Cass. He'd briefly wondered if he should say something to Dee, about the two of them. But what *could* he say? All he knew was he wasn't going to be able to keep up the façade for much longer. Once he laid eyes on Cass, all bets were off. And Dee was no one's fool. She'd been giving Stef sideways looks since the river, and Stef was pretty sure she suspected there was something more between him and Cass than just friends.

Stef had left Tanner and Ethan at the table before the small talk and curious looks got the better of him, and sat on the back deck steps watching Dee move the merinos into another paddock, and the three horses chomp on their hay. Somewhere in all that he found a little peace. Eowyn regularly popped her head up to check the driveway, as if waiting for Cass, or maybe Gandalf and Arwen, to reappear.

You and me both, Stef mused, and briefly wondered what Arwen had thought of being left at the river. He hoped that neighbour, Hoff, knew she liked her hay spread in a line and not dumped in a single heap.

Jesus, listen to me. Only two days and he'd turned into a country sap. Move over, Farmer Brown. That is if you liked your farmers with eyeliner.

Tanner bumped shoulders with him. "So, you wanna tell me about it?"

Stef snorted. "I wouldn't even know where to start."

Tanner stared at the parched lawn already beginning to flush green from the rain and pursed his lips. "Well, how about with why you're sitting out here on a dirty step staring at horses, chewing your fingernail and brooding, when we could have you home in a hot bath with a cold Sauvignon Blanc in your hand. Dee said she'd keep us in the loop."

He cocked an eyebrow Stef's way. "And just in case you missed it, let me repeat that bit about sitting in the dirt, because the Stefan Hamilton I've known for too many years to count would rather throw out a pair of his Jimmy Choos than sit on a dusty step when there's a perfectly good chair two feet away."

Stef narrowed his eyes. "I am not brooding. I'm just... worried. It was kind of... intense up there. You wouldn't get it. And I only have one pair of Jimmy Choos, so... understandable, right?" He absently brushed at the dirt on the step and then wiped his mucky hands down the front of his clean jeans, only belatedly catching Tanner's arched brow and matching smirk. *Shit.*

Tanner stared at the grimy smudge on Stef's thigh. "I rest my case. This is not you, Stef, and it's not simply because you're worried about some tour guide you barely know, even if you helped him out. Or that you've had a scare. And just let me say right now how fucking proud I am of what you did. That was no easy thing. The closest you get to the challenge of the great outdoors is finding a parking space at Sylvia Park Mall the week before Christmas."

Stef snorted. "Truth."

Tanner nudged Stef with his shoulder again. "But from what Dee heard from the SAR guys, you fucking aced this, Stef. Aced it, when a lot of guys wouldn't have. And just so you know, I for one am *not* surprised. There's more to you than credit cards, cocktails, and fashion—a whole fucking lot more. You just don't trust yourself to try it and not get shot down. And while I'm at it, fuck Paul Johnson. I'm gonna social media the shit out of this and tag his arrogant arse in every one."

Stef reached for Tanner's hand and squeezed it. "I love you, you know that?"

Tanner squeezed back. "Just as well. So, what's all this about, then? And don't tell me you're worried. I know you are. You care about people, even if you hide it well. But I'm your best friend, Stef. And I was expecting at least a 'Pleased to see you,' or maybe even an 'I am never ever doing that again, Tanner,' or more likely a 'You owe me a shitload of brownie points.' But I wasn't expecting this devastated, I-want-to-be-anywhere-but-here vibe we've been getting off you since the minute you arrived. And not just anywhere, but—holy shit." Tanner's eyes widened comically.

Fuck. Stef dropped his head to his chest and waited for it. Tanner was nothing if not perceptive.

"You've fallen for him, haven't you? You're fucking crushing on the hot, straight tour guide. Holy bejesus."

"*Pfft.* Don't be ridiculous."

"You are. You fucking are." Tanner shook his head. "Look at me."

Stef reluctantly met Tanner's eyes.

"Oh. My. Fucking. God. How many times have we laughed about men who break their little gay hearts on het dudes who are never gonna look at them the way they—"

"He's not straight." Stef pitched his voice low and watched Tanner's eyes widen further.

"He's gay?" Tanner leaned close.

"Bi."

"Huh? And you know this because..."

Stef's gaze slid away towards the stables, where Gimli was chewing on Eowyn's mane while the mare calmly stood and let him.

"Holy shit. You fucked him?"

Stef's cheeks heated. "Well, technically he fucked me—"

Tanner gaped. "On the tour? How the hell—"

"There was this barn, lean-to... thingy... away from the hut... with hay bales—"

"Hay bales? How very... rustic of you."

Stef shrugged. "Besides, it was night." He risked a sideways glance to find Tanner staring at him like Stef had lost his shit completely. *Yeah, about that.*

Tanner shook his head in disbelief. "Son of a bitch. Only you. This could only happen to you. I send you off on a perfectly innocent horse tour of your favourite movie locations for one night, *one* night, and what happens? You end up fucking the *straight* tour guide hottie, get stranded by a freak storm, and have to be saved by search and rescue."

Stef fiddled with the hem of his T-shirt. "He's *not* straight. And you make it sound so... dramatic."

Tanner stared at him.

Stef sighed. "Okay, maybe it was a bit dramatic. But we clicked. I don't know how to say it better than that. And I *really* like him, Tanner."

Tanner patted his knee. "I get it, I think. But he's not out, right? Ethan would've known if he were—and, oh my God, Ethan's gonna kill you if you've fucked things up with his go-to horse guy."

"I haven't. It's all fine. I just... fuck, I don't know what the hell I want. It's so fucking ridiculous. I've known him two days, and one of those was after he'd been hit on the head and was mostly uncon-scious... which, truth be known, was probably the best way to get to know me, right?"

Tanner snorted and kissed him on the head. "Don't sell yourself short. I liked your sassy, short arse in about as long."

Stef waved the comment off. "Yeah as a friend, not in the 'I wanna fuck you, have your babies, and buy a cemetery plot together' kind of way."

Tanner looked like he'd swallowed one of those botflies that kept hanging around Stef's legs.

"Too much?"

Tanner coughed hard and nodded.

Stef sighed. "Figured. But you see what I mean? I'm going batshit here. I can't decide whether to dismiss it as lust, go back with you, and forget about this whole thing before I embarrass the shit out of myself even more or go see him and, I don't know... hang around a bit longer. See if maybe there's something real there."

The slam of the screen door had Tanner spinning in his seat.

"Oh." Ethan stopped in his tracks, a bucket hanging from one arm. His gaze flitted between them. "I interrupted something. Should I leave?"

Tanner glanced Stef's way and Stef only hesitated a second before waving Ethan to a seat on the step. For a young guy, Ethan had a solid head on his shoulders and Stef didn't expect Tanner to keep anything from his boyfriend. Ethan might as well hear it from the horse's mouth, so to speak.

"It's a council of war," Tanner explained, wrapping an arm around Ethan's shoulder.

"Oh, cool." Ethan snuggled close, draping his hand over Tanner's thigh and sending little shivers of envy through Stef's heart. "Who's the enemy?"

Tanner sat back to let Stef to tell his story.

Oh, goody.

"So, let me get this right." Ethan cut a quick look to Tanner when Stef was done. "I give you the gift of a horse trek with my favourite stables in an effort to win over my boyfriend's best friend—"

Win me over? Stef opened his mouth to protest, but Ethan stopped him with a raised hand.

"—and you fall in love with the owner, the *straight* owner."

"For fuck's sake, he's *not* straight—"

Ethan kept talking. "You take a sexy tumble in the straw with him—"

"Hay, it was hay..." Stef trailed off as two sets of eyes drilled into him.

"What*ever*." Ethan waved his hand in the air. "You take a sexy tumble in the *hay* with him, and then you want to, what... move in and pick out a china pattern with him the next day?" His face lit up in a huge grin. "This is fucking *awesome*. Hell, I thought I had the corner on a soap opera life."

"See, I told you." Tanner high-fived his boyfriend. "Dramatic doesn't even begin to cover it."

"I hate you both," Stef grumbled, and got to his feet. "And I don't need to be laughed at by you two. I'm horrified enough at myself."

"Sit down." Tanner's expression sobered, and he grabbed Stef's hand. "We're sorry. We were just joking."

"Please?" Ethan patted the step, and Stef sat reluctantly. "I actually think it's kind of... sweet."

Stef rounded on him, horrified. "Oh God, it is, isn't it?" He buried his face in his hands. "I'm never gonna live this down, am I?" He peeked out from between his fingers to find both men smirking. "Fuck."

"Yeah." Ethan laughed. "As I said, *awesome*." He ducked and slid sideways before Stef's hand could reach to knuckle his head.

"Your boyfriend needs a leash," Stef told his best friend.

"Yeah, good luck with that." Tanner eyed Ethan with blatant affection. "Although..." He waggled his eyebrows, and Ethan's pupils flared.

"Oh, no." Stef waved a hand between them. "Stop it. I'm in the middle of an existential crisis here. Have some fucking respect. I need to be the centre of attention."

If Tanner had rolled his eyes any harder, they'd have popped out the back of his head and bounced down the stairs. Stef was quietly in awe.

"You *always* need to be the centre of attention," Tanner muttered.

He wasn't wrong. Stef pursed his lips and tried to keep a straight face. Thank God for friends. It occurred to Stef that Ethan had found his way on to that list as well, and not just because he was Tanner's boyfriend—although the young man was everything Stef's more serious friend needed.

It was a thought that poked at Stef's dilemma in a big way. Age aside, Cass and Stef were likely opposites in more ways than Tanner and Ethan. So what did that say about their chances? He knew Cass saw him as a fish out of water in the country, itching to get back to his comfort zone: noise, shops, and caramel lattes. And if anyone had asked that first day, Stef would've been on board with that 100 percent. But now? Now, Stef didn't know what to think. *Could* he live in a place like this?

He scanned the towering mountains and felt the keen sense of isolation and solitude they wrought on a psyche.

He wasn't sure. He thought he could. Queenstown was less than an hour down the road. Though it might be small, the tourist buzz made it feel bigger, and it was well serviced with bars and clubs and all the trappings he'd need to escape to from time to time. Because he *would* need to escape. There was no doubt a large part of his creative mind liked it down here—it thrummed with ideas. But no matter how much he'd loved the last couple of days, Stef knew he also needed the energy of people around him. And Cass had been hurt before. He'd have to really want to try with Stef, enough to take that risk again—because Stef couldn't promise anything, not this early.

"Anyway"—Ethan got to his feet and retrieved the bucket from beside the back door—"Dee wanted us to give the horses the scraps from lunch. Shall we?"

Stef took the bucket from Ethan's hand and the three of them wandered across to the stables. The horses recognised the bucket and immediately trotted over, nickering and throwing their heads up and down.

"So, what do you think?" Stef nabbed a handful of carrot peelings and held them out for Eowyn, who inhaled them in a second and nudged him for more. He chuckled and rubbed her nose affectionately before giving her a second handful.

Tanner stared at him in shock.

"What?" Stef frowned.

"That." Tanner indicated Stef's hand, buried in the bucket. "You.

I'm not sure I can cope with this new, improved version of Stef. I thought you were scared of horses."

"Who, me?" Stef threw him an innocent look. "These precious beauties? Nah, I love horses. You must be thinking of somebody else. And also, improved?"

"Yes, improved." Tanner grabbed a handful of his own and held them out for Gimli, while Ethan did the same with Bilbo until all three were happily munching away.

"I'm still nervous around them," Stef admitted. "But Cass is a good teacher—"

"I bet he is—" Tanner squawked as Ethan elbowed him in the ribs.

"Turns out horses and I actually get along okay." Stef upended the bucket, and the animals pounced on the remaining scraps while the three of them leaned on the railing and watched.

Stef's cell rang and he jumped, tearing it out of his pocket as if Cass might miraculously materialise on the other end. It was Benny. His father had let him know Stef was safe, and Benny was checking in. God, it was so good to hear his voice. Benny scolded Stef for yet again getting into trouble without Benny there to watch out for him, and did Stef know what a pain in the arse he was? It was the closest Stef had come to a real laugh since everything had gone to shit. He reassured Benny he was fine and promised to call him back when he had news about Cass. He pocketed his phone and looked up to find Tanner eyeballing him.

"So you're really serious about this thing with Cass?" Tanner stood with his sneaker resting on the bottom railing. His checked lumberjack shirt hung open over a white T-shirt and loose jeans. He looked like he fucking belonged there—a lot more than Stef, who was down to the last two of his T-shirts, the current one sporting the tag line "I expect more than 8 seconds" written on the chest, accompanied by the image of a pink-chapped bull rider.

"He's a good guy, Tanner," Ethan chipped in, much to Stef's surprise.

"I'm not saying he isn't." Tanner eyed his boyfriend. "I just... I don't want to see Stef hurt again. It's really quick, that's all I'm saying."

"How long did it take you?" Ethan pressed. "'Cause I knew *you* were trouble for me a few seconds after you walked into my café."

The lines around Tanner's eyes softened, and he reached out and brushed a thumb across Ethan's lips with heart-rending tenderness. "Same. It just took me a bit longer to get my head out of my arse and do what I needed to do."

Ethan's eyes misted. "And what if you'd only been down here for two weeks and not six months? Would you have trusted that instinct? Would you have still pursued me?"

"I didn't pur—"

Ethan arched a brow.

"Okay, I totally pursued you. Maybe, I don't know. I might've chickened out."

Ethan blinked slowly. "Then we wouldn't be here now, would we?"

Tanner rubbed the back of his neck. "Yeah, missing out on you would've been the worst fucking decision ever." He pulled Ethan up on his toes and kissed him soundly.

Stef was pretty sure Ethan's knees wobbled on the landing, and God, he wanted that sort of connection more than he wanted to breathe. His stomach clenched. *Cass.*

Ethan cleared his throat. "So, what you're saying, *sweetheart,* is that Stef is actually a step ahead of you. He knows he feels something more, and he's at least wanting to see where it goes, right? He's not running away and pretending it's nothing he can't get over."

There were a few seconds of pointed silence between the two, and Stef threw Tanner a smug smile. "Have I told you I *really* like your boyfriend?"

Tanner flipped him off. "Okay, so if you want my opinion, here it is. I think it's hella soon, and there's all kinds of complications—like he's not out, for fuck's sake, you live in Auckland, he's in the middle of big surgery with no guaranteed outcome right this very minute, and you're about as country as Metallica. Plus, you have a business to run, and in case I didn't mention it before—he's not out."

Stef bristled. "He *was* out. When he was in Wellington, he was out... for years. I think he just hasn't had a good enough reason to officially come out here... yet."

Tanner cocked his head. "And you think you could be that reason?"

Could he? Was Stef imagining what he saw when he and Cass looked into each other's eyes? "Maybe. I hope so. I'll soon find out. I wouldn't even try if I thought he was closeted. And if the surgery doesn't work out, we'll handle that then."

Tanner stared at him as if he'd grown a second head, and Stef couldn't blame him. *Holy fuck.* It seemed outrageous, *was* outrageous, to be thinking about long term with a man he'd only known for a few days. But Stef couldn't shake the idea... or the overwhelming sense that if he left without even trying, it would be the worst decision of his life.

But he was also thirty-seven. He didn't want a long-distance relationship, and he didn't think Cass would either. Yes, he had a business. But that business didn't need him to be based in Auckland. And Tanner, his best friend, lived here now. Stef could do his jewellery anywhere. His gaze fell idly on the barn, his thoughts kicking up dust.

He could rent his Auckland apartment like Tanner did and get a flat in Queenstown while he and Cass dated—tested the waters, whatever. He could also likely get a local jeweller to rent him some workspace for that time.

He'd need to travel, sure. He'd need to sell and market his brand. But that would also give him the opportunity to get that city injection he'd need. And then he could come back here, back to Cass, back to this place, and create more. It *could* work. If he and Cass worked out, the rest could work too. Stef just didn't know if Cass would be prepared to stake his bruised heart on hopes and maybes.

Jesus, was he setting himself up for heartbreak? "You think I've lost the plot, don't you?" He studied his best friend.

Tanner took two steps and wrapped his arms around Stef. "To paraphrase the words of someone very dear to my heart when I was acting apeshit not that long ago..." He pulled back, keeping his hands on Stef's shoulders. "You're a smart man, Stefan Hamilton. You can find a way, if that's what you both really want. You don't have to have all the answers. If it doesn't work out, you deal with that then."

Stef's throat squeezed tight. He pushed Tanner away and pressed the heels of his hands to his eyes. "Goddammit, you made me cry, you sappy bastard. But thanks, that was good advice. Terrifying, but... yeah, maybe I'll just stop at terrifying."

"Well, don't thank me too quick. Remember, those words came from the same man who only seconds before said, and I quote, 'Dammit, Tanner, what the fuck would you do in Queenstown? You can't keep mooning about a guy you had a fling with for a half second down there. The place has nothing to offer you.'"

Ethan gasped and whacked Stef on the biceps. "You said that to him?"

Tanner grinned lopsidedly. "Balance is everything, right, friend?"

Stef barked out a laugh. "Fucking throw me under the bus, why don't you? To be fair, you hadn't told me how you felt at that point—and besides, when do you ever listen to me?"

"Lots. I listen to you lots. Why? Because what you have to say is worth hearing, understand me? Now, we're gonna head home, and you're gonna go see this guy who's so damn lucky you're even speaking his name and yours in the same breath, and then we're gonna be there if you need us, okay? Whatever and whenever you need."

Stef was about to haul Tanner in for a hug when the tractor pulled to a sudden stop at the fence and Dee jumped off. She left it where it was, scaled the fence, and ran towards them.

"They called." She headed for her truck. "He's out of surgery and on his way to ICU. The burr hole was enough. So far so good. We can see him in about an hour. Come on, Stef. You other two, stay as long as you want and just lock the door and pull it shut before you go."

Stef pressed a kiss to Tanner's cheek and another to Ethan's. "Thanks. I love you both."

Then he ran to join Dee, heart thundering in his chest for more reasons than he cared to look at.

CHAPTER FIFTEEN

IF HE WAS DEAD, CASS WAS GONNA HAVE A FEW CHOICE WORDS with the boss upstairs, because it was too fucking cold to be heaven... and no one ever mentioned taking your damn headache with you into the afterlife. Balls of fire pulsed through his right eye, while some fucker wound the steel trap on his head that much tighter every second.

And would someone turn off that bloody alarm?

"He's awake."

Who's that? His eyelids flickered but stayed closed. *Open, damn you.* Nothing.

"His blood pressure's spiking. Get John back here."

Who's John? What the hell? Plastic ripped somewhere behind him.

"Hand me that pain relief, and... shit... grab his hand!"

Fucking... suffocating... need to breathe... Cass gagged, bit down on... plastic. *Have to breathe... to get...*

A hand clamped around his wrist, pinning him to the bed.

"Now. I need it now. Hold him down."

Floating...

The rhythmic flow of breath in and out... the only thing breaking the hushed silence. His breath, Cass finally realised. He lay there a minute, focused on the movement of his chest, the quiet pulse in his neck, the glorious absence of pain. Someone had untangled the shit in his head, opened the windows, cleared the fog. He still felt... brittle. A little crumbly round the edges. But alive.

His hand twitched. Something on his finger; the beep of a monitor. Well, okay. Hospital.

Scraps of images in his head. The river, the hut, Arwen on her hind legs... and Stef. *Stef.*

A little turn of his head. *Check.* Cool. A twinge in his neck, the heat of something pulsing above his right ear, a dull ache in his eye. Different. Not great, but okay. Better than... before.

Eyelids. Fucking heavy bastards. Like lifting an industrial roller door when the power's out. One would have to do. Oh no, there goes the other one. Small mercies.

Right then. What've we got? Beige walls, concrete bed, white cardboard sheets, mouth like a sewer. Definitely hospital. A soft snore. Not him. Long, glossy strands across his fingers. Eyeballs down on the count of three and.... His heart stuttered. *Stef.*

Relief.

With supreme effort, Cass lifted his fingers, and Stef's hair fell through them like a waterfall of silk. So beautiful. His thumb brushed across the faint web of lines that had fallen soft in sleep at the corner of Stef's eye.

His own lids wanted to slam shut, but nothing was going to steal this moment from him. Jesus, what was wrong with him? To let someone so close—someone who could only bring him pain. But Cass had no regrets. He might not be able to have Stef for long, but he could have this moment—and maybe a few more. Relish the knowledge that Stef hadn't disappeared from his life and taken all the colour with him.

A pair of sleepy hazel eyes rose to meet his then flashed wide. "Cass! Oh my God, you're awake." Stef shot forward on his seat. "Do you need a nurse? Are you okay?" His gaze ran the length of Cass's body, concern etched in every line of his face—his very exhausted face.

Cass shook his head slowly, fought off a wave of nausea, and made a mental note not to try that again too soon. "Nah, no nurse, just you. Stop fussing. I just want to look at you."

Stef's expression softened and he relaxed. He returned an almost shy smile, and Cass had to look twice to be sure he'd got it right. Shyness and Stef were two words that rarely appeared in the same sentence, but it was there in the way he tucked his head and straightened the creases in the sheets over Cass's chest. And if Cass hadn't already been hopelessly smitten, that one look would have done it right there.

"You can't say shit like that." Stef slumped back in his chair. "I don't... I never... ugh, whatever." He waved a hand between them.

Cass bit back a smile and tried to reach for Stef's hand. His body took a second to respond but got there in the end. Stef enfolded his fingers eagerly and leaned in.

"They said you could have a few ice chips if you woke and made sense. You want some?"

"God, yes."

Stef shook a few from a small thermos and slipped them between Cass's lips. He crunched through them like mana from heaven and his mouth came alive.

"How long have I been out?"

Stef's thumb drew circles over the back of Cass's hand. "Since the surgery yesterday afternoon. You've woken a few times, but you've not really been with it."

Yesterday? Shit. "Surgery?" Cass's head jerked up, and the throb above his ear went nuclear. "Ow... shit, shit, shit..." He fell back on the pillow.

"Take it easy." Stef placed a restraining hand in his shoulder. "You've got a fucking hole in your head. You need to be careful."

A hole? "A hole? What the hell?"

Stef gave a sheepish smile. "Yeah, well, everyone needs one, right? At least when I tell you you're talking out of a hole in your head, you'll be able to ask, which one?" His laugh had a nervous edge. "Too soon?"

Cass rolled his eyes and wished he hadn't.

Stef frowned. "Yeah, too soon. They warned us you might not remember..."

"Just tell me." Cass shifted so he was a little more on his side. "The last thing I remember was coming down the track, then it all gets fuzzy. Even before, it kind of comes and goes."

A flicker of fear passed through Stef's eyes. "Do you... um... do you remember—"

Oh. "Us?" Cass squeezed Stef's hand as tight as his useless muscles allowed. "Yes, I remember us. I remember talking by the fire. I remember how amazing you were with the horses. I remember being dazzled by you in the hay shed..."

Stef's cheeks brightened adorably. "Dazzled, huh? Well, of course"—his gaze slid off Cass—"I mean, it's not as if anyone could forget *me*, right?" He pulled his lower lip between his teeth and chewed on it.

Cass stretched his hand to free the poor abused thing and ran his thumb over it instead—no lag that time. His body was coming back to him.

"As if." He tilted Stef's chin up till they locked eyes. "I will never forget that, ever."

A slow, sexy smile stole over Stef's face. "Well, that's good, then. Long as we're clear."

"So, tell me about this hole in my head."

Stef glanced at the door. "I don't think I should be the one... I mean, Dee's just gone down to the cafeteria... and your dad's due any time. The doctor will be here soon—"

"Stef."

Stef's gaze jerked back.

"I asked *you*. I trust *you*. It's fine. Please?"

Warmth bloomed in those tired eyes, and Stef's mouth curved up at the corners. "Oh, okay."

God, he was adorable, and Cass wanted nothing more than to haul him on to his bed, slide his tongue between those lips, and then tuck him into his side for safekeeping as they both caught up on some sleep—about a hundred years should do it. But the razor slice of pain through his temple reminded him he wouldn't be doing any such thing, not even close.

Stef's account of what happened, how spaced out Cass had become that second morning, and on the trip down to the river, was sobering to say the least. Cass remembered very little of it, and nothing at all of his collapse at the river or getting winched across. Everything was blank until he'd woken. What was clear—from the way Stef's voice wavered and the moments he struggled to form the words—was how very frightened he'd been for Cass.

"But they said you did really well," Stef continued. "As soon as they drilled the hole and released the pressure, all your vitals improved. They sent you to ICU for a few hours until you stabilised before they took the breathing tube out, and then you were shipped down here." His gaze flicked to the door. "Look, I really need to let them know you're awake. Dee will kill me if she comes back and finds I haven't." He reached over Cass and pressed the call bell.

The nurse came quickly, smiled, took some vitals, and then bounced off to let the doctors know. When the guy was gone, Stef pulled his chair close, and only then did Cass see the T-shirt.

He snorted. "Eight seconds, huh?"

"What?" Stef glanced down. "Oh." He grinned sheepishly. "Well, you know. Better to lay all your cards on the table from the start, right?"

Cass grinned, which only served to pull on the stitches around the fucking *hole in his head*, and ow, fucking ow.

"Not that *you* have anything to worry about on that score," Stef added with a heated look that somehow managed to bypass all the pain and drugs in Cass's system and tickle his balls. His dick raised its head for just a second, decided nothing was gonna come of it, and dropped back to sleep. Was nothing sacred?

"The staff think it's hilarious."

Cass read the slogan again and sighed. Of course they did. He wondered what else they thought and tried not to let the concern show on his face. He failed, at least judging by how the smile fell from Stef's face. *Dammit.*

Stef was quick to reassure him. "I, um, didn't say anything... about you... or us. It's just... well, I'm kind of obvious, right? But they know I'm just a friend... or something. Anyway, Dee got me on the approved list."

"She did?"

"Yeah. I, um, was a bit of a wreck when they took you away, and she figured we'd... bonded"—his gaze tracked back to Cass—"or something."

Cass chuckled, and another wave of nausea circled his stomach. He added laughing to the "don't" list. "Bonded, huh? That's what the kids are calling it these days?" He squeezed Stef's hand. "Hey, it's fine. When did you get here?"

Stef squirmed. "Uh, yesterday. Dee brought me in with her. I wasn't sure if it was the right thing to do, whether you'd—I just thought—" The words tumbled from his mouth. "But maybe it's too awkward. I understand—I can go—I don't have—"

Cass squeezed his hand. "I want. I very much want."

Stef exhaled slowly. "You do? Well, that's good, then... that I came, I mean." He beamed.

And Cass felt like he'd won the fucking lottery. "So, you stayed at the hospital last night?"

Stef nodded. "Dee got to stay with you in ICU, since your dad isn't getting here till this morning. Tomas and Andrew rang to see how you were and to pass on their good wishes and hope it all goes well. Tomas said he'll come visit when you get home. Dee got me into ICU there for a quick look at you, but they only let one person stay, so..."

Cass frowned. "Then where did you sleep?"

Stef yawned and rubbed at his eyes. Every nail on his right hand was bitten to the quick. "In the waiting room."

Cass gaped. "In the—"

Stef waved away his concern. "It was fine. I shoved a couple of chairs together. Vending machine coffee is absolute crap, by the way... though they did have Jelly Tip ice creams, so that was a bonus."

Cass could only stare at him.

Stef's brows crunched together. "What?"

"You did all that, just to see me?" He wouldn't let himself think about what that might mean.

Stef looked confused. "Uh, yeah? Of course. I mean, I thought we —" He broke off, frowned, and bit his lip. "I just thought you might want to see me when you woke up. You know, fill you in on stuff... in case you forgot... stuff."

Oh. Of course. "Right. Well, I did. I do." He brushed the back of his hand over Stef's cheek. "And there's one thing in particular that I'm in urgent need of a reminder about." He attempted an eyebrow waggle that likely came off as a rabid tic, since one eyebrow refused to cooperate.

Stef snorted and laid a warm hand on his chest. "And what would that be?" The brown flecks in his eyes glowed gold in the reflected light, and Cass had to blink hard to get past the lump in his throat.

"Kiss me."

Stef smiled and leaned in further. "With absolute pleasure."

Their lips brushed, and all Cass could do was melt. It was sweet and chaste, just the tip of Stef's tongue riding Cass's crease before disappearing as he pressed soft kisses from one side to the other, his long lashes brushing Cass's cheek, their noses pressed together, sharing breath and... something more, something Cass couldn't get a handle on.

"Morning, boys."

Fuck.

Stef jerked back, a horrified look on his face, as Dee slid past and delivered a kiss to Cass's stunned cheek. "Glad to see you're awake, darling boy. Your father's on his way, and your mum said she'll call again as soon as the doctors have been. She's been blowing up my phone, in case you wondered." She smirked like the cat who'd stolen the cream, her gaze flicking between him and Stef. "Hungry, anyone?"

Oh boy. The witch. Cass wasn't going to poke that loaded question with even the longest stick. He'd never thought Dee would have any problems with him being bi, but he'd also not expected to out himself in quite such an obvious way. So he ignored her question, which only earned him another smirk.

"Here." Dee pushed a paper bag into Stef's hand. "Pastries and a breakfast bun. Eat."

Stef peeked in the bag and sighed with pleasure. "You keep feeding me like this and I'm gonna need to book two seats on that plane—" His gaze jerked to Cass.

Cass acted like he hadn't heard. It was a timely reminder that this thing they had was temporary. *Enjoy the moment. He'll be gone soon enough.*

"Is this a private party, or can anyone join?" A beanpole of a doctor with a thin grey comb-over and smiling eyes strode into the room and across to Cass, followed by the same nurse who'd been in earlier. "Well, you look a whole lot better than last night. Let's take a look."

The nurse motioned Dee and Stef to leave.

"No." Cass wanted Stef in the room, needed him there. "I'd like them to stay, please."

The doctor nodded absently. "Fine."

Dee looked surprised but took a spot on the other side of the room, and Stef joined her, equally surprised but also... pleased. *Good.*

The doctor poked and prodded, checked his abdomen with a

comment that the scans around there had been clear, shone a light in Cass's eyes, mumbled something about pressure readings, asked the nurse about urine output, checked with Cass about any pain, and asked a hundred other questions until it all blurred into background noise and Cass couldn't keep up. Dee and Stef were hanging off every word, so Cass figured he was good.

When he was finally done, the doctor told the nurse to remove all the tubes except the IV access for antibiotics and warned Cass to start eating and drinking. He'd need to stay in hospital another couple of days, but as far as the doctor could tell, Cass was apparently a star patient and any immediate threat had passed.

But that bubble of good news was then popped unceremoniously, balanced by a serious discussion about how dangerous his injury had been, and how, if Cass hadn't received treatment when he did, he might've suffered irreparable brain damage. And even with that treatment, no one could promise he'd be free of any long-term repercussions—recovery would be a process. Cass had suffered a traumatic brain injury, the doctor explained. The burr hole relieved the pressure, which relieved the immediate symptoms. But that didn't mean there'd been no damage. The brain would need time to heal, and Cass could expect to struggle with intermittent headaches and some balance, memory, and concentration issues at the very least. Riding horses, let alone leading tours, was out of the question for the immediate future.

Fuck.

When the doctor left, a heavy silence filled the room.

"Well, that was fun." Cass closed his eyes and fell back on the pillow. "Just take my fucking livelihood away with a smile, why don't you?"

Stef was instantly by his side with a poke to his good ribs. "Hey. You're alive, arsehole. By the sound of it, things could've been a lot worse. You'll figure it out."

Cass cracked an eyelid open. "Your bedside manner could do with some work."

Stef grinned and stroked Cass's cheek. "My bedside manner is just fine, thank you very much."

Cass smiled up into those twinkling eyes. "It is indeed."

Dee cleared her throat from where she'd sneaked up on the other side of the bed, and Cass pulled away from Stef's hand. He couldn't ignore the elephant in the room forever.

"Dee, I—"

"Hush." She turned that perceptive gaze to maximum volume. "All I'm gonna say is, you need to talk to your dad before he stumbles on the two of you like I did."

"How long have you known?"

"Oh, my dear boy." She patted his hand. "If the number of times I caught you checking out some film crew guy in my café didn't do it, getting an eyeful of you behind the barn with your tongue down the throat of that little hottie horse trainer you had hanging around here last year certainly sealed the deal. I was looking for some baling twine, by the way."

"Hottie horse trainer?" Stef arched a brow.

"Oh. My. God." Cass burnt with embarrassment. "You saw that?"

Dee smiled widely. "Saw it, took notes, and lost a few years of my life. If only I'd had a camera. And yes"—she glanced across at Stef— "he was delicious."

Stef snorted, and Cass fired him a glare.

"What? It's kind of funny."

Cass intensified the glare.

"Or not." Stef cleared his throat. "Nope. Definitely not funny."

Cass swung back to Dee. "Why didn't you say something?"

Dee shrugged. "Not my business."

A hundred questions ran through Cass's head, but only one was important. "So you're okay with it? With me?"

Dee kissed him on the cheek. "Of course. Why wouldn't I be? But just to clarify—gay? Bi?"

"Bi."

She gave a satisfied nod. "Good. I'd hoped for Tricia's sake that was the case."

He understood. "It was. And it had nothing to do with the divorce. She always knew about me. Does um, Dad—"

Dee laughed. "Completely in the dark, I suspect. So tread lightly there."

"Do you think he'll—"

"To be honest, I don't know. But you know your father. He's not one for a lot of emotion. Unless you're a merino with poor wool quality taking up his precious grazing space, he's fairly laid back about most other stuff. But I'm here if you need me."

"Need you for what?"

Cass nearly choked on his tongue as his dad strode into the room, still dressed in his musterer's long oilskin. Ignoring everyone else, he walked straight over to Cass and pressed a soft kiss to the bandage on his head, before enfolding him in a gentle hug—a surprise to everyone, not least of all Cass. He soaked in the warm attention until over his father's shoulder, he noticed Stef slinking towards the door. He quickly wriggled from his father's grasp. "Stef."

Stef pulled up short with enough acid in his expression to flay the skin from Cass's back.

"Yes, Cass," he hissed, conveying just how badly he wanted out of that room and how pissed he was at Cass for interfering with that mission.

Tough cookies. Cass ignored him, knowing he'd likely pay for it later. "Stef, I'd like you to meet my father, Sean Martin. Dad, this is Stefan Hamilton, the guy who got me off the mountain."

Sean's gaze landed on Stef's T-shirt first, and his eyes widened slightly. Then his face broke into a huge smile, and he threw out a hand.

Stef stared at it like you would a rabid dog before sighing and shaking it firmly.

"I can't thank you enough for looking after my son."

"I didn't do—"

"Nonsense. You stayed with him and got him down safely. He couldn't have done it without you. Visit any time you like."

Stef mumbled his thanks. And then, before he tore out the door like his arse was on fire, he sent Cass a look that spoke very clearly about what Cass's father *might* say if he truly knew how much, and in what way, Stef had actually looked after his son.

Cass merely grinned and added that to the list of things he'd undoubtedly pay for later. He could hardly wait.

CHAPTER SIXTEEN

"YOU WANT COFFEE?" HIS FATHER CALLED THROUGH THE screen door to where Cass sat in a wicker chair on the back deck, staring at the corral and feeling like he was only a liniment rub and a laxative away from being booked into a rest home. The cane across his knees only added to the indignity.

The horses stared right back, and Cass swore that was a smirk on Gandalf's face. *Fucker.*

Hoff had been over to exercise them all that morning with Sean's help, while Cass could do no more than watch from the deck.

Three months until he could ride again, and then only after he passed a full medical check. Six months until he could lead a tour. *Son of a bitch.*

Not that he could argue with the logic. Although his head was a million times better than when he'd woken from the anaesthetic the week before, that only lasted while he was seated, quiet, and staring into space with an empty stomach. Change any of those variables, and Cass was in trouble. His balance on his feet was for shit, his concentration gone to hell, and food seemed to hit his stomach on a bungee cord, destined to return and tell of its adventures. He was pissed, bored, and generally cranky.

The only bright spark in his hospital stay had been a certain sexy visitor from Auckland, whose mission, it seemed, had been to drive Cass out of his tree with fruitless desire. Cass might have lost none of his urge, but his body was leagues behind doing anything about it. He could barely hold two ideas together in his head let alone get all hot and bothered with the man who seemed to have become the subject of his every waking thought.

Stef had visited each afternoon, carefully avoiding Cass's dad, who came in the mornings. Even if Cass hadn't been in the mood for company, it never lasted once Stef arrived. His vibrant personality, caustic wit, and genuine concern ensured Cass never had a chance.

Before he knew it, Stef had shared a family anecdote or offered his sassy take on some article in the newspaper and had Cass laughing till he cried, his head exploding all over the place. Or Cass would find himself curled up in Stef's arms as his brain demanded time to heal. He fell asleep without warning, with no respect for time or place. And even though he might be out for hours, he'd wake to find Stef still there, holding him, watching him. More than once Cass had been transported back to the hut, reminded of Stef's warm body behind him on that cot, arms wrapped around him while they stared at the stars.

They'd talked about everything and anything during those visits. With his head feeling somewhere between being wrapped in cotton wool and drowning in treacle, there wasn't much to do *but* talk. Cass had even spoken to Benny again, enduring the speakerphone equivalent of a protective older brother's scolding for having the audacity to get hurt when Benny had charged Cass with the job of looking after Stef, not the other way around.

Cass had listened indulgently to the dressing-down while Stef had looked on in silent laughter. He had managed to redeem himself by painting Stef in the light of saviour and superhero, and with that, all had been forgiven. But when Benny asked whether Cass knew of any nice gay men to introduce his brother to, Cass had mumbled incoherently, and the temperature in the tiny hospital room had plummeted while Cass scrabbled to change the subject.

But there'd also been moments when Cass had caught Stef looking at him like he had something to say, and with such undisguised affection it stuttered his heart and had him wishing for things he had no business doing. It was ridiculous and hopeless, and at times so fucking romantic he didn't know what to do with it. Then he'd remember Stef was on holiday with return tickets to Auckland, and all those silly feelings got wound into a tight ball in his chest and threatened to choke him.

Their lives were so far apart they might as well have continents between them—and Cass knew if he didn't carve out some comparable emotional distance, he'd have no chance of holding his heart together when Stef left. So when he'd been discharged three days before, he didn't let Stef know until he was home, and he hadn't needed to see Stef's face to know how much he'd hurt him.

To make matters worse, Graham had been on Cass's doorstep within hours and not long after, Tomas and Andrew had dropped by the homestead to check up on him as well. They'd been relieved to see Cass up and about. Tomas had phoned a couple of times since the surgery, but it was great to have the chance to thank them both in person for what they did. Cass wasn't so sure he'd still have been there without them. Andrew was noticeably quiet and there was a palpable tension between the two brothers, but Cass didn't ask.

Tomas checked if it was okay to visit again, and Cass gladly agreed, shocking himself in the process. Go figure. Still, he liked the young guy, and maybe Dee was right and his friendship group did need widening. God knew there was going to be a gaping hole without Stef's constant chatter in his ear. How could one guy burrow so far under Cass's skin in such a short time?

So, all up, it wasn't like Cass hadn't had visitors, invited or not. And yet he'd spent two days fobbing off Stef's texts and calls on one pretext or another—the doctors said he needed quiet, his constant headache was particularly bad, or some other dreadful half-truth meant to protect his heart.

But he was out of excuses. What's more, Stef was leaving in three days, and Cass couldn't let him go without seeing him. The mere thought horrified him. He'd been a right prick, and he missed Stef in a way he hadn't thought possible. But he didn't know how to have that conversation—how to say goodbye when he really, really fucking didn't want to. But he owed Stef that and so much more.

He stared at the half-dozen unanswered texts sitting on his phone.

Was he a bastard? Undoubtedly.

"You didn't answer, so I made one anyway." His dad handed him a steaming cup and pulled the second wicker chair close. "It won't be as good as yours, but I'm sure you'll cope."

They sipped on their coffees for a bit as the autumn breeze kicked up the leaves on the lawn. The horses got bored and took themselves into the barn, out of the sun, tails flicking in disgust.

"As if I live to entertain you," Cass muttered, and his dad chuckled.

"So, you wanna talk about it?" His dad prodded Cass's shoe with his own.

Cass's head jerked up. "About what?" Because no, he hadn't come out to his father. *Coward much?*

"About whatever stick you've got shoved up your arse."

Surprisingly apt.

"I thought that would've been obvious," Cass answered crisply. "I got my head trashed by a horse, had a hole drilled into it, and can't work for six months. Oh, and I have the mental agility of a slug... on a good day. Good thing I've got enough accountancy clients to keep my head above water for a bit, so bankruptcy isn't on the cards... yet—at least once I can work on a computer for more than three minutes without losing my complete train of thought, that is."

His dad rocked back and sipped on his coffee. "Hmm. That's a deep well of self-pity you've dug for yourself there, son. Do you need a rope to get out or just hang yourself with?"

Cass shot his father his best don't-fucking-mess-with-me glare, which only earned him an indulgent grin. Parents.

His phone buzzed with another text. He glanced down, sighed, and shoved it in his pocket.

His dad frowned but said nothing.

Arsehole, thy name be Cassidy. Well, he might not be able to solve the Stef dilemma, but Cass could at least get things out on the table with his father.

He cleared his throat and shuffled his chair around so they were face to face. "Okay, so, um, you remember that guy Evan I knew in high school? I used go riding on his family's farm past Jackson Point. You dropped me there a few times."

His dad thought for a moment, then nodded. "I guess. He the one who dyed his hair every colour under the sun for about two years?"

Oh God, Cass had forgotten that. He couldn't help the grin. Evan was hardly a shrinking violet, and he'd been an awesome first kiss—not to mention a few other things. He cleared his throat.

"Yeah, him. So anyway, I, um, didn't just go there to ride horses."

Sean Martin arched an impressive brow. "Is this where you tell me you got his sister pregnant and I have a twenty-year-old grandchild?"

"Wh—" Cass choked on his coffee and sprayed it all down the front of his shirt. "Aw, shit." He brushed at the mess, only spreading it further. "No, Dad. No. No grandchild. Jesus."

Sean smiled in amusement. "That's a relief. I might have liked them more than you, and then I'd have to bump you down in my will."

Cass stared at his dad in disbelief, then shook his head. "Can I just finish?"

Sean waved a hand. "Go ahead."

"Thank you. No, Dad... the *other* reason I went riding with Evan was that—" He paused and took a deep breath. For God's sake, he was thirty-six years old, yet somehow he felt all of fifteen. Coming out to your parents sucked regardless of age.

"The other reason was that I had a huge crush on him." He waited a couple of seconds for that to sink, then followed with, "I'm bisexual, Dad. I like men *and* women... romantically speaking."

Sean Martin sat like a rock, frown fixed in place, blinking fast, his cup locked in his hand. Cass didn't know if it was because he was shocked, disgusted, or just trying to get his head around it. He sighed. "Look, I understand if it's a shock—"

"Just give me a minute." His dad held up a hand, put his cup on the deck, leaned forward on his knees, and dropped his head in thought. He sat there swaying slowly from side to side as Cass waited, heart in his throat.

Finally he sat up and faced Cass again. "Okay. You're bisexual. Got it. I don't know why it's taken you so long to tell me, but you'll have your reasons. Maybe you can share those with me one day, if you want. So, do we need a secret handshake?"

A weight of fear lifted from Cass's chest, and his eyes misted. His dad reached for his hand, something Cass had no memory of him ever doing before. It nearly broke him inside to feel that firm, warm grip, assuring Cass things were okay between them. Grateful and proud didn't even begin to cover it.

"Can I ask some questions?" his dad ventured, keeping firm hold of his hand. "Or would that be... inappropriate?"

Cass swallowed hard and sat back, blowing out the breath he'd been holding to try to stop the threatening tears from falling. He gave up and wiped at his eyes as a couple broke free. His father saw, and Cass swore the man blinked rapidly himself.

"Ask away," he said.

They talked for about twenty minutes, until car tyres on gravel caught Cass's attention and his heart skipped. He didn't need to think too hard about who it was, given all the unanswered texts, and when a van with "Southern Lights Coffee Company" on the side rounded the corner of the barn and pulled on to the grass, his fear was confirmed. The face behind the wheel was achingly familiar.

"Fuck."

His dad's gaze jerked from the van to Cass. "What's that all about? To be honest, I'd expected him sooner. Thought you two were friends."

Cass blinked slowly, his heart jumping through his ribs. "We are... friends." *And so much more.* "It's just...."

His dad's gaze narrowed. "Something I should know, Cass? 'Cause I have to tell you, you've been wound tighter than a two-dollar watch since you got home. Is Stef what prompted our little conversation this morning? Is he... are you two..."

"No. Shit. Maybe. Dammit..." Cass gritted his teeth so he didn't snap at his dad. "Yes. Look, I like him, okay? Too much, as it turns out. But he's going back to Auckland in a couple of days, and I can't be dealing with that on top of everything else. I just needed some space, so I—"

"So you didn't let him come visit? You pushed him away? Cass, the guy saved your life—"

"I know! I know." *Crap.* "Sorry. Look, I'll talk to you later, okay?"

His dad hesitated, then sighed and put a hand on Cass's shoulder. "I'll be inside when you're done, but I'll say one thing before I go: I'll always regret never talking to your mother like I should have. Use your words, Cassidy. If you like the guy, talk to him."

When the screen door slammed shut, Cass grabbed his cane and walked to the edge of the deck, where he took hold of the handrail for added support. Stef hadn't yet left the van, but that didn't stop Cass absorbing the volcanic level of pissed-off-ness he was exuding.

Here we go. Cass made his way slowly down the stairs and across to the barn for some privacy, knowing Stef would follow. He took a seat on a hay bale, briefly acknowledged the irony of that situation, and waited. He didn't have to wait long.

Stef swept into the barn like he had the proverbial bee up his butt, stopped a few metres away, cocked his hip, and glared. And Cass deserved every withering second of it.

After a few seconds, Stef's gaze wandered and took in the barn and its floor-to-ceiling rows of hay bales. "A bit fucking déjà vu, don't you think?" He rolled his eyes. "And people say *I'm* dramatic."

Stef flung his arms wide, revealing a T-shirt that read, "Bin doin' cowboy shit all day," and Cass didn't know whether to laugh or cry. He'd missed him so fucking much.

"Look, I'm sorry." He struggled to hold Stef's gaze.

"No. You stop right there," Stef snapped, and took a couple more steps towards him. "You do not get to wipe ghosting me with a half-arsed, throwaway apology. When I left *four days ago* you were a bit quiet, sure. But we'd had a few laughs, shared a passable hospital fried rice and an inedible chow mein for lunch, and watched a movie. So when I called the next morning to check how you slept, imagine my surprise to find you'd been discharged not long after I'd left, *and*" —he glowered—"you'd known about it for hours."

"You checked how I slept?" Cass scrunched his eyes and dragged a hand over his face. "God, I'm so—"

Stef fired his hand up. "Soooo, I text to see if I can come and visit you at home. But no—you're too tired, too sore, too anything it takes not to let me visit. And since yesterday, let me see..." He checked his phone. "Fifteen texts and no reply. You have to be dead, right? Because that would be the only possible explanation for you not returning any of my messages and leaving me climbing the walls with worry for eighteen hours, twenty-five minutes and"—he checked his watch this time—"twelve seconds... give or take." He poured out a furious sigh. "*Now* you can talk."

Cass thought he'd rather peel his skin off a centimetre at a time with a blunt blade. "Okay, so I might have fucked up—"

"*Might* have?"

Cass stared at him pointedly.

"Okay, carry on." Stef circled his hand at Cass.

"Fuck, Stef, I like you so much—"

"I think we've covered that chapter." Stef tapped his foot on the dusty floor.

Cass arched a brow.

"Sorry, sorry." He zipped his mouth, and it was all Cass could do not to smile. Then he stepped up to the hay bale, scooted Cass over, and sat so their thighs touched.

Just a brush of material over flesh, and the sparks licked all the way up to Cass's heart.

"Give me your hand." Being Stef, he didn't wait for permission. Just grabbed Cass's hand and threaded their fingers together. "I need to fucking touch you already, okay? No, don't answer that."

Cass could do nothing but stare, and feel, and crave, and... *oh Christ*... ache. For more... for everything. It was too late to protect his heart. This was going to hurt like a motherfucker.

"Right, I'm listening." Stef fired him an innocent look. "What? I *can* listen, you know."

Cass sent him a long-suffering look, snorted, and shook his head, all the long-winded explanations he'd practised flying out the window. "You said it to me back at the hut. What are we doing here? You go home in a few days, and you're here, with me, doing... this." He lifted their joined hands and let them fall.

Stef stiffened. "You don't want to hold my hand?" He loosened his grip, but Cass held on.

"Jesus, Stef. Yes, I want to hold your hand. I want to touch your face, and kiss your lips, and wrap you in my arms, and turn you over this damn hay bale and bury myself so deep that I can't feel anything but you, inside and out, filling every goddamn empty space in my life. I want you. I want your heart... goddammit," he broke off, wondering who the fuck had taken over his mouth.

Stef sat for a second in shocked silence, and Cass wondered just how badly he'd fucked everything up. Then two fingers dipped under his chin to tip his head up, bringing them eye to eye. Cass didn't know what to expect, but tears weren't on the list.

"What a coincidence." Stef pressed their foreheads together, taking care to avoid Cass's healing wound. "I just happen to have a heart going spare with your name on it. How about that?"

What? "But... you're leaving." He blinked slowly. "You mean, you... like me... like, like me like *that?*" His mouth fell open, a state he was becoming accustomed to whenever Stef was around.

Stef scrunched up his nose. "That's a lot of likes, and I'm not quite sure what '*that*' means, but I'm gonna take a wild guess here and assume it means something along the lines of—not only do I want to fuck your very delectable arse into next year every time I lay eyes on you, but I also want to wake up to you, laugh with you, talk and watch ridiculous westerns with you, dance with you... even that fucking line-dancing crap, and holy shit I cannot believe I just said that. I want to brunch with you—crap, do they do brunch down here?"

Cass hadn't got past the gaping bit.

"Nah, of course they do. Thank God for that. Almost hit a hard limit there."

Cass figured this was what it meant to be thunderstruck. They were beautiful words, but... "I love it here, Stef. I can't leave again. I don't do well..." He drew away a little.

"I know." Stef turned sideways and tugged Cass back around to face him.

It was harder saying the words to his face, but he owed Stef that, at least. "You have to believe that I'd want to. I'd make all the right promises, and I'd really try to make it work, but—"

"Shh." Stef got to his knees, straddled Cass's hips, and pushed him slowly to his back. "I'm not asking you to leave."

Cass shook his head. "But... but this whole thing between us... it's ridiculous, right? We hardly know each other—"

Stef pressed a firm kiss to his lips, silencing him. "Don't we? Really, Cass? I'd say we know each other pretty well, actually." His tongue teased for entry, and just like that Cass opened, lost to the taste of the man who filled his every thought, the demand of the kiss, the overwhelming sense of the man who covered him, wanted him—

lost to hope and maybe a promise—until Stef pulled back, and Cass's heart touched ground again.

"Look." Stef licked his lips. "God, you taste good. This is what I know about Cassidy Martin. I know you love horses, you live for these mountains, you care about your family, you're good with business and money, you like to help people, you're super smart, you're kind, you're good with kids, or at least my brother—which is pretty damn important to me to be honest—you've been hurt but you mended, and you know yourself, know what you need. You took care of me, helped me grow and believe a bit more in myself, in what I can handle—and you fuck like a trouper. I'm not sure there's any more I need to know about you to decide I want more of *all* of that and I'm willing to fight for it. I was waiting to tell you how I felt. Waiting for you to recover a bit more. But then you went and fucking ran on me."

Cass cradled Stef's face and pulled him down for a kiss. "I'm so sorry I did that."

"Forgiven. Look, I know it's fast. Do you think I haven't had the same argument with myself? I'm not entirely without a brain. So, this is what I thought. I thought... *maybe* I could move down here—"

Move in? Shit, he'd said that aloud.

Stef barked out a laugh. "God, you should see your face. No, you fool. Get a flat down here is what I meant." He grinned and peppered Cass's face with kisses. "*Move in* with you? *Pfft.* I don't even know how much you snore—could be a deal-breaker."

He kissed Cass some more, and Cass was beginning to feel like he'd bought a ticket on the spinning teacups only to find it was the roller coaster instead.

"But your business." He turned his head to give Stef more room to work on his neck.

"Is portable." Stef found the soft flesh below his ear and drew it into his mouth, sucking hard enough to leave a mark. "I can rent space locally."

Cass finally pushed Stef away so he could see his whole face. "But you love the city. It's your life. You've said as much. 'Born-and-bred city boy,' I think, were your exact words. I can't, I *won't* ask you to move. There's nothing for you here. You'd hate it, and then you'd hate me."

"You're not asking." Stef tried to grab another kiss, but Cass held him off. He sighed and pulled a frustrated face. "Besides, *you're* here for me, and that's a big load of very enticing *something*, right there." He sighed. "I think we have something, Cass, and it could be more. It could be... everything. I want to do this. I want to find out. Don't you?"

Just like Tricia. It hit Cass like a ton of iced water. "It won't work." He pushed Stef aside, landing him unceremoniously on his arse on the floor, and sat up.

"Okay, so that was unexpected." Stef got to his feet and brushed himself off.

"Fuck, sorry." Jesus, could Cass make any more of a mess of things? "Tricia said the same thing, you see. She said she'd try coming back—try to make it work. It didn't."

"I'm not her." Stef pushed Cass back down before crawling up his body once again. "So how about you let *me* decide what will work for *me*?" He sat down hard, and Cass's aching cock performed complicated and painful origami. He grunted and tried to get some wiggle room.

Stef arched a brow, daring him.

Cass stopped in his tracks.

"Look." He stared down, tucking Cass's hair behind his ears. "I know I can't make any promises and maybe it's not fair to make comparisons. But right from the start, Tricia never wanted to come back, she never wanted to live here—that's what you said. Her plan from high school was always to leave. Well, that's not me. I'm *choosing* to come here, to try this. Yes, I love the city, but I can still visit there. There's such a thing as planes, you know. Plus, this is hardly the middle of nowhere, after all. Queenstown is just down the road, and so is my best friend. I love this place, Cass. I love this valley.

I even love those great hulking horses. But maybe we can get some chickens, huh? 'Cause I *really* like chickens."

Chickens? It was all Cass could do not to tell Stef there was a coop tucked round the back of the barn, empty since his mother left. An image of Stef stumbling out in his sleep pants in the morning to feed and talk with a dozen hens ripped the air right out of his lungs. *Jesus, could it really work?*

"This place fires my ideas, *different* ideas, and lots of them." Stef's hands worked in the air as he got more and more excited. "I have a notebook jammed full of sketches in my bag. Colours, metals, bars, bracelets"—his dancing eyes flashed at Cass—"leather, harnesses."

The man was fucking incendiary. Cass's hands found Stef's arse, took a grip on each cheek and began to knead.

Stef bit his lip and stared down at him. "I just need to know if I'm the only one flying this plane or if I've got a co-pilot. If you really want to try. And don't humour me here, Cass. I need you to be honest. Anything less and we haven't got a chance in hell of making this work. So, in the words of Gandalf the White..." He paused meaningfully. "'All we have to decide is what to do with the time that is given us.'"

Cass lifted his hands to Stef's face. "You know, for a late-thirty-something man, you are so fucking adorable at times." He took a breath. "I know what I want, Stef. I have since that first night. You, it's always you. I don't want you to go. I don't want to lose you. But I'm so fucking scared of doing this, of trying... and then losing you anyway."

Stef nodded, dropped to his elbows, and kissed Cass gently. "So am I. If only you knew. You're the first man I've trusted in a long while. But I'm more scared of not trying and never knowing if maybe you were the one."

They stared at each other for a few seconds while Cass absorbed the inescapable truth of those words, a truth equalled in Cass's heart. "Okay. Let's do it."

Stef groaned and lunged forward on to Cass's aching cock, one of the few parts of him that seemed to be working good as new. Shocked the hell out of him.

The question must've struck Stef at the same time, because he suddenly pulled off, looking slightly horrified. "It's alright for us to be doing this, right?"

Who the hell knew? But Cass wasn't about to let that cat out of the bag. "Doc said to let my body guide me with most things. Nothing too strenuous. I'll let you know if we need to stop." He snagged Stef's lower lip between his teeth, sucked on it, and let it go. "He also said no riding"—he grinned—"but nothing about being ridden. If you can work with that?"

Stef's smile turned wicked. "Ride a cowboy, huh? I'm sure I've got that T-shirt somewhere. But I think we should set the bar lower to start with." He dropped his lips to Cass's mouth and hummed contentedly. "So, I'll get a flat, and then you can date me."

Cass smiled against his lips. "I can, huh?"

"Yes. We'll do it properly. No cheap shit. I want flowers and everything."

Cass's hands travelled under Stef's shirt, up that long, lean back, hot skin shivering under his touch. "Flowers, mmm, got it." He fingertips grazed over Stef's nipples, earning him a surprised hiss.

"And doughnuts," Stef groaned, arching back, eyes closed. "I want cherry doughnuts—extra for Arwen."

Cass held on as Stef ground down on him, slow, lazy circles, and if he didn't get his sweats off soon, his dick was gonna need a splint at the very least. Then Stef pressed down hard, and Cass nearly went lights out.

"Holy fuck." He pushed Stef back. "Just give me a sec. I'll make a list, okay? Chickens, flowers, cherry doughnuts—check. Now get your goddamn clothes off and stop strangling my damn cock or I'm gonna need another burr hole to relieve the pressure."

Stef scrambled to the floor. "Oh God, I'm sorry. Fuck, I wasn't thinking." Then he glared. "You were supposed to let me know."

"Oh, right, so it's my fault," Cass struggled to get his sweats down. "Newsflash: this is me letting you know." He finally got one foot out and kicked the other free, sending the offending item flying to the floor before starting on his T-shirt. "Hey." He clicked his fingers at Stef, who was standing there staring at Cass's fully engorged, bobbing cock. "Clothes off, now."

Stef's gaze jerked up. "Huh? What? Oh, right." He delved into his wallet, threw a packet of lube on the bale, pulled his shirt off and began tugging at the buttons on his jeans. "Are you sure they didn't give you something to enhance that monster while you were under? 'Cause holy shit, Cass, I gotta tell you, it looks bigger in the daylight." Stef got his jeans and briefs off in one go.

Daylight. Shit. Cass froze. "Hey, um, check for Dad, will you? He knows I'm bi, by the way."

Stef's mouth dropped open. "What? He does? How'd it go? And no! I'm fucking naked here, Cass."

He was, deliciously so—cock swinging at full mast.

"I'm not walking out of the barn to see if your *dad's* coming while I'm stark fucking naked. Are you out of your mind? You do it."

"It went fine. He was cool about it. And yes, I'd check myself, but you know I'm not supposed to get up and down quickly..." He fluttered his eyelashes at Stef, who stared back, clearly trying to work out if Cass was yanking his chain.

"Oh, for fuck's sake..." Stef grabbed his T-shirt from the floor and balled it in front of his junk. Then he stalked across to the edge of the barn door and peered around it.

It was funny as shit and it was all Cass could do not to crack up— a sure-fire way to lose his balls. Then it suddenly hit him that this was only the second time they'd been together, like this. It should've been a stark reminder of how little time they'd known each other and how fast they were moving, but instead it was just—he caught sight of Stef's pert arse flying starkers in the wind—fucking awesome.

"Coast is clear. I can see him in the kitchen." Stef pushed the huge barn door closed, stalked back, and threw his T-shirt back with the rest of his clothes on the dirt floor. Then he grabbed his sweatshirt and biffed it at Cass, who laid it out on the bale behind him. "And if I find you were just fucking with me, you're dead meat." He pounced on to the hay bale. "Now, lie that gorgeous arse of yours back on that sweatshirt and stand aside while I blow your mind."

Cass did as he was told, thankful for something between him and the prickly hay. "I'd say you have a very high opinion of yourself there, *Mr* Hamilton." He was about to say something more when Stef knelt between his legs and swallowed him down whole—and all conscious thought evaporated.

Before he knew it, his hands were wrapped around Stef's head, fingers fisted in all that sleek, dark hair while his head pressed back into the hay, nonsense pouring from his mouth. Holy moly, Stef was good, his tongue dragging the length of Cass's cock, sweeping around the head, playing with the frenulum. He sucked the flared crown into his mouth, dipping into the slit, and then slid back down to repeat the whole thing while Cass could do nothing but hold on for the ride.

"Have I told you how much I love your cock?" Stef kissed the end of it, gaze sliding up to meet Cass's, lips red and swollen. "It's fucking perfect." Then, keeping his eyes on Cass, he opened his mouth and took the length down the back of his throat, never hesitating even as his eyes watered, and it was the sexiest, filthiest thing Cass had ever seen. When Stef swallowed around him, Cass saw fucking stars.

He pushed to his elbows to get a better view.

"Stay flat." A hand landed on his chest, and all that wet heat was suddenly gone. Something too close to a mewl for comfort sprang from his mouth, and Cass winced. *Oh God, kill me now.*

Stef's face appeared above him, wearing a smirk from ear to ear. "Would you like to repeat that, *Mr* Martin?" He grinned and licked a path up Cass's throat. "I told you I'd blow your mind."

Cass waved a hand in the air. "The evidence isn't all in yet. Continue."

"Mmm. Is that right? Then you better open that lube."

Cass did, while Stef kissed and licked his way back south, over Cass's stomach and slowly, slowly down to his swollen, desperate cock. Then Stef pushed Cass's thighs apart, lifted his balls and ran his tongue from their underside to Cass's hole where he nipped and sucked and probed with shameless gusto.

Cass gave up on the lube packet and simply moaned. That was until clicking fingers caught his attention, followed by Stef's grabby hand in his face. And while the man's tongue was still buried and otherwise occupied in his arse, Cass dumped some lube on Stef's fingers and then crashed back on the bale, bundling the sweatshirt under his head to help him catch what he could of the show.

Seconds later, a fingertip breached his hole alongside that wicked tongue, and then another. Cass pushed back to draw them deeper, shifting his hips until—"*Oh, fuck*"—he lit up like a Christmas tree.

Stef sat back onto his heels to watch, and started working his own cock with his free hand as Cass slowly fucked himself on Stef's fingers. After a minute, he leaned forward and swallowed Cass down once again, keeping his fingers buried, working, working—tongue, fingers, throat, swallow, suck, press, nip—until Cass could barely remember his own fucking name.

And then with Stef's dick bobbing wet on Cass's calf, the warm buzz that had been building at the base of Cass's spine suddenly exploded in a rolling wave of pleasure that sent shudders through him from head to foot. He spilled deep into Stef's throat, muscles swallowing around him, drawing every last drop until he was done. The world fell away leaving nothing but Stef outlined in stark relief as he freed his fingers and pulled off Cass with a soft kiss to his sensitive cock. Cass couldn't move. Hell, he could barely breathe.

"Fuck, Cass." Stef put his knees either side of Cass's long legs and shuffled up till he straddled Cass's stomach. Then he took himself in hand and worked his cock with a vengeance while Cass watched, transfixed. He looked like a damn angel with his head fallen back, throat exposed and hair flying.

"Fuck, yes." Cass held Stef's thighs as Stef worked himself to the edge. A few more strokes and he came apart, unloading all over Cass's chest and as far up as his chin. And Cass loved every damn second of it. Then he collapsed astride Cass, elbows propped either side of Cass's head, gasping for air, perspiration running down his face and onto Cass.

Cass gave him a few seconds to come down before reaching up for a sweaty kiss. Stef nuzzled for more, licking Cass's chin clean before moving down to his chest to complete the job there. When Stef was done, Cass pulled him back for a more lingering kiss, his tongue sweeping through Stef's mouth to grab another taste. Then Stef slid to his side on the hay and lay still, one arm thrown over Cass's chest. Cass tucked him in close, and Stef hummed contentedly.

They lay there for a few minutes catching their breath, and Cass was caught in how perfect it felt to have Stef in his arms, in his barn, on his farm. He didn't dare fully believe yet, but man, his hope soared.

"Did any of that brain of yours squeeze out that hole, or are we good?" Stef mumbled into Cass's armpit.

Cass reached for his head and patted it thoughtfully. "Nah, we're good."

"Awesome." Stef snuggled closer. "We should measure it for a cork. You know, just in case. Wake me up when your dad walks in and has a stroke. Either that or kills us both for fucking in his barn."

Cass rolled on his side and brought their faces together. "'I would rather share one lifetime with you than face all the ages of this world alone.'"

Stef snorted. "Oh. My. God. You're such a fucking nerd. You do realise that's Arwen's line, which makes you the... you know... in this relationship."

Cass groaned.

"Which, of course, makes me Aragorn. But then, I always knew this to be true."

"Pretty sure Aragorn didn't wear green nail polish."

"Nobody's perfect."

EPILOGUE

"Quit that." Stef elbowed Arwen's inquisitive nose out of the way. "You'll get those velvet lips of yours burnt on this soldering iron in a minute, and then you'll be in trouble."

Arwen nickered and nudged him hard on the back, shunting Stef forward into his workbench. "Goddammit. Now look what you made me do." He held up a large copper hoop with a bar hanging decidedly off-centre. "I'm gonna have to start again. Go annoy your father."

"You were the one who insisted your workbench be situated within equine snotting distance of the stable door." Cass squeezed past Arwen and handed Stef a steaming mug of coffee with the words "I'm pretty sure my death will be caused by making a sarcastic comment at the wrong time" printed on it, while Cass's read, "Oh no, EVERYONE is hot!" Then he leaned back against the newly insulated and lined stable wall looking every inch the deliciously hot cowboy he was: six foot six of denim, leather, and yum.

Stef's gaze dropped to the massive silver belt buckle that hung on Cass's jeans—the single word "Paradise," written in a large, looping font. He smiled—that summed up everything he felt about the valley and his man. He'd secretly designed and made it for Cass's thirty-seventh birthday the month before, and Cass had worn it damn near every day since.

Cass insisted to anyone who'd listen that it actually referred to the anatomy that lay south of the buckle, and well, Stef couldn't really argue with that. A producer on the last film shoot in the valley had taken one look and ordered three for Christmas gifts. It was a creative sideline Stef had never seen coming. Cowboy belt buckles for the rich and famous. Who'd have guessed?

"I think you secretly love that the horses interrupt your work," Cass commented with a wicked grin, dripping sex appeal all over Stef's clean work floor. God, but the man was sexy.

Stef grunted and adjusted himself. He *did* love it. Not that he'd ever admit that to Cass, who thought he was weird as it was—wanting the two spare stables converted into his jewellery workshop when he could've had a room in the nice warm house. It took a month to get them wired, plumbed, lined, heated, and fitted out—including a kitchenette and a couple of armchairs. It would've been cheaper to freight in a ready-made granny flat or convert one of the bedrooms in the homestead, something Cass reminded him about on a regular basis.

But there was something about the smell of horses, and all that muscle and inquisitive energy up in his business, that got Stef's creative juices flowing. One of them was always hanging over the half-door watching him work, and Stef found himself chatting away to them the whole day without even realising it. When he travelled to promote his lines or catch up with his city friends, he missed them almost as much as he missed Cass. Almost.

It was Arwen who most often took the spot—the nosey mare had latched on to Stef like superglue and followed him everywhere. Stef liked to think it was because they had a special bond, but he suspected it was more likely the cherry doughnuts Cass supplied Stef for morning tea most days. He'd had to let his belt out a hole just last week. But he loved the smelly animal. Cass had stopped using Arwen on treks a couple of months back, and she was now officially Stef's.

His sappy boyfriend had put a big bow around her and everything. And anyone who said Stef had bawled like a baby to find her like that when he went to feed her that morning was lying.

Stef noted the shit-eating grin on Cass's face. "I gather Hoff agreed to your plan, then?"

Cass nodded, unable to hide his excitement. It was cute as hell.

"Yeah. And he's gonna ask Dee if she knows of any others who might like to join in."

Stef's family, including Benny, were all flying down for Benny's birthday the following week, Stef's mother promising to bring along one of her Tamarillo Tarts. Stef had a delicious point to prove, and a six-foot-six cowboy to lick it off, if he had his way. Cass had been determined to give Benny a short horse trek to Diamond Lake as his birthday present, and was bummed he couldn't take Benny himself, but he would be providing the support vehicle and lunch. The two got on like a house on fire, texting and talking regularly, and watching them together did all sorts of strange things to Stef's heart.

Recovery from the subdural haemorrhage had been slow and frustrating. Headaches and the occasional lapse in short-term memory were ongoing issues, but they were nothing Cass couldn't handle. The only burr under the saddle—Stef had made it his mission to learn as many annoying cowboy/riding terms as he could, since a riled-up Cass was a glorious thing—was that the persistent headaches meant Cass hadn't got the six-month clearance he'd so badly wanted. He could ride but not lead tours yet, and no one could tell him when that would change. But his doctors were hopeful.

In the meantime, he'd employed Hoff to take the tours for him. It was working fine, but Cass was itching to get back in the saddle, so to speak. He'd upped his accountancy clients to cover the cost of paying Hoff and was using the downtime to plan expanding his business into a riding school—maybe even keeping Hoff on long term so he could focus on the school. Stef was so proud of him.

Stef put his coffee on the bench, held his hand out to Cass, then muscled the bigger man back against the wall. "I've been waiting for this all morning, you shirker. I'm pretty sure that moving-in-together contract I had you sign included a minimum of twenty kisses a day in the fine print." He nuzzled into Cass's neck and nipped at his throat. "Not to mention our secret hideaway hasn't seen any action beyond a wish and a promise for a couple of long-arse days."

The barn had become *their* place, especially before Stef had moved into the homestead—but even after. It didn't take much for them to get naked amongst the hay bales several times a week regardless of the weather. But Stef wasn't silly. A set of old drawers had also made the barn home, with blankets, lube, and a stash of other necessary or just plain interesting supplies, stuffed into its drawers. Before Sean had moved into Dee's house in Glenorchy, Cass and Stef used to hang a Do Not Disturb sign on the barn doors for when they were "grooming"—their secret code word for fucking like rampant bunnies.

Not so secret, as they found out when Sean banged on the doors in the first couple of weeks to inform them they'd forgotten to hang the sign, and would they please stop using that ludicrous word, especially at the dinner table, because if the horses were "groomed" any more vigorously they'd be damn well bald. And could they keep it down, they were scaring the sheep.

Stef and Sean got along fine. Sean seemed to find them as a couple... amusing, but the genuine fondness in his manner towards Stef was undeniable. A man of few words, Sean had never spoken directly to Stef about Cass and Stef dating, other than once in the very first week Stef had arrived back in Glenorchy from Auckland. While the two had been washing the dishes in the kitchen one night, Sean had unexpectedly turned and told Stef to be careful with his son's heart. Stef had nearly dropped the gravy boat he'd been drying. He'd replied he had no intention of doing anything else, and Sean had grunted something that sounded like an approval and turned back to the sink. And that was that.

Sean and Dee had settled in well together, and Cass and his dad had signed an agreement to sell Cass the remainder of the farm over an extended period of time at a ridiculously low price. Sean argued it would've gone to Cass anyway, eventually.

"I'm beginning to think you're avoiding me, Mr Martin. Do I have to invoke the penalty clause?"

Stef tilted his mouth up for a kiss and Cass covered it with his own, tongue diving in for a long, sweet taste. As usual, Stef simply melted. Nothing had changed. Four months dating, four months living together—anytime, anyplace, it was always the same: Cass could do with Stef what he pleased, and Stef would always show up for him. It was that simple. He loved Cass in a way he hadn't thought possible, and he wasn't sure he'd even scraped the surface yet. Lucky for him, Cass seemed to feel the same way.

"Pretty sure I never actually signed that contract." Cass nipped at Stef's lips.

Because yes, there been a contract. Stef was making no apologies. He wasn't going to rely on Cass's goodwill to ensure the flowers and doughnuts kept coming. Or the awesome blowjobs, or the way he stretched Stef's arse just right; the long mornings in bed, or the freezing and sometimes wet-suited moonlit swims in the Dart River with the Southern Lights painting the night sky. That shit needed to be spelled out in detail, because Stef was a complete smitten kitten given the whole ridiculously romantic mission Cass had been on from the minute he'd landed back in Queenstown.

"Pretty sure you did, in fact, sign it." Stef's wandering hands found Cass's impressive cock at half-mast and gave it a couple of strokes through his jeans. "I know this, because it's still sitting in my bedside drawer."

A sudden fluttering of feathers swept the back of Stef's head, and his hand reflexly tightened.

"Ow!" Cass swatted him away and cupped himself protectively.

"Oops." Stef bit back a grin, then turned on the Rhode Island Red busy clucking around his work bench. "Esmeralda, get your scruffy arse back in that coop. You know the rules." He lunged for the chicken, who deftly avoided his hands and made a dash for the kitchen.

"I don't know how the fuck you get anything done," Cass grumbled, heading the chicken off at the pass. "The place is like a damned zoo. Which reminds me, some guy phoned this morning to say Belle and Jasmine would be ready Friday."

"Oh, great, I can settle them before I leave for Wellington on Monday. Don't move, I'll sneak up from behind."

"Promises, promises." Cass arched a brow and made a grab for Esmeralda, who turned tail and scooted under the bench.

"I told you not to move." Stef got down on his hands and knees to flush the bird out. The fact that it put his arse on display for his lover to ponder over never entered his mind. He wriggled it anyway.

"If you stay like that any longer, I won't be held responsible for my actions."

Mission accomplished. Stef shoved a box of scrap metal, which startled the chicken. Esmeralda leapt in the air and made the fatal mistake of flying left, not right, and Stef was able to shoo her out the stable door. He dusted off his hands and was all up in Cass's business in a half second flat, pushing him back into the wall and pressing hard up against him.

"Now, where were we?" He circled his hips provocatively. "Something about that cast-iron contract you signed."

Cass groaned and flipped their positions. "I was under coercion. It'll never stand up in a court of law."

The man had a point. Stef had in fact edged Cass to the limit several times and threatened not to let him come for a week unless he put his scrawl on the bit of paper. "You saying you want the contract made null and void?" Stef eyed Cass pointedly.

Cass cradled his face and leaned in, covering Stef's whole body with his own. Stef arched into the pressure, wanting more, wanting everything with this man.

Green eyes pinned Stef to the wall. "I'm saying, sweetheart, that maybe we could replace that particular contract with another."

Stef rubbed himself up Cass, then side-eyed him with a wicked smile. "Ooh, does it involve toys? Do tell."

"No, it doesn't involve toys, but it would be..." Cass's thumb traced Stef's lower lip, and he pressed a soft kiss on it. "It would be a permanent contract... if you were interested."

Permanent! Stef shoved Cass back, locked eyes, and it only took a second. Everything was laid out for him in that one look. Stef knew Cass loved him; he didn't question that for a minute. And this life they'd been building? Hell, Stef wouldn't change a bit of it.

He trailed his fingers down Cass's jawline and cupped his chin. "Are you asking me to marry you, Mr Martin?"

Cass nodded. "Yes, I am. Will you marry me, Mr Hamilton? Will you make this contract between us permanent?"

Stef beamed. "Yes, permanent is good. Permanent is fucking excellent, Mr Martin."

Cass seemed to almost sag at the knees in relief and Stef realised that Cass hadn't been 100% sure of Stef's answer. He hadn't taken Stef for granted and Stef was pretty sure the grin he now wore could've lit up the night sky.

"That's good," Cass whispered against his lips. "That's very good." He cleared his throat. "So, you being a jeweller and all... I thought you might want some say in the rings."

Stef snorted. "See, this is why I love you. You're a smart man."

Cass grinned. "Yes, and I like my balls where they are, thank you. But I thought we could maybe use a placeholder until you decided what you wanted, so..." He took Stef's hand and slid a ring into place.

Stef glanced down and broke into laughter at the sight of the plastic replica of Sauron's One Ring on his finger. "Holy shit, you ridiculous man. This is fucking perfect." He launched his legs around Cass's waist and they both collapsed to the floor.

"I, um, got two of them," Cass choked out from beneath the weight of Stef on his chest. "The second is um, hidden... some- where... on my person." He waggled his eyebrows.

Oh. My. God. Stef was on his feet in a second, stabbing a finger

Cass's way. "I want you naked in that barn in two seconds flat, mister. And be prepared for some *in depth* and detailed exploration—"

"Fuck yeah." Cass was out the door before Stef had even finished his sentence.

Best. Fiancé. Ever.

THE END

AUTHOR'S NOTE

Thank you for taking the time to read

TAMARILLO TART
Southern Lights 2

If you enjoyed this book please consider doing a review in Amazon or your favourite review spot. I didn't realise until I was an author just how important reviews are for helping an author's sales and spreading the word. I thank you in advance.

Don't miss the next book in the series:

FLAT WHITES & CHOCOLATE FISH
Southern Lights 3

ADRIAN POWELL has a secret, a secret he's guarded for 17 years. But it's come at a cost—few friends, fewer lovers and a lifetime of loneliness. If he's a bit grumpy and a tad pessimistic, who can blame him? So, exactly how he's ended up with a bunch of nosy friends, a beautiful lakeside cottage and a successful business, is beyond him.

It's a life he never imagined, and one that includes a problematic new neighbour, NIALL CARMICHAEL—an irritating, equally grumpy, sexy as hell silver fox, who kisses like a dream, shakes every one of Adrian's walls, and who might just prove Adrian's undoing.

But secrets have a way of catching up with you. And when Adrian's past comes knocking, it might just threaten everything he's built.

ALSO BY JAY HOGAN

AUCKLAND MED SERIES

First Impressions

Crossing the Touchline

Up Close and Personal

Against the Grain

You Are Cordially Invited (2021)

SOUTHERN LIGHTS SERIES

Powder and Pavlova

Tamarillo Tart

Flat Whites and Chocolate Fish

Pinot and Pineapple Lumps

PAINTED BAY SERIES

Off Balance

On Board (2021)

STANDALONE

Unguarded (May 2021)

(Written as part of Sarina Bowen's
True North—Vino & Veritas Series and published by Heart Eyes Press)

Digging Deep
(2020 Lambda Literary Finalist)

ABOUT THE AUTHOR

Jay is a 2020 Lambda Literary Award Finalist in gay romance.

She is a New Zealand author writing in MM romance and romantic suspense primarily set in New Zealand. She loves writing character driven romances with lots of humour, a good dose of reality and a splash of angst. She's travelled extensively, lived in many countries, and in a past life she was a critical care nurse and counsellor. Jay is owned by a huge Maine Coon cat and a gorgeous Cocker Spaniel.

Join Jay's reader's group Hogan's Hangout for updates, promotions, her current writing projects and special releases.

Sign up to her newsletter HERE.

Or visit her website HERE.